RANDOM
HOUSE
LARGE
PRINT

SEARCHING

FOR

PARADISE

IN

PARKER, PA

**Also by Kris Radish
available from Random House Large Print**

Dancing Naked at the Edge of Dawn
Annie Freeman's Fabulous Traveling Funeral

SEARCHING

FOR

PARADISE

IN

PARKER, PA

KRIS

RADISH

RANDOM HOUSE
LARGE PRINT

F
LPE

Copyright © 2008 by Kris Radish

All rights reserved.
Published in the United States of America
by Random House Large Print in association with Bantam Books, New York.
Distributed by Random House, Inc., New York.

**Library of Congress
Cataloging-in-Publication Data**
Radish, Kris.
Searching for paradise in Parker, PA / by Kris Radish. —
1st large print ed.
p. cm.
ISBN: 978-0-7393-2769-2
1. Married women—Fiction. 2. Middle-aged women—
Fiction. 3. Marital conflict—Fiction. 4. Life-change
events—Fiction. 5. Female friendship—Fiction.
6. Happiness—Fiction. 7. Large type books.
8. Domestic fiction. I. Title.
PS618.A35S43 2008b
813'.6—dc22
2008002318

www.randomhouse.com/largeprint

FIRST LARGE PRINT EDITION

10 9 8 7 6 5 4 3 2 1

This Large Print edition published in accord with
the standards of the N.A.V.H.

Paradise is not always a place and finding it is not always easy. This book is for everyone who has the courage to search for their own paradise and it's also for the men and women who love us enough to be patient, to support us, to encourage us while we are looking. If you haven't started your search, get going—the journey is half the fun.

ACKNOWLEDGMENTS

Searching for paradise is a worthy vocation that doesn't always include fruit drinks, a warm breeze, the sound of the ocean, and moonlight dancing across your face. Sometimes, like writing a book, it's hard work.

My search for this slice of literary paradise was supported by a cast of characters worthy of a free trip to any island in the universe.

My beloved editor, Kate Miciak, who has believed in me from the beginning, gets first pick of where to travel. Kate has stretched me, challenged me, and taught me how to be a much better writer. She is wise, generous—terribly patient—and without her fabulous instincts and guidance, paradise would be but a dream for me.

The incredibly supportive, encouraging, and talented Random House team gets an entire island. Starting with Irwyn Applebaum and rocketing through the whole organization, these men and women have patiently guided me and my career through the often-treacherous literary waters of the world and without them I am nothing.

My dutiful agent, Ellen Geiger, is always my champion and her exhaustive work on my behalf has truly turned my writing world into paradise times twelve.

Dr. Rose Kumar is not only a wonderful friend, but her medical expertise was of great value when researching parts of this book. I owe equal thanks to comrade Lynn Vannucci for geographical consultation and her wine expertise.

Trish Washburn and Amy Siewert were invaluable athletic companions and supporters on this leg of my search for paradise. Their professional knowledge was not only an inspiration for parts of this book, but in my personal life as well.

A huge debt of gratitude to Lake Country Cigars and Mary Lynn Smith Kane, president and newly elected queen of Cigar Babes, for bringing me into the fold and educating me on all things cigar.

The women of The Radish Room—supporters, friends, and fans—are part of my paradise as is Madonna Metcalf, all the women who share their intimate stories with me, my beloved booksellers, and every reader who shares my passion.

ONE
Addy hits the wall . . .

Addy Lipton has been nurturing a wild desire for a good twenty-two months to drive her 1988 dark blue Toyota Corolla right through the closed garage door of the lovely two-story white brick and cedar home she shares with a man she vaguely remembers marrying a very long time ago.

The Toyota has not been inside of the garage since 1992, and the last time she opened the kitchen door leading into the garage and stepped inside of what she now calls The Kingdom of Krap was just days before her milestone fiftieth birthday and very close to two years ago. Addy had opened the door to set a bottle of wine in the cool garage so it would chill before her sister showed up to help her celebrate. She placed it next to the bag of dog food left over from Barney the black lab (who had passed without a doubt into doggie heaven in 2001), and then dared to look into the bowels of the garage where she had not bothered to gaze for a very long time.

"What the hell," she said out loud as she raised her eyes and wondered if she had suddenly been transported to a used-appliance store.

The garage, totally her husband Lucky's disgusting domain, was filled to high tide with partially dismantled refrigerators, washing machines, dryers, microwaves, and various other machines that must have been something workable at one time when they could actually be plugged in and turned on.

"Lucky, Lucky, Lucky," she said through a jaw that was as tight as a rusted dishwasher bolt, scanning past the machines and having **a moment.** A moment of desperation, wonderment, tepid fury, and astonishment at what not only her assumed half of the garage but also her entire life in halves and quarters and eighths and sixteenths had become.

"A garage stuffed with crap that my husband will use with his goofyass friends, not to fix, but to spread across each other's lawns like teenagers," Addy told herself, turning slightly in the kitchen doorway to see two piles of old bowling balls, a stack of wire coat hangers, a lawnmower that she knew for a fact did not mow, and the back end of a 1951 Chevy that Lucky had been working on since he found its decaying hulk sticking out of his uncle's old shed and dragged it home when their son was a baby. Nineteen years. The car had not moved, or turned over, or gravitated to the local antique car parade, in nineteen years.

Addy reached over and picked up the wine bottle. She told herself that she would not now wait for her sister, that she would open the bottle immediately and drink it warm. Warm like everything else in her life. Nothing hot or cold or spicy but every damn thing seeming to sit right in the middle as if waiting for something, someone, anything to push it off to one side.

Later, after that bottle was empty and her sister Helen—Hell, as she was aptly nick-

named—stole her away for a birthday dinner where Lucky managed to show up on
time, after she was back home, Addy could
not stop thinking about the damn garage,
which as a birthday gift to herself she began
calling The Kingdom of Krap.

And the garage drove her crazy with wondering.

Wondering what else might be stored
behind ragged cardboard boxes and the as-
sorted stacks of junk Lucky and his ridiculous friends scavenged from behind stores
and each other's garbage piles.

Wondering how a section of the house
and her life had gotten so out of control.

Wondering what would happen if Lucky
spent half as much time with her as he did
with his obsessive collecting and make-
believe restoration projects.

Wondering why she was somehow con-
tent to sit and simply observe as her marriage seemed to drift off to a place where she
could barely see the outlines of what it used
to be.

Wondering what happened to the sensitive, romantic, often wild and terribly lively

man she had fallen in love with when he'd swept her off her feet and into his strong and stunningly passionate arms.

Wondering if she was really prepared to spend the next thirty years lurking at the edge of her garage, and her life, if the family genes held up and she made it that far.

And that's when she started wondering what it might feel like to drive the car right through the door.

She imagined it first as an accident. Something that she did as she bent down to the back seat to grab the papers and books and piles of third-grade projects that she needed to examine for school the following day. Addy would close her eyes during recess duty or a staff meeting and see herself reaching backwards just as her foot slipped off the brake and hit the gas pedal while the car was in first gear.

The car would lurch forward like a large stone that had been pried loose after much pushing. It would jump just as she turned to see the front end of the little Toyota crash an inch below the handle in the middle of the garage door. And then she would see the old

Chevy buckle, the dishwashers spread as if Moses were driving the car, and coat hangers fly like thin birds who have just spotted a large dog at the side of the house.

Sometimes this vision got her through a particularly tough day. One of those days when a sick third grader would vomit first on himself, then on the girl in front of him, and then, on the way out the door, on Addy. A day when the principal would drag a mother into the room who didn't like a comment on a paper composed by one of Addy's students, a paper that was obviously written by the mother, who had forgotten that third graders do not usually know how to spell words that she herself had to look up in the dictionary. A day when Addy's son might call her from his college dorm room and whine about money, or the pressures of his measly part-time job, or the fact that his mother would not give him five hundred dollars to go on a spring break trip to Florida so he could drink cheap booze until his brain pickled.

More times than she cared to remember, Addy had actually edged the car inch by inch up the driveway until she felt the front bumper touch the garage door. She'd put the car in neutral and then imagine the whole scene all over again—flying pieces of the wooden door diving past her window, rocketing wedges of metal, years of precious scavenging being pummeled by the foreign car Lucky sold parts for as part of his job but hated to recognize as a superior model.

But she never did it.

She never did more than nudge the door. Never bothered to tell Lucky she had harbored an overwhelming desire to flatten his hobbies, his haven, his krappy land of fun and freedom. Never told her sister, never mentioned it during the after-work pizza-and-beer gatherings, never told her friends at the YWCA, never asked her son Mitchell what he thought of the garage, never did more than think—just think—about ramming her car from the edge of her world right into the center of her husband's.

Until today.

It is April 1 in Parker, Pennsylvania, and everywhere else on Addy's side of the international date line, and Addy thinks that if

she did it today she would have an excuse.
She would plow through the door in second
gear, which she has also imagined during the
past twenty-two months, and try hard to
make it through the krap and straight
through into the backyard. She could blame
it on the date. "I was just going to dent it a
little and say April Fool's," she'd tell Lucky.
Lucky, she imagined, would either laugh or
rush to check on the fate of his favorite
bowling ball.

There is also the menopause excuse,
which would be a lie because she is dancing
lightly on the brim of menopause—that
joints-aching, two-periods-in-one-month,
fifteen-extra-pounds-last-year, occasionally-
crying-when-she-looks-at-Mitchell's-baby-
photos place—but not in real menopause,
which of course, would be all of the above
times one thousand. She is thinking of saying it had been a hot flash or a fast-beating
heart or the ridiculous urge to shift with her
elbow instead of her hand. Lucky, she knew,
was terrified of the word "menopause" and
so to simply say it out loud might just be

enough to throw him into an instant state of forgiveness.

It is 6:48 p.m. and Addy has plunged into the place of wanting so badly that she has her hand on the gearshift and her mind set on ramming through the door. Addy is exhausted from the pre–spring break tests, from her college son's absent but seemingly ever-present presence, from a marriage that has not so suddenly turned into something that feels and looks and tastes more like a business partnership than a union of two people in love and lust forever and ever.

Sitting in the car, with the tires hovering over the long cracks in the asphalt driveway, Addy this very moment wants lots of things.

She wants to ride a pony and to sleep in.

She wants to do tequila shots with her sister. In Mexico.

She wants to spend the rest of Mitchell's college money on a total house makeover.

She wants to make people laugh—really, really hard and for a very long time.

She wants to go to Italy before she needs to wear trifocals, which is one focal away.

She wants Lucky to initiate a conversation that has nothing to do with "stuff" and everything to do with "them."

She wants to come home, swing open the garage door, and be able to pull her car inside.

She wants to lie in bed naked with all the magazines and books and television clickers on the floor and talk, just talk, with Lucky, only Lucky, for hours and hours and hours.

Addy has one hand on the steering wheel and the other on the gearshift and the car is in first gear. She is trying to decide if she should back up so she can start the garage-door-bashing procedure from the back side of the curb or from where she is right this moment. Her mind is as light as a third-grade song. She pauses to place her right hand over her heart because she is surprised she is so calm, so ready, so eager, and when she feels her heart beating softly, true, regular, and as it always has, she decides that she would like to back up about twenty-five feet, shift into second, and then hit the door with a fresh burst of speed.

She turns her head to make certain some

unseen object has not bounced into the driveway while she has been idling at the lip of her decision. As Addy turns, she feels the smooth seat next to her under her right hand, notices the last glow of an early spring sunset between the two houses at the end of the cul-de-sac, thinks that her training class at the Y is paying off because her neck no longer aches when she turns sideways, and then as she is backing down she stops at the back end of the basketball hoop, which is halfway down the driveway.

Addy revs the Toyota. She takes in a huge breath—a nearly forgotten calming technique she learned in a yoga class long ago— and she closes her eyes.

Closes her eyes to remember the moment, the months of imagining, the abyss she must now cross to take her someplace, anyplace, through the broad barriers of a life that is a garage, a receptacle for dumpage and stagnation, and just as she raises her head and shifts, Lucky is there.

Lucky Lucky.

His head is dipping toward her as if it is a ball that has just passed through the bottom of the ragged edges of the almost-abandoned basketball net.

Addy can feel her heart bounce from her chest, crash through the windshield, and slam against the very garage door that she had hoped to have pushed forever apart—now.

"Jesus, Addy, I've been waiting for you for like an hour," Lucky shouts, pulling open her door.

"What?" she asks him, unable to move, wondering already when she'll be able to drive through the door, now that her plan has been interrupted.

"Honey, you are not going to believe this."

"Try me."

"Ready?"

"Yes!" Addy yells. **"Yes!"**

"We're going to Costa Rica."

"What?"

"I won the company sales incentive prize."

"You're kidding!"

"No. Costa Rica. Do you teach that in third grade?"

Addy slowly shifts the car into park. She

sets the brake, turns the key into the off position. Then she shuts off the headlights and swings her legs out of the car right in between Lucky's legs.

"Yes," she says, as she gets up and follows Lucky into the house. "We study Costa Rica."

And as she passes the garage door she touches it lightly like lovers would touch when they don't want anyone else to see.

TWO
What I should have said to Addy · · ·

Man oh man. I practiced for like an hour on how to tell her about the trip but then when the car pulled up and I saw her just sitting there, doing who the hell knows what women do when they sit in a car and stare, I lost it.

"Lucky," she would have said if I had told her that the thought just disappeared into some black hole behind my eyebrows, which she has been after me to trim for God's sake, men in Parker do not trim their eyebrows, "write it down."

But I didn't.

Now, I remember when it's too late, which is pretty much how my system has been running for a while now.

"Honey," I wanted to say, "I never told you this because I wanted it to be a surprise, but some of those nights when you thought I was out farting around I was working the phones in my office because I wanted to win this trip . . . for you."

There was more.

I wanted to see her walking down the beach in her bathing suit and then I wanted us to have one of those dinners right in the sand by the water for just two people with champagne and I'd watch her read for about five hundred hours in a row by the pool, because she'd rather read than eat, but I got so excited when she pulled up and then impatient, which is another one of my many life curses, and I just ran outside.

And what I should have said to Addy disappeared.

THREE
The smokescream of life · · ·

Addy will pretty much smoke anything. She's breezed through Newports, Kents, gone through a Lucky Strike phase, done the same with Salems and Camels and occasionally lets herself feel exotic by inhaling a pack of international full-flavor Dunhills, which are lovingly made by the British American Tobacco Company. These fabulous babies she lights with an exquisite and very expensive black-and-silver butane lighter that makes her weekday Bic look like a lost shoe in the gutter outside of Kmart.

Behind the Lipton house, in the shadows of a small grove of very tall, very old, and very secluded pine trees, Addy is savoring a Dunhill from the secret stash that rotates from her underwear drawer, to her purse, to a metal box she keeps nested in the thick needles of the tree that she must crawl to and from on her hands and knees because the branches are so thick and so heavy and so wonderfully able to camouflage her secret smoking habit.

And it really **is** a secret.

Addy has concocted a remarkably detailed smoking plan that includes breath spray, clothes that go directly into the washing machine if she smokes on a windy day or rips into her tobacco desire like a starving cat and has two cigarettes in a row. She occasionally smokes cigars, which she is quickly developing a wild and sultry taste for, at her beloved sister Hell's very popular wine and cigar bar, The First National Wine & Cigar Bar, aptly named after the city's first bank which Hell restored and transformed into a destination so unique it has been on the cover of **Midwest Living** magazine. The bar is one of two hot spots in Parker's not-so-lively downtown, the other being Johnson's Bowling Palace—Lucky and the Bobs' favorite hangout, but it's the cigarettes—one pack a month if she's on a roll—that are her most secret and very treasured addiction.

Screw the studies, she tells herself each time she enjoys a cigarette, even if she has been lifting weights and swimming at the Y just hours before her stolen smoke, **this is one thing for me, just me.**

One thing in the sea of schedules and giving and always being there that she has taped to the inside of her arm right where someone else might paste one of those damn nicotine patches so they can quit smoking. Addy thinks of quitting many things but smoking is never on her list.

Costa Rica is what she needs to smoke through her veins while she leans into the stash-box tree and adjusts her glasses. Costa Rica, which fell from a passing plane just as she was to create a lovely insurance claim. Costa Rica, which is a paradise that could make this backyard oasis seem like a slush pond in comparison. Costa Rica, which Lucky managed to pull out of his rear end when Addy was poised to ram her reliable car right into that very region of his anatomy.

The Dunhill is an elegant whiff of a place

Addy imagines every time she indulges in its taste. When she takes her first puff, when the smoke moves from her throat, into her lungs, and rams nicotine into her blood vessels like a side-street jackhammer, she thinks she can hear the ocean rolling against the rocks just outside of the window at the villa where she imagines she will spend ten glorious days with Lucky.

Ten days. She takes another puff and refuses to open her eyes.

"Ten days," she says, swallowing the words with the smoke. "Oh my God."

Addy can feel the Latin American sun burning a lively line of red across her winter-white skin that will be the color of pigeon feathers when she first lies on the beach with Lucky in three weeks. She can smell fresh fish sizzling at the open-air barbecue as she fingers a very long toothpick that has slices of pineapple, mango, and banana on it and that was placed gently into her piña colada by a waiter who looks as if he is in training for the Costa Rican bobsled team.

There will be a boat trip off the coast that will land them on a secluded island for a basket lunch where they will drink champagne and then snorkel in sapphire-blue water as they drift in and out of coral caves, and into a cove where they will slowly float into shore and lie side by side on the hot sand, kiss, and then throw off their snorkel gear and run into the jungle where Lucky will make love to her as if they had been deliberately saving their sexual energy for months and months for just that moment.

The pine tree sways a bit after this thought and Addy opens her eyes and tries to remember when she last made love to Lucky, and then, very quickly, when she last wanted to make love to Lucky.

This is definitely a second-cigarette thought. The dwindling Dunhill supply be damned. Addy reaches beside her to open the cigarette treasure chest and hurriedly lights another Dunhill, which she knows will make her light-headed and giddy and maybe a bit loose lipped. After four drags, and only after four drags, can she admit that it has been too long to remember. Too long to remember the last time she wanted to throw Lucky down where he was standing and melt into him as he melted into her.

Costa Rica may be the smash into life that she needs. Costa Rica, where the fires of her love for Lucky may—please, please, please— be rekindled. A trip to Costa Rica. A journey to paradise. An unexpected adventure, moments of time to talk, to sort through a mess of years that have piled up against her heart so that it is difficult, so difficult, to feel anything but the dull clatter of days turning into weeks, turning into months, turning into years, years that have lost the seductive and sometimes necessary scent of coconuts mixed with lime.

And without giving herself time to turn back from the lifeline of the simple thought that Costa Rica is now the garage door, Addy smokes the rest of the Dunhill with her head resting against the one place on the tree that has a bare spot without branches. She smokes and tries very, very hard not to think, but to just be still for as long as it takes her to suck the cigarette down to the filter, wishing, because it tastes so damn good, that she could eat it.

She finishes, rips the stub of the butt into pieces, and places them inside a plastic bag that she has in her pocket, puts the container back into the arm of the cigarette branch, crawls out of the tree nest, and dashes to the back of the house.

She's also laughing.

Laughing at the absurdity of what she has done, as she laughs almost every time she leaps from the brush with her cigarette breath. Laughing at what she must look like, although it would be fairly impossible for anyone to see her. Laughing at how much fun it is to sneak into the woods in her fifties to cop a smoke, be alone, smell some pine needles, and not be a part of the rest of her world for just a few minutes.

Laughing because when all else fails, Addy has that. She has the sound of her own voice jumping up and down inside of her like an internal caress. Addy can feel the wave of laughter's hands sliding from one end of her body to the next. It's a wave that starts in her throat, passes through her heart, where it self-charges for the descent down her legs, and then back up the other side where it touches her heart once again.

Even with Costa Rica dangling on a tiny mental string in front of her, Addy knows that she may need more than a laughing exit from the backyard to get through the longing she has to bash the living hell out of the garage door and perhaps out of Lucky himself—trip or no trip. Costa Rica had better **rock**.

Costa Rica had better rock because it is there, through that stretch of days and sand and sun, where Addy hopes to peel back the layer of years and find the man who used to stay up until 3 a.m. to talk with her, the man who left her a note every morning on the counter next to his rinsed-out coffee cup, the man who was surely sensitive and observant and who could always make her laugh and who made her always, just always, feel loved. Where are you, Lucky? Is there any part of that man left?

Lucky is next door at Bob's house. Bob Number One, as Addy calls him. He lives on the left side of their house and at the very center of the cul-de-sac circle and two houses away from Bob Number Two, who lives on the right side of Addy and Lucky's house. As far as Addy can tell, that may be the biggest difference between Bob Number One and Bob Number Two, except that Bobbie One is divorced and very single, and Bobbie Two is married and not able to play as much as Bobbie One.

The Bobs in Lucky's world are known as The Bowling Bobs for a variety of reasons, most of which have something to do with bowling, which is not so much a sport in Parker as an excuse to get together and re-member what it was like when the knees were not shot to hell, when most of the guys had hair, when some of them, including Lucky, were great sports stars, and when the world and all its possibilities, even for the bad boys, was longer than Lane 6 at Johnson's Bowling Palace.

This craving for a place and time long past has also given way to a bowling ball fetish on the cul-de-sac. Heaven forbid that the crav-ing for something from the past has anything to do with fortifying a relationship, spicing up a marriage, or romancing a woman you profess to love. The Bobs and Lucky instead collect bowling balls. They keep them, of course, in the Lipton Krap Kingdom, and once or twice a year they erect a bowling ball collage in someone's yard.

The first time Addy saw one of the masterpieces was when she dropped off some teacher evaluation forms at her principal's house and saw the very stack of bowling balls that she had noticed three days before piled in the back of Lucky's truck.

Addy got out of her car very slowly and, without grabbing the pile of forms, walked solemnly toward a structure that looked, even from the curb, like a replica of the Gateway Arch in St. Louis, Missouri. She noticed a bright red ball at the top that she knew for certain Lucky had traded Mitchell's old aquarium for, and she was astonished at the placement of the balls, the way they were strung together with pieces of colored wire and what must be some pretty strong glue, and how the structure looked, well, like the Gateway Arch in St. Louis.

"Like it?" the principal's husband said,

suddenly coming up from behind her and making her almost jump through the arch.

"It's kind of amazing," she said, hoping he wouldn't ask her if she knew anything about it.

"Lucky did it," he said flatly. "I'm sure the Bowling Bobs and a couple of the other guys were in on it, too. My team beat them last week and the week before to knock them out of the semifinals."

"I think you're right," she admitted. "Some pieces of the arch were in Lucky's truck recently. Are you mad?"

He laughed long and hard and told her that he was going to leave the arch right where it was, and he did, and so did the four other guys who had thus far been on the receiving end of the bowling ball sculptures, usually after a bet or an important game was lost or to settle an old or new controversy centering around a useless fact. The statues were not only becoming part of the scenery of Parker, Pennsylvania, they were also starting to become prestigious, which not only startled Addy, but made her wonder if someone was putting something in the city water supply to make the male population go nuts.

Would there be bowling balls in Costa Rica? Addy wonders as she washes her face and hands, sprays some Happy on her neck where smoke may have settled, and picks up the Costa Rica brochures, the plane tickets, and the trip voucher, just to make certain that she is not dreaming, that paradise really is just a few weeks away.

Before Addy can focus, before she can pummel herself with any more garage door questions or uncertainty about the trip, she hears the familiar whine of her sister's Jeep pulling into the driveway, the slam of the car door, the knock that really isn't a knock but a breath of activity before Hell pushes right through Addy's door.

"Baby, are you here?" her sister yells, moving toward the kitchen where Addy is sitting in front of her Costa Rica brochures.

"In here," Addy yells back.

"Let me pee first. I've been cleaning out the cooler all afternoon."

Hell is a vision no matter when she shows

up, which is pretty much at any given moment, every day. The lively receiver of the
family's tall genes, naturally wavy hair, fear-
less attitude, and successful business sense,
she's never married but come close so many
times Addy has made enough money selling
Hell's used almost-wedding gowns to pay for
Mitchell's first year of college tuition at the
University of Wisconsin–Madison. Hell,
who richly deserves her nickname, has a
knack for wildness, for drawing men and
women and unsuspecting children into her
raucous web of a life that Addy simply surrendered to her a long time ago.

The only thing uncertain about Hell is
which pair of cowboy boots, wildly hand-
decorated blazer, boldly low-cut blouse, and
jeans she will be wearing. She has hundreds
to choose from—minus whatever her yellow
Lab and cocker spaniel chew up while she's
out running the world.

"You are not going to believe what happened," Addy says, barely raising her voice
because she knows Hell never closes the
bathroom door.

"Are you pregnant?" Hell asks, laughing before she even finishes her sentence.

"Ha-ha," Addy mocks. "Not yet. But maybe after I get to Costa Rica I will be."

Hell comes running before she pulls up her pants and finishes dressing while she stands in front of Addy. "Talk. Now. Fast."

"Lucky won the winter sales trip and we are going to Costa Rica next month for ten days."

"Holy shit."

"I almost did shit when he told me."

Addy is tempted to let go and tell her about the garage door, but this is one thing, about the only thing, plus the cigarettes, she has decided to keep from Hell, her female soul sister, the only person in the whole world who has always been there for her, someone she loves even when she's an obtrusive pain in the rear end.

"Jesus, all those years at Cooper Auto Systems and he finally does it," Hell says in amazement. "Addy, how do you feel about this?"

Hell knows that Addy has crossed over

the danger line in her marriage. It's a line that is not even visible during the first few years after a marriage, when everyone's tragic flaws are still considered lovely and delightful. The line slowly comes into view only after that, especially if there is a baby, which is exactly what happened with Lucky and Addy. Couples, Hell and Addy have decided, can either start running in the opposite direction from the line or tauten it as they play with the speed of their own relationship. Addy did a little of both, occasionally trying to pep up a marriage that wasn't horrible but wasn't much of anything else either and then running as fast as possible so she could straddle the line, stay on or totally get off the line of marriage demarcation. The Lipton Line has been the heart and soul of almost every serious conversation Addy and Hell have had for the past year. It was the beginning, and often middle and end, of every conversation they have had for three years before that.

"Do you love him?" Hell has asked Addy about three thousand times.

First the answer was "yes" and then it was "sort of" and then it had floated into an "I don't know any longer" stage that was compressed and nourished by Lucky's seeming indifference to what had once been something that could be called a real relationship. He worked, he played with the boys, he spent hours watching local soccer teams and sideline coaching as a way to compensate for the career-ending injury that cost him a college scholarship and a hefty portion of his male ego. Lucky seemed, to Addy, to always be drifting at the edge of his married life, occasionally looking over his shoulder to make certain it was still standing, and then simply ignoring the Lipton Line altogether. But a small part of Addy could not let go of her early and now very old marriage memories of when they talked and played and laughed and loved as if they were the only two people who had ever done such things.

"Well?" Hell demanded, fingering the brochures.

"Maybe this is just what we need," Addy admitted. She avoided a definite yes-or-no answer. "Maybe this chunk of time together and an exotic location and no distractions is just the perfect remedy."

"What if it's not?"

Addy was afraid to think of the **not** part. A piece of her was just as terrified about going as not going.

"We've been married a really long time," Addy said, lightly moving her fingers over a photograph in the travel brochure that showed a man and woman holding hands and walking on the beach. "Don't you think I'd be nuts not to go? It's like an unexpected gift that shows up, a backed-up sewer at the school that gives us all a day off, or you buying me three glasses of wine in a row because I helped clean your bathroom at the wine bar."

"That sounds a bit pimpy, baby."

"Pimpy?"

"Yeah. Like the only reason you are going is because it's free and it's exotic. What if you have to put out?"

"That's not nice," Addy says, throwing a fake punch. "It may be true, but it's still not nice."

By 10 p.m. when Hell needs to swing back and help get her business closed up, because she's training a new part-time manager, Addy has convinced herself, with more than a little help from her sister, that if she's going to go on this trip to paradise, it's going to be the trip of a lifetime. She's going to do some research, plan some side trips, and focus on erasing every notion she has about Lucky that falls into the "dislike" category.

"Lucky is only a big ape about half the time," Hell tells her. "When I come back, let's go through your wedding pictures and stuff. That will help you get all cranked up for the trip."

"Cranked up or embarrassed," Addy says, hugging Hell goodbye. "Oh well—at the very least I may get tan in Costa Rica. Right now I sort of glow in the dark."

"This weekend we are going to drive into Pittsburgh and get you some sexy clothes for the trip," Hell commands. "We'll also put on suntan lotion before we go. The smell of that stuff is enough to get anyone in the mood for the tropics."

The suntan lotion, Addy thinks as she

watches Hell leave, **may have to be swallowed whole for me to believe this trip,
ten entire days, is going to be the magic
potion for a marriage that needs to be
dipped into an entire vat of lotion.**

FOUR
Yes or no to love . . .

Abs afternoon at the YWCA is a refined version of living hell that makes Addy and her fellow penitents want to drink whiskey straight out of the bottle, swear off sweet rolls for the rest of their lives, and question their very existence.

The ninety-minute twice-a-week Life Training class is an experiment that has actually toned and changed more than a few of the limbs and lives in the five-member first-time class that aimed its trial run at midlife women who "want to get **it** back." The real prize, for the group, which has taken to calling themselves the Sweat-Hers, is the thirty-minute free hot-tub time they get, uninterrupted and secluded, at the end of each grueling session.

Getting **it** back has been a wicked but determined uphill climb for Addy, Hell, and
three other brave Parkerites who could commit to a late-afternoon session for six
months. Three months into the plan of pain
and ten minutes into the mega-queen-sized
hot-tub session following abs hell and the
Sweat-Hers are sitting with their legs criss-
crossed and have already launched into what
has become a no-holds-barred twice-weekly
therapy session that never leaves the room.

Heidi, who hates her name and her job;
Debra, who is an excruciatingly happy
mother of four; and Lee, who is so ambiva-
lent about every aspect of her twice-divorced
status that she could float from one side of
the large hot tub to the next for the rest of
her life, are weighing in with Hell on Addy's
Costa Rican adventure as they simultaneously moan with exaggerated pleasure.

"If you don't want to go, I'll go," Lee tells
Addy. "The most exciting thing in my life is
working on the community festival, which
doesn't happen for five months."

"Christ, we'd all go," Heidi adds. "April in

Pennsylvania is about as much fun as the last twenty-five minutes of this damn class."

"I'm going, I'm going already," Addy groans, lying back against the side of the tub so she doesn't have to look anyone in the eye.

"But . . ." Hell adds for her sister and then waits for Addy to finish the sentence.

"Come on, Addy," Debra says. "All you've talked about for weeks is how stale your marriage has become and how you wonder if it's even worth it anymore. And now you have this, this what—trip, adventure, romantic chance of a lifetime—so what's the **but** all about?"

Addy wonders what it would be like to slip under the water and come up in about three months. Would anything have changed? Would Lee, or Debra, or for God's sake even Hell, have gone on the trip in her place and would Lucky have even noticed? Would Mitchell saunter home during his semester hiatus, throw his laundry into about twelve baskets, start phoning all his high school friends, eat everything he could find, borrow money out of the jar behind the stacked noodles, and even notice she was gone? Would all the teachers who count on her to say something hilarious during a particularly tense moment in labor negotiations or during the biweekly "You all stink" lectures by the new and much-loathed school district superintendent, wonder what had happened to her? Would the Bobs and Lucky himself begin looking for her because it was almost time for her to help order food for the end-of-the-season bowling party and get the teams organized for the spring soccer leagues that no one but Addy seems to be able to align and manage and put down onto a piece of paper? And who would bother to design yet another over-the-top bridal shower for all the young, so very young, new teachers who were getting engaged in droves so they could have a wedding before summer was over because they didn't have enough tenure to take time off during the regular school year?

Who? Who? Who? echoes through Addy's ears as if an owl had flown into the soaking room and landed on her face.

"Earth to Addy!" Hell shouts, which totally startles the owl and any thought Addy has of flying away herself.

"What?" Addy questions, trying to play dumb.

"The trip, Lucky, your wavering heart. What say ye?" Heidi asks and then quickly adds, "Oh, by the way, I'm thinking I may change my name to Dakota. What do you all think?"

"Are you frigging crazy?" Hell's voice is just a notch below a bellow. "Why would you want to have the word 'Dakota' near you? People might think about South Dakota, land of women-hating, ancient white men who try and enact laws that are a throwback to the last century; it's the anti-choice capital of the world. What are you thinking, Heidi?"

Addy is so relieved by the temporary distraction that she is smiling as the conversation begins to rage about everything but Costa Rica.

"Well," Heidi says slowly, " 'Dakota' is supposed to mean 'friend.' I was just thinking of that. 'Heidi' always makes me want to put on a long skirt and go find Julie Andrews and the von Trapp family."

The Sweat-Hers have heard how much Heidi hates her name almost every time they have met, and they've been through a gaggle of would-be names and also the tough-love discussion that prodded Heidi to go, for the love of God, and change her name already—if only she could pick one.

"Malibu is the new funky name," Debra shared. "If I have another baby I was thinking that it would be Natalie or Ashlie or Brandie or some other 'ie' name out there. You kind of look like a Malibu, sweetie, especially now that you are all red and everything from exercise and this boiling water."

Addy is now so distracted from Costa Rica and Lucky that she is thinking that her exercise group, which she realizes has morphed into a huge counseling session usually run by Hell, would be a hilarious baby boomer sitcom. Before she can decide which actress would play Ms. Heidi Malibu, already knowing that Sharon Stone and Hell are perfect for each other, Hell manages to swing the name game back to her.

"Addy, you are like three questions behind," Hell says, pushing against her with the entire right side of her body.

"Did I ever tell you how Lucky got his name?" Addy asks, trying hard to stay away from any answers.

"Eighty or ninety times," Lee says. "His name is Harvey, his mother liked it, father hated it, and his mother said, 'You're lucky the baby doesn't look like you,' and so his father never once called Harvey Harvey and they never had another baby and Lucky was called Lucky and then he was truly lucky all of the time."

Lee could go on. She could tell the story Addy has shared about the time Lucky fell out of a three-story window and didn't get so much as a bruise, or the time he scored the winning goal in soccer six games in a row, or how he literally stumbled into Addy's lap at the university the very day he dropped out, or how he walked into the auto parts store on his very slow drive home that same day and they hired him on the spot for a position that to this hour he absolutely loves because he gets to talk about, and occasionally play with, car parts.

"All right," Addy finally says, knowing it's impossible to not only disappear under the water but also hide the truth from these women who know her as well as she knows them. "The truth is that I'm going and that I mostly feel as if it might be a chance to give Lucky my all. But the other part of the truth is that a part of me really wants to just send him off by himself."

Everyone is quiet. Lee, who has vowed to never marry a man, woman, dog, or anything breathing again, knows how Addy feels, how she is straddling that line of long-term marriage and how a soft spring breeze could push her either way. Debra, who occasionally feels as if she's found the last decent man on the face of the earth, wants the whole world to be as happy as she is and she thinks Addy has to try, she just has to try to get back what she once had. Heidi, who has just decided she will be Malibu for a week and see how it feels, thinks at this point that anything is better than nothing, and Hell, Ms. Hell would throw herself in front of the next beer truck making a delivery to her bar if she thought it would help her only sister, her only sibling, the only person who has loved her without question, never doubted her abilities, or pushed her to make a decision that she is not yet ready to make.

"So?" the four women say almost at once, leaning in to form a very close circle around Addy.

Addy, who tells them she thinks she is unattractive and has the most beautiful dark blue eyes they have ever seen. Addy, who imagines herself as a sort-of-simple elementary school teacher and yet has taken the hardest hearts, the meanest souls, the lost minds of dozens and dozens of students and turned them into little geniuses. Addy, who considers her one attempt at motherhood a semi-failure and who has a son who not only made the dean's list his first semester at college and, yes, the drinking-ticket list as well, and who may be uncertain about his educational future, but who is a young man with a heart of gold and a talent he is very close to discovering. Addy, who is always there first when someone needs anything, who looks a bit like Carol Burnett, and who, when she tells a joke, does it very well, and who they now think may need a dose of "Remember when Lucky was . . ." to get her excitement level cranked up not only about the trip but about Lucky too.

"Are you lying just a little bit about not wanting Lucky to go along?" Hell asks her.

"No, I'm **totally** lying," Addy lied, which makes them all laugh.

"Seriously," Hell asks again.

Addy reassures them that the more she thinks about the trip, the more excited she gets. She tells them that Lucky has already yanked out two suitcases from some secret spot in his garden garage that seems to grow whatever he needs whenever he needs it. He's even driven the Costa Rica brochures all over town and showed them to everyone but the six people at the nursing home who were asleep when he stopped by.

"We want you to tell us some nice Lucky stories to help you get ready for the trip," Malibu Heidi suggests. "It's what I do when my own Prince Charming reminds me of something just this side of road kill. I try really hard to remember something good and exciting and wonderful about him that perhaps has slipped away."

"Aren't you a sweetheart," Lee says, patting Malibu on the head.

Addy has already tried this so she's ready to go before Debra and Hell begin comparing men to foreign objects, heated missiles, or strange pieces of excess and discarded scrap metal. She's never really thought of Lucky that way. Other ways, no problem, but he ain't really junk or a throwaway.

He's just Lucky.

He's just occasionally around.

He's just on the other side of the bed.

He's just a distracted auto parts sales manager.

He's just addicted to soccer games.

He's just a fifty-three-year-old man who still likes to play with the boys.

Lucky, she tells her friends, has never really been mean or snarly. He's just sort of disappeared from the important parts of her life.

"When we were younger, for several years anyway, we always had a date night. When Mitchell was little, sometimes that meant just standing in the backyard for a few minutes and holding hands and talking," she tells them as everyone scoots back and lets their legs and arms drift back and forth in the water. "What I miss the most, I think, is the talking. Lucky used to be my friend and now . . . well, he's not really even that."

Every single woman takes in a huge breath. Each knows exactly how Addy feels, even Debra, who admits that her husband occasionally wanders off and she has to pull him back in to reclaim the good parts of their relationship.

"I'm tired," Addy admits. "Sometimes I think I should have backed out of this arrangement a long time ago."

"We all feel that way once in a while," Malibu Heidi says.

"I feel that way most of the time," Addy confesses to her friends, leaning in to wrap her arms around her knees. "If it wasn't for this trip maybe I would have done it."

"It," Hell repeats. "It being the big D?"

"Maybe a little S first," Addy says. "Time apart to see if it matters or if anything at all changes."

"Which, as some of us know from previous experience, almost always leads to the big D," Lee adds.

"Holy mackerel," Debra says softly. "This is something, Addy. Have you ever said this out loud before?"

"Have I?" Addy asks Hell, who thinks she herself could have been divorced four times already if she'd gone through with any of the weddings. She knows for certain the engagements and proposals could throw her way off the scale and into some kind of record book.

"Kind of, especially the past few months, especially when we have the two-for-one wine-tasting special," Hell tells her. "You get a little—well, as the guys would say, ballsy. You start talking about living alone. About buying one of those new condos and being able to do things like park the car in your garage."

"Well," Addy says, holding out her hand. "There you have it. I guess I have."

"But really, though, have you, like, mentioned it to Lucky or anything like that?" Debra presses. "Have you actually had a conversation with him where you said the word 'divorce' or 'separation'?"

Addy shakes her head and longs to dive under the water again. She's been hoping since they slipped into the steaming water that no one would ask her the question she knows is coming next. But there it is, rising like a submarine coming up for air in the middle of their private hot tub.

"Do you love Lucky?" Lee asks.

And the water suddenly feels cold, time stops. There are claws of steel wrapping themselves around Addy's neck and then sliding down to tap against her heart. **Hello in there, is anyone home? Addy, can you feel the love?**

Addy looks from one woman to the next in total wonderment at the unlikely sisterhood that launched itself on the premises of a middle-aged get-your-butts-back-in-shape class. The chance that she would be sitting in this warm water with the lovely budding rippled muscles of four women—three of whom she had never before even seen—let alone sharing intimate details of her life, her marriage, the very core of herself is as astonishing as the fact that she had just told them she has thought of severing her legal and personal and social attachments to a man she once loved so much she'd crawled over a roof so she could sleep with him on a night when the dorm was locked.

"The question seems simple when you ask it, I bet, doesn't it," Addy replies, not as a question but like something she knows for sure and is simply repeating out loud. "But this is what I see now."

And she tells them.

She tells them that she sees years and years, twenty-eight altogether, lined up to form a tight circle around her entire life. Addy says that she sees a certain kind of love, the kind that grows like the leg of a baby, until one day the leg is the anchor for a man and that without it the man cannot move.

"Imagine rolling over after sleeping with the same person for almost three decades and then feeling the empty spot but then wondering if the spot had not been empty for a long time anyway," she explains. "There is a missing already there, a missing that I have already accepted and integrated into my life. Maybe nothing would change if that side of the bed was cold."

Love, she says, is so many things. Always loving Lucky will not be impossible because what is impossible is that she will ever **not** love him. But, Addy adds hastily, the kind of love that offers up reams of desire, that makes you sing in the shower, want to miss this very class so that you can see him or just be in the same room . . . no.

No to some.

Yes to others.

To love, then, to love Lucky, depends on what coat love is wearing, how it tilts its head, where it stands when we pick out wine, how many times it forgets to call, where it parks the car, why it is again late, why things that used to matter no longer seem to.

"Lucky is the father of my son. He once stayed up for two days to help me with a project that I told him was the most important thing in my life next to him and

Mitchell," she explains. "When my father died he baked a casserole, for crying out loud. He let my mother cry in his arms, and then he organized one of the most poignant after-funeral parties I have ever been to in my life. But right this second, if you made me say do I love him like I want to love him, I would have to say, no."

No.

And damn it, just damn it, the workout room supervisor comes in and says they have already gone over the time limit by twelve minutes and can they please start leaving now.

Hell jumps out of the warm water and into the real heat just like that. She pushes the towel bin against the door so it won't open from the outside hall and then jumps back into the water.

"You need to try," she tells Addy. "Do you have anything to lose right now?" she asks her. "Love, because I am such a terrific expert, reminds me of a whip."

"A whip?" they all echo.

"Yes. Love depends on how you hold it. Love depends on what you do with it, how you set it down, pick it up, center it. Even when it cracks and everything is perfect, there still might be a way to make it louder, stronger, sharper."

The other women turn to look at Hell as if they have just found out she's been posing nude for the bowling team. Their eyes are wide. They wonder if she may be close to having heatstroke.

"Honey," Addy says, "that was lovely."

"It's a long time, twenty-eight years," Hell says, "which I realize may also be reason enough to dump your load, but this trip . . . What the hell, Addy, it's Costa Rica, and he's taking you and not one of those savage Bobs and I can't help but think, **why not try?**"

Addy leans over to hug her wild-ass sister. When she imagines one of the worst things in her life it is the loss of this, Hell pushing into her skin at every possible moment, and she tells her, "I love you for sure. I may not know who my own husband has become, but you, you I know, and I love."

And then Addy Lipton, wife of Lucky, decides as she rises, surrounded by her best friends in the world, that yes, she will try, she will go, she will throw herself into packing and planning and she will see what the face of love looks like the day she and her husband back out of the driveway and head to Costa Rica.

FIVE
Life is a beach . . .

April 21 is one of those Pennsylvania spring days that make every soul who lives there ask the all-important and very seasonal question . . . **Why in the hell do we live here?** It has snowed for three days in a row. Not big snow, like in the middle of February when the roads close and the power goes out and everyone gets heart attacks shoveling to just this side of eternity, but a softer snow, snow that laughs at the weary residents who desperately need a ricochet of warm days all in a row so they can make it through the last ravages of winter and into the sweet heart of spring.

Addy doesn't care about the tiny snow deposits that have managed to find their way into her smoking fort. She doesn't care that the hose Lucky dragged out a week ago is now frozen in place alongside of the garage like a dead snake. Mitchell has come and gone and she doesn't even care that he has no idea when he will come back home because he's hoping to find a summer job near the university. She doesn't care about the last stack of grades that need to be turned in, because she can do them the night before school starts again after spring break, which is a bit of a misnomer in this part of the world because spring is usually nonexistent.

What she really cares about is how she is going to look in her new one-piece and fairly low-cut black bathing suit that she got from Land's End because you can order a bathing suit from them that doesn't have the legs cut past the top half of your hips so your entire pubic area shows.

She also cares about the ruby-red sleek nightgown, garnished with ribbons of purple lace, she purchased with Hell in Pittsburgh and is about to slip in between her hiking shorts and a couple of T-shirts so she can surprise Lucky, or frighten him, depending on how she looks on the particular night she decides to pull the nightgown out of its hiding place and slip it on.

Slip it on while they are in Costa Rica, which is what Lucky is yelling to her about because they need to leave in less than thirty minutes for the airport and Addy has not yet showered or shoved the last of her holiday equipment into the luggage.

"Honey, are you not even clean yet?" Lucky asks her as he grabs the bag Addy made him pack for himself and the backpack they have stuffed with tiny wine bottles designed by a brilliant company so they will fit into small plastic bags so travelers don't have to buy an expensive drink on the airplane.

"I'm minutes away," Addy explains. "Come back for these two bags in like five minutes and I'll be in the shower."

"Did you see that the shower at the villa is outside?" Lucky asks her as he picks up his bag. His bag, into which Addy peeked and discovered three pairs of underwear, a bathing suit, twelve T-shirts, one ragged polo, deodorant, socks, and a pair of cotton slacks rolled so tightly they could have fit inside of an empty toilet paper roll.

"Yes, I think I could already find my way around the place in the dark, I've looked at their website so many times," she answers, and then adds, "Lucky?"

"Yes, Addy, **what,** and if you don't mind can you hurry when you answer."

"Nothing," she says, dismissing him as she turns to grab the rest of her cosmetics from the bathroom. "It's really nothing. Go ahead."

"Nothing" was going to be a question. Addy was going to ask Lucky if they could talk a lot on the trip like they used to, about what he would say is "stuff." "Stuff" to Addy meaning their marriage, its direction or lack of it, the smokeless cloud of indifference that clings to everything but this trip to Costa Rica, which has seemed to ignite both of them with a sense of excitement and purpose.

But she doesn't.

Instead she does exactly what Lucky wants her to do during the last twenty-three minutes of the time he has allotted for preparation in order to make his carefully constructed transportation time schedule.

Addy thinks about what holds her back from asking while she leans into the mirror trying to decide if makeup is a necessity or a time-eating commodity and then she simply says "Screw it" out loud, goes back into the bedroom to check her suitcase one more time, throws in her cosmetic bag, and returns to the bathroom and gets into the shower, where the hot water dazzles her into physical submission and allows her not to think at all about what she did or didn't do or say to Lucky.

Her husband.

The man she married.

The man she wonders, as she turns her head into a waterfall with streams of water running in every possible direction, if she loves the way she needs to love in order to stay married. The man who was once in the shower with her almost every single time she turned on the water in the bathroom.

About three-quarters of the way through her almost blissful interlude, Addy hears Lucky in the bedroom, knows he is looking around to see if there is anything she has left on the chair or table, and he's double-checking the way she has secured the nonlocking bags, before he leans into the bathroom and shouts, "Rum shots with a view by 3 p.m. if you shake your ass and we leave five minutes early, just in case!"

Jesus, she thinks, **shake** this, **Lucky,** but she hurries anyway. It's Costa Rica, for crying out loud. Paradise. A snowless landscape where wild howler monkeys scream from the trees to protect their territory so they can munch leaves without being disrupted. She knows this from the weeks of research, and plodding through websites, and launching herself into a travel blog or two, and even whispering the word "paradise" out loud during the Y class. Then whispering that magic word again while she walked the halls of her grade school, or when she cooked, or had her evening wine at the National, or drank her coffee on the way to work in the car and pretty much everywhere during the past few weeks. All the weeks since she totally admitted to her sweating friends that she had finally surrendered to the trip Lucky had won by selling more fan belts, transmission parts, engine starters, and electrical booster connections and floor mats than any other sales manager in the entire Cooper Auto Systems national network.

Dripping wet, Addy steps onto the fluffy blue rug outside of the shower. She runs the towel through her hair, and is about to dry off from the neck down, when she hears the back of Lucky's truck cab open, the tailgate slam down, and then a moment when she will later imagine that Lucky has bent over, grabbed a bag in each hand, then tried to straighten up so he can place them in the back of the pickup.

The fall sounds like a small-caliber handgun, but because no one has ever recorded the sound of a grown and large—not obese, just large—six-foot-one 228-pound man falling into the side of a truck, it's impossible to know without looking what has created the noise.

The sound of Lucky's pain is a sniper's shot that lands in Addy's ears just as she is reaching her waist with the towel.

"Jesus. God. Shit. Addy, Addy, Addy, come help me."

The sound of Lucky's pain is a jolt that rockets through Addy as if she has been set on fire in fifteen different places all at once.

She runs without thinking, without breathing, and without one stitch of clothing on her fifty-one-year-old body. Down the steps, around the dining room table, sprinting for the front door, and into the driveway where Lucky is lying with his arms over his head, his legs tucked to one side, sweat streaming down his face as if he were the one who had just been in the shower.

"Addy," Lucky whispers. "Help me, for the love of God, help me."

"What is it?" Addy asks, bending down to place her hands on his face. "Tell me."

"My back."

"Can you move?"

Lucky closes his eyes. Then he opens them and runs them up and down Addy's body.

"Addy, this is not the time for sex."

"What are you talking about, Lucky?"

"You're naked," he moans.

Just as Addy looks down at herself, Bob One comes loping across the yard with a cell phone in his hand and a look of total amazement on his face at what he sees when he skids to a halt behind the truck.

"Oh my gosh," he says, clapping his hands over his eyes. "Am I interrupting something? I heard Lucky scream, I thought . . ."

"Jesus, Bob, call 911, take off your shirt, throw it to me, turn your head, and then run into the house and get me a couple of blankets. Lucky is hurt and I was in the damn shower."

Bob obeys and Lucky hovers for a minute in that horrific state of forceful pain, wicked, inhumane, violent, nauseating, and totally crippling, and then he aches to slide away into the valley of no return so that he can no longer feel the steel blade that has sliced into all of the nerves in the lower half of his body.

He reaches up to pull Addy by Bob's shirtsleeve, and has barely enough energy left to say, "Addy, come here."

Addy leans lower and it is not enough. Lucky pulls her down farther so that she is four inches from his face and she suddenly wonders if Bob Two, on the other side of the driveway, could be looking out the window at her rear end.

"What is it?" she asks Lucky, cupping her hands around his face. "The ambulance is coming, can you hang on, Lucky? It's going to be okay."

"I'm sorry," he mouths.

"It's not your fault."

"Sorry for the trip . . . everything."

"Shhh," Addy says.

"Addy . . ."

"What, Lucky?"

"Can you search for paradise **here** until I'm fixed?"

Addy stops breathing. Her heart swings as if it has been pushed into the eye of a hurricane. It is tossing wildly like a dump truck being whirled through the air when the storm touches land.

"Sure, Lucky," she promises gently, pushing back his hair. "I can do that."

He smiles, drops his hand, closes his eyes, rolls his head to the side and passes out just as Bob tears out of the house, flings a blanket over her backside, and the deafening ambulance siren wails from three streets over, reminding Addy of an Irish wake she once attended that lasted almost as long as a ten-day trip to Central America.

SIX
What I thought
Addy was thinking . . .

I'm on the ground and there she is saving me again and I know she is thinking that I am an ass and a loser and that I probably did this on purpose because I don't want to spend all those days alone with her.

She is thinking that I'd rather be in what she not-so-lovingly calls The Kingdom of Krap and that now, because I'm probably dying, she can blow that part of the house off and build a library and a little greenhouse like she's always wanted.

"Lucky," she is saying to herself. "You rotten pig."

And maybe I am a rotten pig because I knew this was coming. I've felt the twinge for a long time.

She's thinking she hates me.

I know it for sure.

SEVEN
The smoky dead-end valley of tears . . .

The Lipton-and-Bobs cul-de-sac, plus the across-the-street Swensons and the Zeland clan who guard the entrance in lovely split-levels and are semiactive members of the fun and games that occur at the bend of the lively street, is extremely quiet three days after Addy and Lucky were supposed to be lying naked on a deserted beach in a place so far away the people who live there may never have even heard the phrase "cul-de-sac."

"Dead end, you guys," Addy has yelled more than once when the Liptons have been on the receiving end of the local tomfoolery. "We live on a **dead end** and you are all living up to the name with this nonsense."

Nonsense like the sixty-five real estate For

Sale signs that were strategically placed all over the yard (Mitchell took the credit for this one, saying that it was a sign of great status if your yard was hit like theirs was with so many signs from the high school junior league of young male pranksters), a fully inflated and filled king-sized water bed in the huge oak in the yard, a giant wooden rhinoceros that usually sits outside the abandoned art center that looked as if it was urinating as it was propped up against the side of the Krap Kingdom, and about a thousand—make that three thousand—balloons tied together (How long did that take when someone could have been working on world peace and saving the whales?) on Lucky's fiftieth birthday, which was apparently cause for a yard-decorating celebration that lasted for several months.

Addy is sitting behind her house, not in the trees but in plain sight of everyone who would care to look, and she's chain-smoking. She's on her third cigarette following her husband's back surgery, following three hours of real sleep in forty-eight hours, six bowls of tepid soup, fifteen cups of the lemon tea they serve for free in the waiting room of St. Michael's where it's possible she has logged close to twenty miles pacing, one stolen shower after the nurses left and Lucky was still in la-la land, a lovely phone call to Mitchell who promised he would come right home if she needed him even if it meant missing a major psychology exam, and Addy's very loud "DO NOT COME NOW" response, that she quickly followed by the almost forgotten word—"sweetheart"—and so many phone calls, plant deliveries, and guys wanting to visit that Addy finally threw the weight of it all onto Hell who was now giving her a few hours to, well, sit in her backyard and smoke.

"If half of them have seen my ass, my breasts, the entire me naked, it just may be time to smoke in the open," she told herself as she returned to the house three days following the back siege and discovered that her Y friends had not only unpacked the luggage from the doomed Costa Rica trip but had cleaned the house, put some fresh food and beer—thank God—into the fridge, and left her—**her,** not Lucky—a bouquet of roses the size of El Paso with a note that said, **Get back to the hot tub—We are working on Plan B.**

Jesus.

Shit.

What the holy hell.

Plan B.

Perhaps a miracle in the suburbs.

Addy needs a cigarette almost as much as she needs to cry and as she sidles up to the rusty barbecue, where she is using the bottom of the grill for an ashtray, on the tiny patio that Lucky is probably never going to enlarge and enhance now, she thinks that if she keeps smoking she might be able to avoid the crying portion of what she knows she needs to do.

If only there were enough cigarettes.

When the tears do threaten, Addy is on her fifth cigarette and feeling like she may need to lie down or stick her head into the freezer. She's nauseous, frozen stiff, beyond ready for a good meal and for several hours of sleep all in a row uninterrupted by blood-pressure checks, the administration of pain medication, or the hollow whistling sound of her own breath that seems to have filled her up to overflow with more questions, questions Addy knows she cannot now answer.

Addy makes it into the house and almost into bed before she explodes with emotion. For the past three days she has held on to her fear, anger, loss, desperation, and maybe, just maybe a small bit of love so tightly that she has been a controlled mass of shaky strength. She's instructed nurses, called insurance companies, talked to Lucky's boss, and watched close to collapse as Lucky was first moved onto the stretcher—which she followed with Bob One driving as she pulled her clothes on in the back seat and during which Bob, to his credit, did not say a word—then into the ER, where Lucky came to screaming because of the pain and promptly passed out again, through a three-hour tortured hiatus in the family waiting room, which she was more than familiar with because of an assortment of broken and sprained arms, legs, ankles, fingers, toes, and one ruptured appendix each from Lucky and Mitchell who seemed to be as far from grace under fire as possible on the athletic fields and who were so alike she often wondered if Mitchell, who was adopted, had actually been passed magically through a uterus Lucky had all along and never told anyone about, and then into the moments, long, long moments when the doctor took her and Hell, who arrived shortly after Addy got there, into a private room to tell her what might happen next.

"It's two ruptured discs and it looks like mashed potatoes in there," the doctor told her. "I've seen a few backs this bad, but this— Well, it's bad, Addy."

"How bad?" Addy asked while Hell held her hand and Bob One, who had now been joined by Bob Two, paced outside.

"I'm going to call in the neurosurgeon from the university hospital," the doctor answered. "He will probably fly in because we need to do this as soon as possible," she explained. "Lucky's nerves are totally jammed and we need to get the pressure off of them right away."

Nerves. Surgery. Pressure. Addy closed her eyes and imagined what it must now look like inside of Lucky's back—a tangled snarl of bloody veins and discs that now look like strands of shredded wheat—and how it must have felt when the discs finally said to hell with it and let go.

"And," the doctor added.

"And what?" Hell almost shouted. "Is there more?"

"Has he hurt his back before this? Had any prior falls?" the doctor wants to know.

"He's been falling for years. He played soccer, a little football, but serious soccer in college for a while, plus he has a fetish for lifting heavy objects."

The doctor smiled when she knew she shouldn't and said, "He's a good-sized man, but years of movement like that can add up. It's like pulling on a rubber band. It holds for a while like it's supposed to but one day, it just snaps. Several things snapped for Lucky today."

"What else?" Addy questioned.

"He's got some fractures along the bottom of his back that may or may not be part of the problem," the doctor said. "We have to fix the ruptures but I'd like to do a more detailed MRI to see about those fractures. It might make sense to take care of those when we operate—but it could mean some extensive recovery time and serious rehab."

Hell takes in so much air she could lift off her chair if she had a hand over her nose.

"Extensive," Addy whispered.

"Time is important, we realize," Hell said. "But could you just elaborate a bit on what we are looking at, Doctor?"

Months. More months after that. Bed rest. Hospital for a good week or more. A little more bed rest. Visits to the doctor. Slowly moving to physical therapy. Acupuncture for pain and a variety of other positive effects. Massage therapy. Possible occupational therapy if . . .

And here the doctor hesitated.

Hell and Addy looked up at the same time and leaned toward Dr. Patricia Christopher who looked extraordinarily brilliant and awesomely competent in her half-glasses, with her hair up in a twisted bun, and with her tiny made-for-surgery fingers folded against her chest as if she was praying, not only for

Lucky, but for his sad and terrified family members as well.

"Sometimes with cases like this there is nerve damage," Dr. Christopher told them. "We won't know until we get in there, and you look like two women who might know what that means, but here it is anyway. Loss of feeling and control, for starters. And, as you also know, any surgery—all surgery—is risky."

"Thank you," Hell said with a shaking voice.

"What do we do now?" Addy asked, sitting up straight, ready to pace herself for what will end up to be a seventy-two-hour bedside vigil, and banking her well of emotions behind a dam that won't break until the moment she finishes smoking five cigarettes.

"All you can do now is wait," the doctor said, adding, "I'm sorry."

Addy knew what she was supposed to feel while she waited during surgery and she felt most of that. She felt each second of the damn clock in the waiting room tick against the inside of her wrist and then move up to her head so it felt as if there was a heavy pen tapping against her temples. She felt frightened at what could, but most likely wouldn't, go wrong in surgery. She felt Lucky's hand clutching her sleeve before he slipped away. She felt helpless and extremely sad and she felt a longing to feel more.

Addy wanted to feel more.

She wanted to feel more when they let her come into the pre-op holding room where Lucky was strapped to a portable bed and where so many tubes were hanging out of him that he looked like a very large marionette. She wanted to feel more the few moments when he fluttered like a lost bird back to reality and tried to whisper something to her that made absolutely no sense because his tongue was as thick as the drugged fog racing through his mind. She wanted to feel more when the nurse came in, touched her on the shoulder, and told her to say goodbye because it was time to take him down to surgery.

"Goodbye, my Lucky," she said, kissing

his cheek, and then his lips, and then the very top of his head.

Addy said goodbye and braced her heart. She stood right where she had kissed Lucky and watched his big feet as they went out the door and he was gone. She braced her heart to feel more than it did but the jolt did not come as she picked up Lucky's bag of clothes that seemed ridiculous now—a flowered tropical shirt, baggy shorts with enough wide pockets to hold half of the Costa Rica they would not now see, and his old leather sandals that she thinks he may have been wearing the week Mitchell started to walk. Addy put her hand into the bag to touch Lucky's shirt and she braced herself to feel more. And she didn't.

She tucked the bag under her arm and walked slowly to the waiting room where Hell and the Bobs were sitting and wondered if Hell would recognize the look on her face—the startled, depressed look, not of someone whose husband was at this very moment undergoing a long and very complicated surgery that could leave him crippled, roasted, fried with a blood clot the size of one of his favorite oil caps moving up from his spine and into his cortex like a fast snail heading for a pond—but of a woman who had a secret the size of the entire waiting room, the whole hospital, and half the town of Parker, Pennsylvania.

And of course Hell knew the minute she looked at her.

"Honey, do you need to eat or something, take a walk, lie down on the floor, I could see about getting one of the private waiting rooms and you could lie down . . ." Hell said in a run-on sentence that would have gone on for at least another five minutes if Addy had not stopped her.

"No, but thanks. Just let me sit," Addy told her sister, pushing back every thought that was now about to explode in her bedroom, which reeked of cigarettes, because she had climbed into bed with all of her clothes on.

When Addy Frances Lipton starts to cry the dam that has wedged a steel girder between her and her emotions lets go, resulting in a riptide that would have a hyphenated name as long as the Mississippi if the weather people were in charge. It rises fast and sharp and takes her breath away so that she finds herself crawling the last few feet to the bed.

Addy drops back into the pillows, curling up tight on the side where Lucky always sleeps. When she puts her hands on the bed they sink into the spot where his hips roll sideways every night, and then as she reaches over she knows that is exactly where his knees jut out and occasionally gouge her lower back and this fact makes her cry harder.

Lying on the bed, Addy knows that another woman, someone who feels more than she does, someone who does not want to drive her car through the garage door, would have slept right there burrowed into the sheets that smell like her mate, wrapping her arms around the pillow where he had slept, placing her hips gently into the same mattress dent created by his wide hips before everything changed.

Another woman would have been crying for missing Lucky, for what might still happen, for what Lucky had lost and might never get back again.

Another woman would have taken the tropical shirt out of the bag and slipped it on, after she took off her dirty blouse, and then slept in it for the rest of her life.

Another woman would have crawled into bed without the nauseating scent of cigarette smoke that has already soaked into the blankets and that clings to her hair, her skin, every inch of her flaming lungs.

Another woman would have gently packed a new bag of Lucky's favorite objects—the photo of Mitchell when he was on the soccer team in sixth grade, the book he was reading about an artist from someplace in Denmark who became famous for making objects out of recycled tire rubber, his bowling shirt, the coffee mug that he used religiously because some soccer star he met at a playoff game in Detroit gave it to him sixteen years ago, and the watch Addy gave him on his fiftieth birthday.

Another woman would not have even been in the goddamn bed. She would have stayed at the hospital for one more night and the night after it and only come home when Lucky had been out of bed for the first time.

Another woman, but not Addy Lipton.

Addy crawled over to her side of the bed as if there was an invisible fence that would go up any moment. She pulled the blankets up over her head so she could barely breathe and she fell asleep that way, sobbing like a baby who is hungry and has to cry itself to sleep, because the one person who might listen is not even in the same house.

EIGHT
A kick in the teeth · · ·

They have a meeting without her.

Hell, Malibu Heidi, Debra, Lee, Bob One, Bob Two, Shaun and Barry from Cooper Auto Systems, and two of Addy's fellow teachers, Carla and Mimi, meet at The First National Wine & Cigar Bar the night before Lucky is going to come home from the hospital. They meet to coordinate a plan they all hope will help their two friends ease back into a world without full-time nurses and the dripping of the automatic pain machine, Addy being able to leave the room and the entire hospital when Lucky gets really testy once he realizes what he is in for when the hard part of recovery begins, and the necessary transportation of Lucky to appointments from one end of Parker back to the other and sometimes to see the head honcho surgeon in Philadelphia.

Bob One, who has been through three prior knee surgeries and finally a replacement a year ago, takes the lead at first. He comes to the meeting, which starts with a round of coffee and very quickly moves into pint glasses of the seasonal tap beer, Holly's Revenge—a lively darker-than-usual amber ale from a micro-brewery in Vermont—that is a perfect fit for a discussion about hauling Lucky, saving Addy from a potential nervous breakdown, and taking out the garbage on Monday evenings.

"Lucky may be a pain in the rear end for a while," Bob Two declares, and very quickly and honestly adds, "I sure as heck was the last time I was sick."

"Was?" Hell asks, smiling.

"Do you think I'm a pain in the rear end?" Bob Two asks, sincerely thinking that Hell, whom he knows from a few backyard barbecues as well as his own forays into the cigar bar, might be serious.

"Just occasionally," she replies, bumping his leg under the table.

"Kids," Debra says, clapping her hands together, "it's Lucky-and-Addy time here! Let's get the chart made before one of my children sets my house on fire."

The chart is a list of anticipated house and yard chores, possible trips to a variety of medical facilities, the bowling alley, the spring soccer games, the Sweat-Hers sessions, and a mess of potential recreational outings that will all depend on Lucky's pain level for that particular day.

"Hell, do you think you can be the one to present this to Addy?" Bob Two wants to know. "We don't want to assume she'll accept this. But I think if it came from you, being the sister and a regular, make that an almost daily, at the Lipton household, well—it just might sit better with both of them."

"I've seen **enough** of Addy lately or I'd deliver it," Bob One says, covering his eyes. "If only I could just get it out of my head."

"Knock it off," Hell yells, throwing a napkin at him. "Promise me you will never ever bring that up to Addy! She's hanging by a thread right now."

A thread.

More like a slightly frayed piece of fishing line that has a whale on one end.

At the very moment the ten best friends she and Lucky have ever had are busy plotting ways to help them even more, Addy— who is sitting in the physicians' room at the hospital going over discharge protocols, medications, the schedule for follow-up doctors' appointments, physical therapy, three-times-a-week massage, range-of-motion exercises, weight-carrying restrictions, blood-draw checks, and details for everything from how to go to the bathroom to how to bathe—would much rather be lying on a table at First National with her face inside of the largest martini glass in the joint.

"You should probably be writing some of this down," Dr. Christopher suggests. "It's a lot to remember."

"No kidding," Addy mutters. "This is overwhelming. Totally overwhelming. Did you go through all of this with Lucky?"

"Yes," the doctor says. "But he didn't take notes because he said you'd do it and that you'd help him remember everything."

"Of course that's what he said," Addy groans, sitting right on the edge of a place that could knock her into a dark abyss if the wind blew just a little bit. "You don't plan for something like this, do you?"

"We all think about it now and then but, no, an accident, something that suddenly changes everything, it's hard to focus on that, isn't it?"

Addy admired Dr. Patty. She has seen her handle Lucky and his "poor me" yelping, his endless questions about playing sports and how soon he could start hefting washing machines and lifting large round balls over his head again, with the grace of a professional woman who has pretty much seen and heard it all. Following the surgery, she was there with a diagram, endless patience, and a promise that the hands that had just worked to put Lucky back together again were as good as it gets.

"God," Addy moans, covering her face with her own hands.

Dr. Patty gets up and walks over to sit next to Addy. She puts her hand on her shoulder.

"Do you have someone to talk to?" she asks, very gently.

"I'm tired of crying and feeling sorry for myself," Addy confesses. "I'm exhausted, not just from this but from lots of things. I have friends, you've seen them, but the whole damn thing feels like being dumped into the middle of the ocean and swimming for shore, which is about a zillion miles away. On top of everything else that I am, now I get to be a nurse, and the part-time physical therapist. Lucky has his moments but he's a big baby."

"Let's finish with you for a second," the doctor interrupts before Addy can tell her about the time Lucky had the flu and she thought he'd been run over by a cargo plane. "Would you like to talk to someone here? I could arrange it right away."

Addy imagines herself lying on a long slender couch on the third floor and complaining about having to take care of her husband, the man she married in sickness and in health, the man she is supposed to love and care for no matter what. The way her luck is running, the psychiatrist would be the mother or father of one of her students who would accidentally tell someone how Addy is a cruel beast and she'd be ostracized from not just the entire teaching community, but from the gossip-riddled village of Parker, where everyone knows everything about everybody.

"Well, really, if I talked to someone, and I assume you mean a counselor-type someone, it would be a marriage counselor, because that's what this is all about," Addy confesses. "I'll figure it out somehow. Lucky's broken back and bones and everything else he's broken just made the whole mess fly into my face, I guess."

The doctor hesitates. She's resting on a narrow patient-client bridge that leans toward Lucky but she's been where Addy is and she knows if there is trouble in the Lipton household that the tender care and feeding of an injured man will not necessarily keep the marriage floating until Lucky can get down on one knee and propose again. Actually, it may be a very long time before Lucky can actually bend anything but his index finger.

She says, very carefully, "What happened to Lucky won't make any of your decisions any easier."

Easier was the packed bag for Costa Rica.

Easier was smoking her lungs out in the pine trees.

Easier was ignoring the silence.

Easier was yapping in the hot tub with her gal pals.

Easier was sticking a pin in her eye and then running with scissors barefoot over hot coals.

"I know that, too," Addy says. "That's what's so damn depressing. But..." She hesitates.

"But what?"

"I suppose this is bad to tell a doctor but I've got my cigarettes and vodka and my girlfriends."

Dr. Patty laughs and asks if she can be invited to the next party. She confesses that she loves—and she says the word "loves" with her eyes closed—those little cigars in the blue tin that Hell sells at the bar that go really well with a martini so dry it's hard to get a drop of it out of the glass.

"You know, Addy," she adds, "the next couple of weeks will be bad, and then the next four after that a little worse, and maybe two more after that are going to be totally horrible, and probably a few more weeks beyond those weeks as well, so whatever you need to do to keep yourself sane is okay with this doctor—as long as you keep the vodka away from Lucky until he's off the meds."

And she makes Addy promise that if her sanity meter drops below the dip and sway of the Pennsylvania horizon, she will let her know so she can get her the help that she needs. "It's not just about Lucky now," the doctor says, moving for the door. "He needs you now, probably more than ever. Which is a kick in the teeth, if things have been rocky before the accident."

"I'll figure it out," Addy promises. "I'm really not as bad as I look."

"You look fine and one thing I do know is that getting the hell out of this hospital makes everyone feel better—even the people who aren't patients."

This just when Addy is thinking of moving into the waiting room she discovered on the fifth floor that has an espresso machine, a long couch where she has been napping, and lead walls so her cell phone doesn't ring and where she can hide, momentarily at least, from the rest of the anxious world.

Lucky is asleep when she goes back into his room. Addy scribbles him a note, touches him lightly on his right big toe, and then bolts for the elevator just as her cell phone vibrates. She clicks the phone on in the middle of Hell's message.

"—you on your way home?" Hell demands.

"Yes. I need a hospital break."

"I'm going to meet you there for just a few minutes."

Addy cannot remember the last time she said no to her sister. Maybe she has never said no to her sister. No one says no to Hell Sinkman and why should they? Hell's a brazen, open, kind, generous, wild thing of a woman who has always seemed to know who she is and where she is going—unless, of course, she's dating a man. She's on every volunteer committee in Parker, runs a hugely successful breast cancer fund-raiser not once, but three times a year, and she's always been there for Addy.

Sagging up against the side of the elevator, Addy looks down at her tennis shoes and starts kicking the edge of the carpeting. Can she say no? No to Hell?

"Hell—" she begins and Hell catches on right away.

"Tired?"

"What would be three words beyond tired?"

"Dead, I think."

"Well, one word before that, maybe. I just met with the doctor and got the first wave of discharge information, schedules, appointments and a sort-of timeline for Lucky's recovery."

"Oh, shit."

"Hell, this is not going to be pretty."

"That's what I wanted to talk to you about."

"Listen, Hell, you know, I'm never alone at home. It's so rare. And after tonight, my house is going to be like a waiting room and not a place where I can sit in the quiet. You know?"

"So you just want to be alone tonight?"

"Yes. Please."

"I understand, babycakes. And I don't blame you. But listen—the gang got together and we worked out a schedule to help you. Everyone is taking a day to sort of be on call, so you don't have to take off of work and so you don't have to shoulder this whole thing by yourself and there is a community festival meeting tonight anyway."

"Really?" Addy says, not quite certain she's understood her sister's words.

"Really. Now go home, pour yourself a cold beer, take a long hot shower, and climb into bed. What time do you pick up Lucky tomorrow?"

"After lunch, and Hell—thanks, thanks so much. You know I love you?"

"Shucks. I love you, too. I'm going back to work, so call me if you lock your keys in the car or anything."

Anything. Hell was good for it, always good for it, and as Addy passed the First National on her way home she beeped, three times, something she had been doing with her sister since high school. Then she turned

at the far side of the city and into the cul-de-
sac and the driveway that will forever be
called Lucky's Folly.

The house is a dark soldier, a solid hunk
against a sky that has gotten progressively
lighter every night as it has climbed up the
ladder of spring, and Addy pulls up close to
the garage door and stops. There's no way
she can even think about ramming the car
through the door now. Without hesitation
Addy gets out of the car and walks right over
the spot where Lucky fell, does not look
down, and walks quickly through the front
door that has been locked only a handful of
times in all the years she has lived there.

Inside, her feet echo on the tiled foyer, her
car keys hit the small table that was put there
precisely as a home for all small objects that
can fit inside of a pocket. Without turning
on a light, Addy opens the refrigerator, grabs
a beer, and pushes back her desire to
smoke—again. Her routine since Lucky has
been in the hospital the past eight days has
been to come home the nights she didn't
sleep in a chair in his room, grab something
to drink, and then sit smoking in the back-

yard unless Hell or one of the Bobs or someone from work or any one of about three
hundred other friends or neighbors stopped
by—which was often, very often. And then,
when they'd left, she would slip back into
her seat beside the grill and smoke, feeling
sorry for herself.

This night—the last night—Addy wants
nothing more than to be still.

She can count on one hand the number
of nights she has spent alone in this house
during the past ten years and the silence is
almost as good—almost—as the way the
cigarette smoke curls through her entire
body like one of those long snakes Lucky
uses in the bathroom when the drain clogs.

Addy sits in the dark, on the couch that
she never really liked, but bought because it
had a wide back and was high enough for
Lucky's legs and then Mitchell's, too, and
she thinks how lovely it is to be in the quiet.

No television.

No shouting from The Kingdom of Krap.

No ringing phone.

No one asking her to do anything.

And for the very first time in twenty-eight years, Addy Lipton, on the eve before her wrecked husband comes home, looks around the living room and begins to wonder what she would change in this very spot if she were living alone.

NINE
What I should have said to Addy · · ·

She is standing right there, signing the discharge papers, and it was a big chance for me.

I should have said "Thank you, honey" about a thousand times.

Just when I thought of it, I moved too fast, and it felt like I had fallen backwards on a **Star Wars** sword or something and that was it.

That was it.

TEN

*The poker rumble on
Saturday night . . .*

The word "Mom" sounds at first like an echo from across the street where the two neighbor kids, both still in grade school, make Addy swing her head at least once a day when she hears them shouting, and then usually screaming, for their mother who has the same name Addy does when Mitchell is around.

He calls her **Mom**. Never Mother or Ma or Mommy—just Mom. Addy is in Mitchell's room wishing to hell she'd realized sooner that it would be impossible for Lucky to climb the steps to get to their bedroom. "Mom?"

Lucky spent his first night home from the hospital on the couch. He was all ready to set up camp there permanently with a TV clicker, a tray of food, the telephone, and an assortment of handheld video games that his co-workers had dropped off to keep him company when Addy assured him that she could indeed shift a few things in Mitchell's room so the living room, which she might occasionally want to use, would not look like a triage center.

"Mom, are you here?" she heard again and knew that her son, her only child, the boy turned man, the hot university freshman, was somewhere in the house.

"Mitchell!" she yelled. "Mitchell?"

And there he was, in person, standing in the door with a small pack over his right arm, a paper bag in the other hand. His totally irrepressible dopey smile knocked against Addy's heart in such a physical way that it made her catch her breath.

"Hi, Mom," he said, dropping his bags and stepping toward Addy with his ropelike arms ready for a hug.

"What are you doing here? How did you get here? How are you?"

Mitchell laughs as he hugs his mom and

tells her to slow down a second. A guy from school, he tells her, was heading to New York for his sister's wedding so he hopped a ride. He'd catch the same ride back in two quick days.

"I was worried about Dad, Mom," he admitted. "Is he okay? Is he here? Is everything going to be all right with him?"

Sometimes, Addy thinks, the mystery of life and timing and love is amazing. Not only does she need help moving Mitchell's bed away from the wall, but just when she decides she's raised a no-good, worthless, lazy, selfish slob of a son, he shows up at precisely the perfect moment, to not only do some heavy lifting, but to give his mother a hug.

"Take a breath, Mitch," she says. "Bob Two took your father to the doctor for a day-after-dismissal visit—he came home yesterday—and then my guess is that if your father is up for it they will drive around and look at all the male highlights in Parker . . . you know, the soccer fields, the car lot, the back end of the bowling alley . . ."

"Mom . . ." Mitchell sighs. "Are you still on that males-are-pigs kick?"

"Yes, I am," Addy says firmly, grabbing Mitchell just so she can reach her arms around him and feel his skin under her fingers when they loop behind his neck. "You are a little piggy too, and a spoiled brat, and I think I almost missed you once about three weeks ago but then I looked into your closet, which has been condemned by the Pennsylvania State Department of Health, and I didn't miss you anymore."

Only children, Mitchell knows, are supposed to feel the weight of both parents across their shoulders 24/7. And if they are adopted it's supposed to be worse, he read someplace along the trail of his nineteen-year-old life, but Mitchell wouldn't know which parent to save if the boat tipped over. He knows his mom loves him by the way she looks at him as if he is a garland of hope every time she sees him and drops everything—almost all of the time—for him. He cannot think of one mean, horrible—unless you count the time she actually sat him

down when he was fourteen and asked that
he confine his masturbation activities to one
specific area of the house, that area being his
bedroom, and then launched into an embar-
rassing, but kinda cool, lecture about how it
would be wrong not to masturbate—or bad
thing she has ever done to him. His father is
also totally there for him. Lucky has shown
him how to do everything from change the
oil in his first car to play soccer, and his
mom doesn't know this, but Mitchell and
his dad also smoke some of Auntie Hell's cigars and drink beer together when they go
camping or bowl or hang out in The
Kingdom of Krap, where they blow the
smoke out of the back window and then just
ignite the propane torch and burn something stinky to get rid of the smell.

Happy Mitchell, with his curly hair and
dark eyes, looks so much like his father that
Addy finally stopped bothering to tell people he was adopted when Mitchell was five
years old, because it really was never a necessary part of any conversation anyway and
because from the moment he touched down
in their lives he was simply—their son. Now

he helps his mom move the bed, a dresser, and clears a few hallways while he briefs her on the last month of his life, which includes enough pauses so that Addy knows he surely is not constantly studying until midnight at the university library and helping elderly Wisconsin ladies cross the street on the way to church.

And Addy does feel her heart leap when she looks at her son, who, yes, is floundering in some ways, but who got into a top-ten school and who has realized since tenth grade that the world does not stop in Parker, PA. And when Lucky finally shows up, exhausted and looking as if Bob has dragged him home behind the car and through a field of upright nails, the look on Mitchell's face gives her even more reason to feel totally breathless.

Which she does.

"Mom," Mitchell asks, "are you okay?"

"Just catching my breath. This has been a hell of a time, Mitchell. I think a touch of anxiety is warranted."

Lucky has limped to his new bed, and Mitchell, who now also looks as if he has seen a ghost, helps Lucky lie down and then runs back to find his mother, wanting to know immediately and step-by-step what exactly did happen at the hospital, and will Dad ever get better, and how did this happen.

Addy sits him down and tells him everything in great detail because Mitchell may sometimes act like he is in third grade but he is actually old enough to have babies, get married, fight in a war, live away from home, and know the truth. He listens to the news about ruptured discs and what the weight and pull of all those years of lifting and falling and running in place can do to a back and all the tender passageways that hold it together. She spares Mitchell nothing because it is time that he hoists his own portion of the load even though he now lives several states away. Because he is, and will always be, part of the family.

Mitchell sits with his long arms across his equally long thighs and his mind drifts from his father, to his mother, and to that sort-of-innocent place of wondering if any old friends are in town. The seriousness of his father's injury, of what has happened, is there, but his first real taste of freedom and life beyond Parker and curfews and his mother calling his cell phone to ask what time he might consider arriving back at the home where he really lives even though he thinks he lives at Jeffrey's, Chad's, Nick's, Paul's, and Brad's, and his father sometimes asking him if he will ever have a girlfriend for longer than one date, has made him about six paces behind cocky.

His dad is tough, he thinks, he'll lick this surgery and this therapy stuff. And his mom will be there because she is always there. He is thinking that, even though his father has lost ten pounds since he has last seen him, which he needed to do anyway, and that he moaned in pain when Mitchell helped him roll onto the bed, it will all go away.

Mitchell James Lipton is nineteen years old and he thinks that everything bad will go away.

He thinks that his father is a rock.

He thinks that his mother is a savior.

He thinks that he is ready to make brave and lasting decisions.

He thinks that his seven months away from home have earned him the right to swagger just a bit.

He thinks that he knows so much more than he did a year ago, it is an amazing feat that his head has not exploded.

He thinks he is so far **there** that he will never ever get lost or stumble or ask for help when he is stranded alongside of a road in the middle of nowhere at midnight without his wallet, money, or a clue to the next point of salvation.

"But he'll be okay, won't he?" Mitchell asks his mother. "Dad will get back close to where he was, won't he, won't he be okay?"

Addy looks at Mitchell and sees right through him. She has watched his fast walk move into a swagger and she's bitten a hole in her tongue that is large enough for an entire fleet of Navy ships to pass through without touching its sides. She's seen her son stumble through the door drunk when his friends dropped him off at 3 a.m. with a note taped to his shirt that said "He wouldn't drive." and she's shown him how to wash the floors with lemon-scented ammonia, how to gently clean out his ears with a Q-tip, rotate his head just a bit to the left side for photographs, write thank-you cards so people can actually read them, and pace himself while eating at buffets.

And now, she lies.

"He'll be fine, Mitchell," she tells her son, not knowing for sure herself but wanting to believe it so bad the insides of her legs and every tooth in her mouth ache. "It won't happen overnight, and it will take a bit of work, but he'll be fine. Maybe not trying-out-for-the-Pittsburgh-Steelers fine, but walking, talking, living-close-to-how-he-has-always-lived fine. He will."

Mitchell wants to believe her so bad that he jumps right up, asks his mother if there is anything she needs to have him do. "How about if I drive the car downtown, clean it out, wash it, and then I will come back and do a yard pick-up for you?"

Addy is stunned.

"Is this a trick?"

"Not really."

"What part is the **not** part?"

"I'll probably see who is around when I'm

out. Some of the guys going to State might be home for the weekend."

Of course.

Addy gets up, whispers "It's the thought that counts" into Mitchell's ear just before he bolts out the door after going back in to check on his father.

"Mom, he wants you," he throws over his shoulder as he flies out the door as if he's a volunteer fireman and the siren is blaring.

Lucky wants a television set, a pain pill, a glass of orange juice, and some cream for his feet, and oh, maybe a pillow.

Shit.

Addy props him up and gets him a pill before she fetches juice and then fishes around in the bathroom for some kind of cream that will stick to the feet of a man who has appendages that could have been transplanted from an alligator. When she gets back to Lucky's new room, he's snoring with his mouth wide open in one of those drug-induced coma-like positions that would allow for a car or maybe even a truck to be driven right through the center of the house without the snores skipping a very tiny beat.

Lucky, Lucky, Lucky.

Addy sits and stares at her husband. Really, she thinks, they've been, well . . . lucky. Beyond the scrapes and bruises and broken bones inflicted by a variety of playing fields and hard balls, they've been healthy. They've always made the mortgage payment, they both have a pretty decent retirement policy piling up dollars, and she's pretty certain that Mitchell has never spent a night in jail. Sure, they've wrestled with the heartache of losing friends and family members, but the level of uncertainty in their lives has been a steady line of remarkable goodness. There's actually been more chaos in her third-grade classroom the day before a holiday than there has ever been at the Lipton household.

This, then, this back mess and learning how to bend and walk and lift a whole new way, should be a breeze, a life lesson of humble gratitude for the rest of the years filled with minor abrasions.

It should be.

But Addy knows that ignorance is bliss and that so is keeping busy with bowling balls and maybe grading papers and volunteering too much for school committees and hanging out in The Kingdom of Krap and at the First National and every other place that is a distraction so that one day a husband and wife pass in the hall of their own home, bump shoulders, and say, "Excuse me, but do I know you?"

"Do I know you, Lucky?" she whispers, settling back into the old futon chair that served as Mitchell's spare sleepover bed, boxing bag, and the make-believe gymnastics mat. "Lucky, do you love me? Do you **really** love me?"

Lucky is a stone that moves only when his breath fans out for such a long period of time it's a wonder to Addy that he is not totally deflated.

And just as Addy is about to reach back, way back, for a lovely memory of Lucky and Addy, **any** lovely memory of Lucky and Addy, something to charge up her own loving batteries, she hears her cell phone ringing out in the kitchen. She slips out of the bedroom, quietly closing the door, to catch the phone.

Mitchell, Mitchell. Mitchell.

"Hey, Mom."

"Hey."

Addy knows something is coming. She's tired and every other adjective that has to do with caretaking, depression, motherhood, wifeliness.

"Just ask," she says.

"I know Dad is recovering and everything, but I ran into some of the guys and I was wondering—well, we are all wondering—if we could come over and hang out in the basement and play poker."

"Poker."

Addy says the word as if she has never heard it before and she is trying to learn to pronounce it. She says it and she can hear Mitchell breathing and the shuffle of feet in the background and car doors and she realizes she was a fool to imagine that this part of her life ended last September when Mitchell left for college. The part that was a revolving door for the Parker boys and a handful of girls who are so familiar with the Lipton family they all stopped ringing the doorbell when they came over and Addy would find them in every room of the house twenty-four hours a day.

And she knew she was supposed to miss this part of her life, too, but she didn't and she couldn't bring herself to say no either.

Addy said yes and then she lined up all of Lucky's pills in the order in which they were supposed to be taken. She filled the refrigerator with drinks, took out the garbage, checked the answering machine, started a load of wash, double-checked the grocery list, which was now covering almost three pages of paper, went downstairs to put salt in the water softener, changed the smoky sheets on her bed, left her sister a message, wrote down the next three doctors' appointments on the calendar, and then went to stand by the window in the spare bedroom on the far side of the house.

The window gently draped with green curtains that has the best view of the oh-so-terribly-solid Lipton garage door.

ELEVEN
On pins and needles . . .

The woman has hands that look as if they have been severed off of a small child who has never played in a sandbox, stuck her hands inside of a bucket of dirt, or launched a mess of fireworks into the air that went off before they were supposed to hit the backside of a low cloud.

Lucky is glad for the beautiful hands because he is so nervous that he has for the very first time in his life almost peed in his pants while waiting in the office of Sandra Giesma, an acupuncturist whose very presence in little Parker, and now in Lucky's life, is all the proof anyone needs for the existence of miracles in the modern-day world.

His fifteenth day post-op and Lucky dis-

covers that his lovely—make that border-
line-hot—doctor, Dr. Patty, is into what
Lucky calls "cool medicine," like whatever it
is Ms. Giesma is about to do to him the moment he composes himself, lets go of Addy's
hand, and tries to get off of the chair and
step into what probably is a dark room with
burning incense, pictures of Buddha on the
walls, and women with silver bracelets ush-
ering willing and unwilling victims up and
down the halls of the Parker Wellness
Center.

"Addy, have you ever had acupuncture?"
Lucky asks as he wiggles like a little boy, but
just for a second, because if he moves wrong
he will most definitely collapse on the floor
in a shower of pain.

"No, but I have read about it and it is
good, especially if you remain open to it, for
everything from menopause to your back
pain and leg pain and every other pain you
have."

"Don't say 'menopause,' baby."

Addy looks at him as if he's just tried to
strangle her and decides to let it pass.
Menopause is a breeze compared to this

stuff, she wants to tell him. Menopause is better than going bald and throwing an extra mile or two of blood vessels into your body via the weight gain in your stomach. It beats hitting your sexual peak when you are thirty-five and not seventy-five, which is exactly where I plan to peak, she wants to say, but she does not say one word.

"Addy."

"What?"

"What do you mean by being open to it? I mean how can you be open to a woman with tiny hands who wants to poke needles into your body? How does this work?"

Addy's sigh could knock out a fleet of ships. When she turns to look at her husband, she digs deep and what she wants to do is ask him what he has been doing for ten years while the rest of the world has taken vitamins and purchased treadmills and rediscovered yoga and removed hunks of lard and grease from their diets and realized that preventative medicine is surely not just the wave of the future but the wave of the past, and the present as well, but she sees that Lucky is in distress yet again, possibly scared, and so she does not ask him. Instead, she asks, "Lucky, are you okay?"

"Jeezus, honey, I almost peed in my pants. Now I know how you feel."

He leans in to whisper in her ear and Addy wants to pee in her pants, too, because this conversation is about as intimate as she's been with Lucky in the past three years.

"You have to like squeeze **everything** or you will just **go,**" Lucky whispers.

"Yes, that's how it works, Lucky."

"So . . ."

"So what?"

"What do I have to be open to?"

Addy has imagined many things in her life. When she drinks too much at the First National she imagines that someone will flirt with her again. She occasionally thinks about what it would be like to redo the entire house, start over and get rid of all the Early American junk she bought to make her mother happy. She imagines Mitchell calling one day and saying he's going to take the train home and could she pick him up so he could take her out for dinner in Pittsburgh and then go see a play with him?

She's recently thought about Costa Rica and living alone and changing the locks on the door, and smoking in public.

But not this.

Never.

Not sitting in the office of an acupuncturist with Lucky telling her he knows now what it feels like to have loss of bladder control and then that same man leaning over to ask her what it means to be **open**.

Open to the universe.

To change.

To the healing powers of the human heart.

To the knowledge that the body can heal itself.

To a parallel knowledge that the mind is a powerful place.

To falling into the power of another person who is way ahead of you.

To relaxing your inner demons so that your own energy can flow.

Addy turns toward Lucky just as another man walks into the office, tips his head toward him in a kind of "Yo, here we are, man" type of greeting and Lucky quickly lets go of her hand, shifts ever so slightly away from her, and puts his elbows firmly on his knees.

"Lucky, just think it can work, that's it, think it can work and it will," she says, thinking of everything else she could say, and does not, and feeling only slightly offended by Lucky's macho move.

Addy is stretching hard. She knows that Lucky is in a world of hurt and that Dr. Patty's goal is to wean him from his doses of pain medication as quickly as possible and that the doctor's also big on movement, which has not been easy for Lucky, who has been bemoaning the fact that he never went on the Atkins Diet when the rest of the world did and could not bring himself to think about the South Beach Diet or the eat-dog-food-for-lunch diet or the lie-on-your-side diet because he knew his weight-gain balloon had started to inflate about the time he blew his knee out and stopped playing and started watching.

"Don't be so hard on yourself," Addy told him each day when he was forcing himself to walk around the cul-de-sac and through a hoop of pain that seemed to have latched on to his body like a mad dog. "It's only been a few days, Lucky. This will take time."

Lucky was pissed. Angry that he had ignored the warning signs in his lower back that snarled at him when he twisted, got up too fast, or bent down to pick something up without his knees touching the ground. One afternoon when he was at work and the guys in the back needed help unloading a truckload of boxes, he'd jumped in to help and then spent two hours on the couch in his boss's office with an ice pack the size of an Alaskan glacier. He could no longer wear his favorite boots because the pain that ran down his leg seemed to back up against a bank of nerves tucked inside of some attention-starved body part that was so agonizing he once took off the boot in the middle of a sales meeting and was so close to crying that he got up to leave the room, limping with one boot off and one boot on.

But he'd never said anything to Addy and he'd never gone to the doctor, subscribing, of course, to the "suck it up and get up" philosophy that had seemed to sustain his father, brothers, and most of the men he hung around with. Except that damned Bob One, who had turned overnight into a vegetarian, started power-walking, and had even enrolled in an online writing class at the university about six months after his divorce was finalized.

"Bob," Lucky had said, astonished at and just a bit jealous of his friend's new life. "You are sort of disappearing and this writing-class thing—where the hell did that come from?"

"When Vicky and I decided this was never going to work, I just sat down one day and made a list of everything I have always wanted to do and never did because, well, just because things slip away, Lucky, you know?" Bob had told Lucky as they were driving to pick up Mitchell from school so they could all go to see yet another soccer game. "Let's face it. I look like shit. I've gained weight, I feel like an old man and I probably never told you this, but I wanted to be a newspaper reporter once."

You could have pushed Lucky over with the reverse-suction power from a shop vacuum. It got him to wondering for just a bit what he might do if things, if life were different. And so one day when Addy was out pumping iron or doing whatever the heck she did with those women at the Y, he'd sat down at the kitchen table, made himself a cup of tea, because that was what Bob One drank most of the time, and he started a list.

He wanted a big fishing boat.

He wanted to get back into shape.

It was so hard to think like this. Lucky sipped his mint tea and wondered what it would taste like if he put in a shot of whiskey. He looked out the window and decided he should top off the old pine tree and wedge its side in a little more to get it higher and maybe give it a few more years. He got up to get a cookie and he actually slapped himself really hard on the cheek so he could concentrate.

What else had he always wanted to do?

He wanted to clean out The Kingdom of Krap. Honest. It drove Addy nuts not to be able to park the car in there. And it would give him more room for his bowling ball art.

He wanted to think more seriously about

the meaning of art, read more art books, talk to some artists.

He wanted to coach again.

The list stopped there because Mitchell came home and Lucky never had the urge to drink more tea after that, although the mint had made him feel light and determined, and then he forgot where he put the list anyway and then Bob One gained a little weight back and then one day Lucky's back snapped, his discs ruptured, and there he was trying to get up to shuffle down a hall so that a woman with long dark hair who had hands the size of a baby doll's could take pins and stick them all over his body.

"Do I have to get undressed?" Addy heard him ask as he went down the hall and disappeared.

Addy waited.

She thought about Lucky taking about ten minutes, because of the pain, to slide onto the practitioner's table and how the woman might then cover him up with a warm blanket, maybe even use one of those heat lights, and how she would explain every single thing that she was doing while Lucky tried not to wet his pants. She thought about the unusual combination of needles and pain and then the expected release and knew that the body could heal or harm itself depending on which direction you steered it.

Then she noticed that her leg was thumping. One of those nervous habits that other people had, never her, where they had to constantly move something—an arm or a leg, or a finger, or even their heads back and forth if they were really into it.

Addy, Addy, Addy.

The other man had left the waiting room and Addy got up because she did not know what else to do. During the past month she had read more magazines than in every year of her life put together. Apparently, there were magazines for everything from how to raise a vegetarian baby to how to manage your wealth and income so that you can retire after sixth grade and open up a sub sandwich shop. Her favorite was a knitting magazine, apparently a huge new fad—

make that resurrection art, which had intricate wall hangings that had been knit from the collected hair of a woman's pets. Yikes.

The woman behind the desk didn't look up when Addy picked up one of the office brochures, and without sitting back down, she walked around the waiting-room table and stood in front of her chair with her heel tapping on the floor. Then she lost herself in reading about acupuncture, about how many people who have chronic pain find relief with the ancient Chinese method of opening up obstructed channels within your body and she closed her eyes for a moment and tried to imagine how many of her inner channels were blocked. Blocked and obviously backing up her system so that she was sometimes choking on her own words and everything else that was working hard to crawl over the top of the dam.

When she opened her eyes they settled on the section that said "Promotion of Health and Well-Being." That's what wine and the Y and friends are for, she told herself, but then again would having one more weapon in her war to keep the car away from the garage door hurt? Would it?

Addy walked over to the receptionist. She made an appointment for the following week, and not for the same day that she made another appointment for Lucky, and then she sat back down with one foot tucked under her and picked up a bicycling magazine that was filled with people who looked really, really good in those tight little spandex shorts and tops.

"Pigs," she said out loud just as Lucky came limping back down the hall with the help of Ms. Giesma.

"Here we go," said the acupuncturist. "Make sure he lies down, get him lots of fluids, and did you make an appointment for next week?"

Yes, on everything Addy said yes, and yes and yes again. Lucky was the fluid-and-rest king of the cul-de-sac. He was the monarch of the television clicker and he now had first right of refusal on access to the downstairs bathroom at all times. He had a menu that in some parts of the world might require a full-time cook, and the constant look of someone who has been broadsided and cannot remember his name, how to get home, or what he's supposed to do next.

He walked to the car holding Addy's arm as if he were trying to avoid an invisible minefield, and when she got him into the car, lifting his legs up for him, pushing the seat back, hooking his seatbelt, and then shutting the door, he managed to roll down the window, push his head out before Addy walked to the other side of the car and he said, "Addy, I tried to be open but I think I just fell asleep."

"Sleep is good, Lucky, it will work anyway," she lied. "It's okay."

And by the time she got him home, back into the house, gave him some pills, and started dinner she was too damn tired to go sit by the barbecue and smoke so she climbed into bed alone, decided to sleep right in the middle of the mattress. She put an unlit cigarette in her mouth, made believe she was smoking, and flicked the nonexistent ashes on the pillow Lucky would be using if he was not a temporary cripple.

TWELVE
What I thought
Addy was thinking · · ·

The lady with the needles put me as close to the edge of losing it as you can get without falling over and I didn't want to say anything to Addy because I am sure she was thinking that the woman should have just stuck a large pin through my heart and put us all out of our misery.

If only.

THIRTEEN
Girls gone wild · · ·

Mason Unser is standing on top of Addy's desk as Addy walks into her classroom and when she sees that he's about ready to dance on top of her notebooks, a photograph of Mitchell that he must have knocked down when he jumped up there, and an assortment of teacher gifts from last Christmas including six cups decorated with apples and the word "teacher" on them, a flower vase in the shape of a ruler, a set of colored pencils in a hand-carved wooden holder, and four paperweights, she steps into the room and clears her voice.

"Ahhummm."

When he turns, Mason has his hands on his cute little blue soccer shorts as if he is going to pull them down, and the rest of the class, except for the gang of book freaks who are lying on the floor reading and oblivious to everything else in the entire world, are holding their breath in the hopes that they will see the class clown's round rear end probably for the fiftieth time.

"Mrs. Lipton," Mason squeaks as he freezes in place.

"Could you please get down?"

"Okay."

Mason saunters over to Addy, who has not moved. He stands very close to her, looks up, and says, "The usual?"

The usual, Addy thinks, has not worked with this seemingly attention-starved, usually totally wonderful, but occasionally insanely wild boy whose parents seem as baffled as Addy by his spontaneous behavior. Now, in less than thirty seconds, Addy has to pull some remarkable and brilliant potion out of her magic teacher's hat. Something that will not be like everything else she has already done to try and keep Mason off her desk, the windowsill, the top of the closet, and every chair in the classroom.

A tonic of tameness for a nine-year-old.

A magic solution that will not shame or harm.

A wise word that can turn a heart.

A life lesson to rock the universe.

When Addy closes her eyes for just a few seconds, she imagines Mason as a grown man. This is a trick she has created during her twenty-nine years of teaching that always seems to change everything. What she sees this moment is Mason on the stage that he so loves. He's worked his way through acting school as a waiter, where his interactions with people have given him a sophisticated glaze that he can take with him to the stage. An actor, an intensely popular young man who really is harmless, but simply wants to make everyone else happy, Mason could charm the pants off a rodeo clown.

"Mason, my man," she says, setting down her papers and books so that she can get down on her knees and look him in the eye. "Today is not the usual, standing on the teacher's desk is not the usual, making believe you are going to pull down your shorts is not the usual, so today what you must do is **not** the usual."

Mason's eyes have expanded about an inch. This may be the first time he has stood still since he began to walk.

"What?" he pleads.

"Shhh," Addy answers. Addy who never raises her voice in class, who has loved this, this real teaching, moments like this when she can turn the key to someone's future in seconds, loved it all since the moment she walked into the classroom her first full day of class and felt her heart sway in an entirely new direction.

"Class, first of all, good morning and you are all looking extraordinarily handsome and lovely today," she says. "Second, we all know that Mason loves to entertain us before class, just as we know that getting on top of desks and dancing on the windowsill is not appropriate."

No one else is moving now except Sammy Sutherland, who could not sit still if she were tied to her desk.

"Mason will now be in charge of prepar-

ing a special greeting for us every morning
so that he will not have time to step on the
desks," Addy announces. "He will deliver an
important speech or put together a short
play or act something out for us every single
morning."

About six hands immediately shoot up as
if they have been attached to triggers and the
voices beneath them are all clamoring, "Can
I help? Oh, please, can I help?"

If it were possible to see inside of someone's head, the interior of Mason's fast-
roving mind would look like a shower of
rainbow-colored confetti. It would look like
a dream come true, the northern lights in
late August, and millions of clapping hands.

"Really?" he asks.

"Really, Mason. But this is serious business," Addy admonishes him. "You may
work with anyone who cares to work with
you, but this is your show and you must
prove to us every day that you deserve to be
doing this. Understand?"

Mason nods his head up and down and
then walks quietly to his desk where he immediately starts writing in his Warrior

Notebook, a special book each one of Addy's students is required to keep on top of their desk at all times, so that random and wild thoughts and ideas can be written down for use at a later date.

During the next quiet period, when math minds are busy working on a series of problems, Addy finally allows herself to take a break and to run through the morning's events. She turns to look at Mason, who probably already has three acts of a play written, and imagines that her life would have been a bleak forest if she had not chosen this professional path, a path that has occasionally been a minefield of learning and growth for her as well as her students. And she remembers that it was in fact a teacher who turned her away from a ludicrous degree in financial management, which she surely could have excelled at but would have driven her insane with its sameness.

Professor Joyce Dorothy had corralled Addy following a mentoring session when Addy was a sophomore in college and informed her that her skills in finance were beyond question but that her personality, her ability to create workshops and planning sessions for the class, led to an obvious question: "Have you thought about teaching?"

Determined not to fall into the "woman's limited career choice" category, Addy fought the suggestion at first. But when Professor Dorothy told her she would flunk her if she did not go spend a day in the experimental teaching class on campus, Addy literally ran to the class and her entire life changed during the next eight hours.

Even now, when the heat of an entire school year is pressing in on her, when the students are antsy for summer break, when her school leadership roles, her teaching responsibilities, and her work in the teacher's union make her shoulders stoop, she cannot think of one other job or profession that would have made her this happy, this glad to pull open the door every day, this impatient to find out what Mason Unser will become when he grows up and stops dropping his pants in public.

The panic in her heart starts to rise when she turns back to her desk and realizes that in just three weeks the school year will be over. That is usually a glorious gift of time in which she can work occasionally at the First National, sleep in, catch up on house projects, and do whatever the hell else she feels like doing or not doing. But this year, in twenty days, both she and Lucky will be home 24/7 and Addy now longs to get on top of the desk just like Mason.

She rides out the panic for a few moments by dropping her head to get some blood in the valleys of her brain. Then she rotates her shoulders and breathes through her nose very slowly.

"Mrs. Lipton, I think some of us have to go to the bathroom."

This from Mary Petzonsky, who has seen Addy drinking wine at her kitchen table, lying in her backyard in a jogging bra, and sleeping on the living room couch. Mary Petzonsky's mother is Debra from the Y Sweat-Hers. In twenty-nine years of teaching, Addy has had about 850-plus students, and in a town the size of Parker, PA, that means she has had wine at the kitchen tables of lots and lots of her students' mommies.

Addy jumps up, picks up papers, gets the

students to the bathroom. And then much to their surprise and hers, she takes everyone outside for an extra recess. She does this so she can call Hell.

"It's, like, one-thirty, where are you?" Hell wonders.

"Next to the swingset. I'm desperate, Hell."

"What?"

"Is there class tonight?"

"Yes. Are you coming?" Hell asks, frozen in place in her office, where she is wishing that her money-minded sister would be at this very moment so she could help her balance the books and find someone to fill the part-time shift at the bar.

"Come or die," Addy vows. "Is there someone on the schedule you wrote up with the gang who can go tend to Lucky for a few hours?"

"It's right here and it's . . . Shit! Me."

"Well, this is a good one." Addy laughs.

"Go to class," Hell says without hesitation. "I'll go get Lucky some dinner and whatever else he needs and we'll meet back here after, okay? I may even be able to catch the last part of class. Addy—are you having a nervous breakdown?"

"It just dawned on me that school is over soon and Lucky will not be going back to work anytime soon and that means . . ."

Addy can barely say it. She can barely acknowledge that the idea of being with her husband 24/7 for 2.6 months makes her feel as if she's been hammered in the head by a sack of rocks.

"Tonight," Addy begs her sister, instead.

"Does he need anything special?" Hell asks just before she hangs up.

Addy could spend the next hour answering Hell's question but instead she tells her sister to IFM Lucky. "Ice, Feed, and Medicate," she explains. "It's not like he cannot get up and walk to the kitchen. And the neighborhood is loaded with Bobs who should be home soon."

"Such tenderness," Hell snorts.

"Hell," Addy whispers as she waves her hand to bring the mob on the playground back to earth, "thanks."

"Get out of here," Hell says, hanging up and wondering if something really, really bad is about to happen.

Malibu Heidi may now be stuck for life.

When she walks into the First National with Addy, three out of four people say hi, not to Heidi, but to Malibu.

"Cool," Malibu whispers in Addy's ear as they walk to the back of the bar where Hell always keeps a table for her private gang. "If I would have known it was this easy to change my name I would have picked something new a long time ago."

"Wouldn't it be something if the rest of life were like that?" Addy replies. "Just get up in the morning and discard whatever it is you don't want or like anymore . . . kids, husbands, the living room couch."

Hell catches the end of the conversation as she swings by the table and drops off a pitcher of beer and a small pizza.

"Ladies, sorry I missed class but I was IFMing," Hell announces.

"How did that go?" Addy asks, falling into her chair.

"Fabulous. Bob One came not so long after I did and he made Lucky dinner, we talked for a while, and when I left there was a wild discussion going on about how most doctors have no idea what they're doing," Hell said.

"Bob **cooked**?" Malibu Heidi says in astonishment, grabbing the first beer.

"He's a real magician in the kitchen, you'd be amazed," Hell answers.

"And he's kinda cute, isn't he?"

Addy looks at Malibu Heidi and then at Hell, as if she is trying to decide who disgusts her more.

"I need a cigarette," she finally says.

"Do you smoke?" Malibu Heidi asks her.

"Yes, I've been a closet smoker, a backyard smoker, a rooftop smoker, a blow-it-out-the-car-window smoker, an anywhere-I-can-sneak-it smoker, for the past twenty-five years."

"Jesus, Addy, are you kidding me?" Hell exclaims, sitting with her hands on the edge of the chair so she won't fall over. "We all smoke cigars—but cigarettes? Are you frigging kidding me? How could I not know this?"

Addy gets up, goes behind the bar without asking, takes a pack of Salem Lights, rips off the top, lights a cigarette, and says the very first thing that comes into her mind.

"I am in big trouble."

Malibu drinks her entire beer in one gulp and Hell gets up, grabs a bottle of tequila, three glasses, three Rocky Patel vintage 1990 Robusto cigars, dumps it all on the table and commands, "Talk to us."

Malibu Heidi who has been more Malibu than anything else her entire life cannot stand the suspense. She wants to know what **kind** of trouble—is it Lucky, something at work, probably not, most likely the husband-sick-maybe-not-in-love thing, but could it be Mitchell? She asks all of this while pouring herself another beer, grabbing one of the shot glasses, and putting some salt and lime on her hand.

"Malibu," Hell scolds gently. "Addy will talk to us as soon as you give her a chance."

Addy has not moved since Malibu started talking but now she slowly moves her fingers toward the shot glass. She raises it to her lips and for a moment Hell thinks she may swallow the entire glass.

"Okay," Addy says, wondering herself what she is going to say. "Hell, light me a cigar, Malibu Heidi, pour me one more shot, everyone else stand back."

Hell is biting her lip so hard she can taste blood. Crap. Addy smokes? How could she not know this? This about-to-happen nervous breakdown is a piece of cake, it's the smoking that has Hell fried.

Fishing for a word, a way to start, Addy takes all of her thoughts and pushes them from the corners of her mind where she has been storing them and sees what falls off of the top. She dips her finger into the shot glass, sticks it in her mouth, and starts talking in a way that may as well be Spanish or French because she has never heard herself speak like this before and the last thing, the very last thing, she wants to do now is to stop.

"When someone you love is sick, and sort

of helpless, it's the way of the world and the heart to want to help, and sacrifice, and to take away the pain, and it's supposed to be a kind of test of love," she begins. "I am failing the test, the only test left, the test that would give me my 'Married for Life' certificate and wake up my desire so I can get my 'Love to Be with Lucky Every Second of the Day' diploma."

Addy cannot stop herself. She talks while she drinks four more shots, finishes off the cigar, has another one—a Moontrance CAO that is so good it makes her want to lick the wrapper, especially after the third tequila shot. She does a wonderful job of helping the other women drink two pitchers of beer, and then she skips through a litany of complaints that could cause an avalanche if she was near a mountain.

The impatience at the slow recovery.

The empty pause when she should want to kiss him.

The anger at every single little flaw.

The ache of missing that is required yet absent from her heart.

The torture of waiting for Cupid to knock on the door.

The sigh of relief when she doesn't have to go home.

The sordid anticipation of what might come next.

"What?" Hell asks, still dying to know about the cigarettes. "What do you **want** to do, Addy Lipton?"

"More shots would be good," Malibu innocently suggests.

"Malibu Heidi, that is a very good suggestion, and after that I think I will always do what I have done, and that is to take one step at a time but maybe call and see if Bob One can have a sleepover because Hell, I need to stay with you tonight, that is if we can find someone to drive us to your house. We're too smashed to drive."

"That's it?" Hell asks.

"I just had to say it," Addy says. "I just had to get those words out of me and it had to be now, and it had to be today, and, yes, that's all I can do for now."

When Greg Jensen, the bartender, drops

off Malibu, and then Addy and Hell, he is worried that the women might want to moon some cars or go skinny-dipping because they make him drive through Parker three times with the windows down, stop at the all-night drive-thru for really greasy cheeseburgers, and then listen while they sing four hits from the Supremes before they finally surrender and stagger through Hell's front door.

The last thing Addy remembers is Hell rolling over to say "Are you okay?" and her answering "I'm going to still try" as she slipped away to a dark and very lovely place where there are Mexican dancers, open windows that stretch from floor to ceiling and carry the salty scent of the sea, and huge bowls of spicy guacamole which she never has liked but eats anyway.

FOURTEEN
Boys gone wild . . .

There is something about the absence of anything remotely female in Bob One's house that makes Lucky feel as if he is standing in the center of The Kingdom of Krap, a locker room, an antique-car lot, the storage center for Snap-on Tools, and in one of those huge steam rooms where men sit naked, read the sports pages, and hope to God that when they leave after steaming their brains out they have miraculously lost ten pounds.

It's a male paradise that Bob One slowly created following his divorce, when he began reconnecting the dots in his own life. It also helped that Vicky, his ex-wife, pretty much took all of the furniture, left nail holes the size of small boulders in the plaster walls, and as part of the divorce decree even took the blinds, the shower curtains, most of the linens, and, at the last minute, Bob's beloved restaurant-sized refrigerator—because they all fit in her new house and it was legal—in other words, he got the house and she got the stuff in it.

Bob One wallowed for a good five months before anything happened. He slept on the ratty couch he hauled up from the basement that smelled like the very corner it had called home for 10.3 years. He ate out of some plastic bowls he stole from work, kept his food inside of his camping cooler, and taped newspapers to the bedroom window so that he could sleep past sunrise.

Bobbie was in post-divorce, "I had no clue what was going on, why did she really leave me" shock, until one day when he caught a glimpse of himself in the one mirror left in the house that was not sitting in the lovely three-bedroom condo that Vicky shared with her new dog and an occasional boyfriend, and saw someone he did not recognize.

"Holy shit," he said to his reflection. "You are a big fat slob with bags under your eyes and a beer belly big enough to host a foreign exchange family for a year."

He stood there for such a long time just staring at himself that his macaroni and cheese burnt and his beer got warm.

"No wonder she left you," he told himself. "Jesus. Holy hell. Get a grip, Robert, just get a grip."

Which is exactly what he started to do immediately. Bob got dressed as fast as possible, lest any unsuspecting neighbor children or women were passing by the uncurtained windows, took a shower, shaved, threw out the macaroni, drank the beer, balanced his checkbook, went online to see if he had any money, and realized that he was in much better shape financially than he thought.

Bob One became a machine. He tossed out every single piece of leftover furniture in the house, ripped up the carpeting—right there he lost six pounds—started going to the gym, went to a salon and not a barber to get his hair cut. Then he went to see Burt

Francis, the local furniture store owner who is a closet interior designer and who helped him turn his house into a manly man's retreat. Instead of taking back his old life, Bob started all over again.

"Bob, are you, like, gay or something?" Lucky asks him as the Bobs and the rest of his support committee sit at the poker table that Bob One had specifically designed to be the center—the **center**—of his new living room.

It's five weeks after surgery and it's Lucky's Get-Out-of-the-House Male-Bonding Therapy Night and Lucky Lipton, the bowling ball sculpture king of Parker, has hit a major recovery slump. His pain in recent days has accelerated instead of subsided. His physical therapy sessions seem to be going nowhere. His mind is in a state of chaos and depression so thick it's made his brain seem like a tar pit. It's a wonder he can remember where Bob One lives, and Addy, that horrid bitch, had made him **walk** to Bob's house, which is just steps away, but still—

Lucky, who has weaned himself from his

pain meds, is drinking whiskey on the rocks and baring his turbulent soul.

Bob One is looking at Lucky sideways and wondering if he's lying about being off the pain meds.

"Gay?" he repeats. "Would there be something wrong if I was gay?"

"So you are?"

"Do you know what, Lucky, you beautiful hunk of a man, I believe that there is a piece inside of each man that is gay, that is feminine, that really wants to reach out to another man the way women do. And if that means I'm gay, brother boy, then bring it on."

Lucky is frozen in place. He's got a great hand, four cards to a straight, and he's betting the house that the last card he needs will pop into his hand from the river, but Texas Hold 'Em be damned, because suddenly he feels like crying.

Crying like a baby.

Crying like he never cried before.

Crying into his whiskey and on the cards and almost into the bowl of pretzels.

"Lucky . . . ?" Barry, a fellow Cooper guy, asks, concerned, dropping his own cards onto the table.

"Hey," Bob One offers. "Lucky, I'm not really gay, just trying to prove a point here. Are you okay?"

Lucky has not cried for so long that when the flood begins it feels as if huge boulders are falling from his eyes. He drops his own cards, exposing himself suddenly on all levels. He just starts talking—talking as if someone else has jumped inside of him and is moving his throat and lips with tiny fingers that only require him to push air in and out so the words will come spilling out. Words that come from a jungle so deep and dark and old that Lucky Lipton is lost.

"I wouldn't care if you were gay, Bob," Lucky says, raising his hands to his eyes. "I get what you are saying, I'm just . . . I'm just a mess."

Lucky's unexpected confession has everyone staring at each other—Bob Two, Barry and Shaun from work, Jim Zeland from across the street, and Bob One, who leans over to put his hand on Lucky's arm.

"It's been the shits, buddy, lots of things have happened to you the past few months," Bob One offers. "We are here for you, buddy, you know that, don't you?"

Lucky looks up and wipes his eyes on the edge of his shirt but he is still crying. He grabs his glass, gulps it down, motions for Jim to fill it again, takes one more drink, then says: "There's more."

"Did you get some tests back?" Shaun asks. "That can be a pisser if you still have a ways to go. My uncle John, hell, it took him two years before he could even lift his tackle box."

"I wish that was it." Lucky sniffs. "They say it will be at least a year, **an entire fucking year,** before I can do more than sit at a desk for a few hours."

All the men say "Oh" at the same moment and then Lucky tells them. He launches his words quickly so they will not get lost in the jungle of his life, so he will not lose courage, so he can put it out there before the whiskey simmers down in the lining of his bloodstream.

"It's me and Addy," he almost shouts.

"She **hates** me, I know it, and maybe I feel the same way about her. Things haven't been right for a long time and I thought this damn Costa Rica trip would help. It's not all her, it's been me, too, but now, now this shit happens to me and I'm around all the time and it's like I'm a baby and she has to take care of me, which I know for a fact she hates like hell, and she stays away a lot and I'm **glad** when she is not there."

"Christ," Bob Two whispers.

But Lucky isn't done.

He's on such a roll he may never stop or slow down. He takes a deep breath in between waves of tears, taps his glass with his finger, and tells his friends everything.

Everything.

How sex has become nonexistent.

How it just got easier not to talk.

How he gradually moved his entire life into The Kingdom of Krap.

How he has slowly stopped thinking about Addy.

How he has all these things to say and no one to say them to.

How maybe the direction of his life needs to take a new direction.

And finally how he would be lost without them, his buddies, the men around the table, his lifeline to humanity in all its masculine (and feminine) forms.

The silent pause is deafening until Bob One gets up. Bob One walks behind Lucky, gets on his knees, wraps his arms around his shoulders, and says, "Lucky, I'm always here for you, I know what this feels like, we won't let you down."

Barry, Jim, Shaun, and Bob Two are holding on to their glasses of whiskey and bottles of beer so tightly that it's a wonder one of the glasses has not shattered.

"Here's to you, Lucky, here's to your journey, here's to terrific friends and all kinds of talking and drinking, and cards and . . . hell, even bowling balls," toasts Barry. "We miss ya at work, we, well, hell, we're here for you."

The first toast turns into dozens more. The cards are left in little piles, most of them faceup, as the men grab a fresh bottle of whiskey, literally pick Lucky up in his chair, and lift him into the backyard patio where Bob One has created a sensational smoking patio with built-in ashtrays, high screens designed with some kind of imported flowering trees, because he "likes to sit back here naked and watch the sun and stars and the neighbors' lights go on and off" and where he fires up the grill and begins cooking what he calls Testosterone Tenders—hunks of top-grade steak for his friends and tofu for himself, dipped in a secret batter and grilled in piles of onions seasoned with spices Bob One bought online from a place that usually sells directly to restaurants.

While they smoke and drink and the meat cooks, Bob One decides it would be a good idea for all of them to go to confession. He starts by waltzing through his own divorce, his own walk back to life, his resurrection as a gay man in a straight man's body who still wonders if his transformation would have occurred sooner if Vicky was still in his life.

"No," Jim advises. "She's the reason you changed. You would have been like Lucky, plodding along, doing everything the same, not bothering to work on the relationship because you'd let yourself go for so long."

"Jim, Jesus, are you in therapy?"

Jim hunches down in his chair and looks at Bob One as if he's been caught taking a sip out of Bob One's drink when Bob wasn't looking.

"Yes, I am."

Shit.

Jesus.

Goddamn it.

What the fuck.

"It's not all peachy at our house, either, but I'm telling you, just talking, even like this, well, Bob, you are right, we should all be more feminine. Half the goddamn time I have no idea what my wife is thinking, or what I did wrong, or when the hell was the last time I did something right."

"Well," Lucky says, "I'm in every other kind of therapy. Do you guys think I should see a shrink?"

"You aren't very happy," Barry says. "And it does seem like the unhappy started before you broke your ass."

"Maybe you could just do it and not even tell Addy."

"It would be a good step," Bob Two agrees. "Lots of people do it, Lucky, and hell, look what's all been going on."

Lucky does look. He sees the lines of his life fading into some unseen sunset and he starts crying again. Mitchell is gone, Addy is half gone, he's worked so long at Cooper he could probably get early retirement, and he can barely walk, let alone kick the soccer balls that he so very much loves.

The men talk so long that the coals in the barbecue fade to black and just before midnight, when they all realize they are drunk as skunks, they take turns calling their wives to let them know they are having a slumber party at Bob One's house.

And not one wife volunteers to come pick up a husband.

And not one wife thinks there is something weird about grown men having a slumber party.

And not one wife asks what time the husband might come home.

And for the very first time since Boy

Scout camp, Lucky Lipton falls asleep next to another male, and when he dreams, everything appears in light colors and he's constantly worried about the way his hair looks, if his teeth are clean, and whether or not he is going to be late.

FIFTEEN
What I should have said to Addy · · ·

Addy looks at me with my hangover, which has set a record for the number of hours I have had a continuous headache, like she wishes it would last for the rest of my life.

We are barely speaking but I should have asked her this one thing. I should have just gotten up and walked over to her and asked her if she wanted to try.

"Addy," I should have said, "do you want to go to therapy with me?"

But I didn't ask.

I didn't ask Addy.

SIXTEEN
Shrinking hearts on Lipton Lane . . .

Mitchell calls three times in one day, missing Lucky and Addy every single time he calls. Their son has been a quiet oasis since his spontaneous weekend visit, and the fact that he does not try to call either one of his parents on their cell phones is the tip-off for Addy, who has been wondering since the last visit if something, anything, one thing or a dozen things, were not up.

"Mitchell called again," Lucky yells from the couch when Addy gets home from school.

"What did he want?" Addy responds, not even caring if she sees her husband, and secretly hoping he will not get up so she does not have to look him in the eye.

"I missed the call because I was at an appointment."

"Which appointment?"

"Therapy," Lucky answers from the living room where he is praying to God that Addy does not walk in and ask him what kind of therapy.

"What did Mitchell say?"

"He called three times actually. He just said he wants to talk to us."

"Us?"

"Yep."

"Shit," Addy says, throwing her books on the counter. It's past crunch time at school, the grades are in, and it's the last week of classes and Addy does not want to go into the living room, she does not want to look at Lucky, she wants to get the hell out of the house as fast as possible.

"I ate," Lucky tells her, as if he is reading her mind.

"How are you feeling?" Addy finally asks, appearing at the opening of the living room.

"I'm sitting on ice."

"Oh."

"I had muscle spasms all afternoon."

"Oh."

"Barry came and got me on his lunch hour and took me back to work for a little while," Lucky shared. "I sat in my office chair for about fifteen minutes and then asked Barry to shoot me."

"Didn't the gun go off?"

Lucky looks at his wife, thinking he is supposed to smile, but he can't, and she is, but it isn't funny because he thinks that Addy would have liked the gun to go off.

Addy senses that something so large has moved in between them it may soon be impossible for her to see over the hedge of what has grown there.

Unspoken words enough to build a fence around an entire marriage.

Misplaced emotions.

Hearts grown weary with the strain of trauma.

Expectations ignored.

An off-key serenade of longing.

Disgust as wide as the goddamn garage door.

And all tied together with a very large knot of anger.

Addy decides to do what she has been doing for months and months. She ignores Lucky, and what he is saying. She skips right over the gun business and goes back to Mitchell.

"Do you know what Mitchell wants?"

"No. But it seems kind of funny that he would call so much and not ask for money or something, doesn't it? He knows he could get us on our cell phones."

"He'll call back," Addy says. "Maybe he has a girlfriend or wants to switch majors again."

Lucky shrugs his shoulders, winces, picks up a magazine, and wonders if Bob One would mind if he came over to sit by the barbecue. If Addy doesn't leave, he decides he will just hobble over there, do some stretching in the backyard, and start working on his therapy exercises.

The real therapy exercises. The ones Dr. Tecal Mensky gave him a few hours ago when Lucky went in to see him for the first time.

Write down what you want.
Write down what you want back.

Write down your wildest life dreams.

"Really?" Lucky had asked the psychologist in astonishment. "I was just thinking about that not so long ago and I sat down, put a sheet of paper in front of me, even made some tea, and then it was just like an empty room up there."

"It doesn't have to all come at once," Dr. T, as he prefers to be called, told him. "Most people, especially men, never stop to run through their emotions like this, and we need to wake yours up, Lucky. It may take a while but the fact that you came in here, that you know something isn't right, that you want to change it—well, that is more of a start than you might think."

It was **a start,** Lucky told himself, holding on to this therapy secret as if he was hiding the last bag of food in the entire city. It was his own bold secret, even if his friends knew, but Addy did not know and he was not yet sure if he would ever tell her. Lucky had such a craving to be alone that he did not even wait to see if Addy was taking off to work out or to go hang out with Hell. He simply got up, yelled up the stairs where she had disappeared leading to what he was now calling "Addy's bedroom," said, "I'm taking a walk," and left without waiting for an answer.

Addy heard him, paused by the bathroom door, and then waited until she heard the door close behind him before she rushed to change her clothes, threw on a pair of shorts and a shirt, grabbed her bag, and without leaving a note or shouting after Lucky, drove to Hell's.

Lucky watched her leave, smiled, then crept into Bob One's backyard with his pad of paper, a bottle of water, two pens, and a notion that he might just ask Bob if he could spend the night again, only this time in the spare bedroom.

"Space," he said out loud as he happily put down that first word on his list.

Less than a mile away Addy pulled into Hell's driveway so fast she ran over the exact same bush at the edge of the asphalt Mitchell hit every time he slid into her driveway too fast. Hell, thank God, was not there and Addy stamped down the ground after she backed up and let herself in through the side door which had not been locked since the day it was hung onto the side of the house.

"I'm losing my mind," she mumbles. "Absolutely losing my mind. How can I hate someone that I once loved so much? How in the hell did this happen to me? How did I go from wanting to be with this man constantly because he made me feel precious and beautiful to hoping he would not even come back home?"

Addy paces herself through Hell's kitchen with its low windows that offer a view of her sister's backyard gardens, filled from edge to edge with late-spring blossoms. Hell's dogs are delighted to have an unexpected romp in the yard. Addy is almost running through the open living room, through the library—which in every other house on the block is a dining room but to Hell, every room, including the bathroom, is a dining room—circles down the long hall, past Hell's bedroom—a huge master suite that had been two bedrooms and a small bath before a massive remodeling project that kept a somewhat bewildered freelance carpenter busy for an entire year.

She opens the refrigerator. She brings in the mail. She lies down on the couch for less than two minutes and gets back up and rotates through the house three more times before she starts to make a pot of coffee. She tries to call Mitchell.

"Mitchell, it's your mom. You keep calling the house and you know we are hardly ever there. Call me on my cell phone. I'm at Hell's now but I don't know where I will be later."

He doesn't pick up and Mitchell, especially after 5 p.m. EST, was always at the end of his cell phone.

By the time Hell gets home after she has kick-started the dinner crew, Addy has downed three cups of coffee and her face is the color of Santa Claus's backside after a rough ride through the tundra.

"Hey," Hell calls from the kitchen. "What's up, sister?"

Addy comes around the corner with yet another cup of coffee in her hand, takes one look at Hell, and although she wants to cry, cannot bring herself to the edge of tears because she is too angry.

"I should talk to him!" Addy exclaims. "I know I should talk to him but I can barely stand to be in the same room with him for more than five minutes. It's like something toxic has seeped out of him and I'm breathing it in and it's making me sick to my stomach—"

"Jesus, Addy, sit," Hell commands. "**Can** you sit?"

"I don't think so."

"What happened?" Hell asks, grabbing herself a beer.

"I just looked at him," Addy laments. "I walked into the house, knew he was sitting in that goddamned chair, had to go past him to change my clothes and, well— Shit, Hell, I cannot stand to be around him."

Hell sits but Addy won't.

"You have to go talk to someone else, Addy," Hell demands. "You know that, I think. You can't avoid him, you can't keep running away like this, you have to figure this out, for God's sake."

"Christ, Hell, who can I talk to?"

"Like a shrink. Like someone who has a degree. I can just keep telling you the same things. I can tell you that I love you. That men are assholes. That marriage is an outmoded institution. That Lucky is a fat pig who spends more time in The Kingdom of Krap than in a serious discussion with you. But none of that matters when the curtain falls."

Hell is up and she is talking with her hands and a teeny tiny part of her wants to put those hands around her sister's neck so that Addy will really listen.

"How do I do this?" Addy not so much asks as pleads. "How?"

"First you go to see your doctor, which is not a bad idea anyway. When was the last time you had a physical?"

Mammogram. Yearly Pap. Tetanus shot. Procrastinating the colonoscopy. Flu shots. Addy admits it's been a while.

"Don't you need a referral with your insurance anyway?"

"Yes."

"Well, call. You could get an appointment

in like ten seconds. It's not like people don't know you. It's not like there is a waiting line in the shrink's office."

"How do you know?"

"I'm guessing. Actually, he's probably busy as hell."

"There's only **one** shrink in Parker?" Addy wails.

Hell laughs. Addy, queen of the education system, sometimes seems to know about as much as one of her third graders.

"There are a couple, unless you hoof it into Pittsburgh. I'll get some names. Addy, you have to deal with this. This is what you call a crisis."

A crisis.

Turmoil.

A shakedown in paradise.

Addy finally sits down. She sits down and she pushes away the coffee cup because her hand is shaking from the caffeine and she reaches for Hell's beer and asks her to open some wine and then she takes in a huge breath of air and she asks her sister the big question.

"Hell, do you think I'm crazy?"

Addy's sister has never been able to lie but
she's always been able to be there for her sister, always been able to pick up a small piece,
if not all the pieces, has always watched her
sister closely and loved her but never, ever
imagined herself living the same kind of life.
So Hell tells Addy the truth. She can do it
no other way.

"Anyone in a serious relationship is
crazy," Hell tells Addy.

"You think that? That relationships are
crazy?"

"Some of them. Life gets crazy and things
get in the way and you have kids and there
are 'issues,' " she says, using her fingers for
make-believe quotation marks. "It's not like
there is a map for this, Addy. Look, I see this
all of the time. My business is more psychology then booze and cigars, you know that.
People come to the First National to escape.
They get something they think they want
and then they open the package and say, 'Oh
shit—is this what it really looks like?' "

"Maybe."

"Maybe my ass, honeybunch. It's the
truth. You and Lucky have been plodding

along like those damn horses in the parade they have in the big city each year. They follow the horse in front of them and always turn at the right corner. You've been lost for a long time. It's a wonder this did not happen sooner."

"Oh, Hell. Hell."

Hell does not back down.

"Get the referral. Get it in the morning. Stop this shit. Do you hear me?"

"It's not shit, it's my life!" Addy cries.

"You're right. But you have to move a bit, do you know?"

Addy knows. She's known since the day she parked her car by the basketball hoop and was three seconds from ramming through the garage. She's known for weeks and maybe weeks before that.

She slumps on top of the table and asks Hell if it will be okay if she sleeps upstairs in the guest suite for one night.

And Hell, of course, says yes, Addy, you have the key even though the door isn't locked, you have anything you want here, you have everything you can possibly want when you want it.

The two sisters sit at the table for a long time, until Hell has to rush back to her own kind of marriage—her business—and make certain the new night manager knows the ropes and the outer door is locked and everything is where it is supposed to be.

Addy sits and drinks some wine and then takes a very long shower. She checks her cell phone about fifteen times, but Lucky does not call and Mitchell does not call and she finally decides to stop trying.

Then, sucking in enough air to fill a beach ball, she calls the house. She calls her house and no one answers and she leaves a message. She tells Lucky that she is staying the night at her sister's and that she will see him in the morning. That is all she says. She makes no excuse, no explanations. Nothing else at all.

Addy's message comes two minutes after the message that Lucky leaves on the same machine. He's called from Bob's kitchen, where he has helped Bob One cook a light pasta dish sautéed with a touch of sweet wine, fresh vegetables, and a hint of garlic so light it's barely noticeable.

"Addy, I'm staying at Bob's tonight," Lucky said into the machine and then hung up very quickly.

And at the Liptons' house the hall light stays on all night but absolutely no one is home.

SEVENTEEN

The pressure is on · · ·

Margarite Sanchez is seemingly the only doctor left in the United States of America who refuses to throw her hat into some large HMO pot and herd her patients like cattle when an invisible alarm sounds every fifteen minutes so she can meet her performance quota that will ensure all the insurance executives can get a billion-dollar bonus, and she has been known to make house calls—especially for elderly patients.

Margarite Sanchez has a devoted array of patients who are so loyal they will wait for hours if she has an emergency. Dozens of them even volunteer to help at her office so she can spend more time working—although she does not call what she does work. She

calls it a "personal spiritual labor of healing."
Dr. Margarite Sanchez has been the Person
of the Year in Parker for five years in a row.

And she's mad at Addy Lipton.

"You have not been in here for a very long
time, Addy," says Sanchez, as she prefers to
be called because she tells her patients, her
friends, everyone she knows that her last
name reminds her of her lovely childhood in
Mexico before her parents immigrated and
started over so she could go to medical
school with her four siblings, all doctors, all
"healers."

"I know," Addy admits. "But I've been to
every other doctor and to the hospital and to
the clinics and . . ."

"What happened?" Sanchez asks her,
holding tightly on to a file with missing
records from the appointments Addy has
never made. "You look like you've been
dragged behind a Harley, by the way. Get up
on the table while you talk. Off with your
shirt, woman. Move it."

Addy talks while she breathes in and out,
while Sanchez focuses on her heartbeat, her
breathing, the way her face is so red. Sanchez

does not make a single comment on Lucky or on the obvious fact that Addy Lipton is stressed-out, depressed, and a walking time bomb, not even when she tells her doctor that she's a mess.

"Friend, your blood pressure is through the roof—163 over 103—and I think you may have some other stuff going on," Sanchez reveals.

Every ounce of blood but the few drops now cruising, way too fast, through Addy's heart have pooled in her feet. She is so dizzy with fear that she simply falls back, rolls over to her side, pushes her legs up and curls into the very same ball that was her position inside of her mother's womb.

"Addy . . ." Sanchez whispers. "What's going on?"

Sanchez has pushed a chair over to the examining table and she has her hand on Addy's leg. It is a warm connection, a line of heat that keeps Addy breathing and just to the simple side of sanity.

"I came in here to get a referral so I can see a therapist," Addy says, moving only her lips. "My marriage is a shambles, I'm depressed, Lucky and I cannot even look each other in the eye, I am at the point of not caring if he even gets better."

"Okay, Addy, first things first. The blood pressure is a huge problem and I am sending you to the hospital today for a series of tests—no excuses or I will sit on you to get you there, do you hear me?"

This, Addy thinks, is the tough-love shit happening before I even see the shrink. "Yes."

"Heart disease, heart problems, high blood pressure—this is the real curse for women, well, besides men, of course. I can tell you there are so many women walking around Parker with hearts that are time bombs that you'd better start wearing a surgical mask in public," the doctor explains. "We are going to do blood work, a stress test, and I may have them strap on a heart monitor for a bit. Have you felt heart palpitations? Short of breath?"

Addy confesses.

Her heart, she says, is a wicked fiber of bouncing hell that throbs as if it is crying all of the time.

When she sits up the doctor does not move her hand and Addy tells her that her marriage is resting on a long branch that has been falling from the sky during a strong, windy storm for years and years.

"This didn't just happen," Sanchez agrees. "But you owe it to **yourself**—forget Lucky just this second, put yourself first, which is another thing women never do, damn it— you owe it to **yourself** to talk to someone, to settle your heart, to stop this pounding."

"So, my heart—you know, the muscle part—isn't right?" Addy questions as a stream of tears rolls down her face in an increasingly familiar line that curves just to the inside of each cheekbone. "Should I be flipping out?"

"Calm is good, Addy, but starting with this immediate trip to the hospital, you **have** to take better care of yourself. I'm going to get the psychiatrist's card for you, he's a man but he's sort of a girly-man, women love him, he's very, very good, and then you are going to go to the hospital and then you are coming back to my office after the hospital and we will decide on medication or what to do next depending on the tests."

Addy hugs Sanchez, which is a welcome and ongoing occurrence in the doctor's office, on the street, in the grocery store, and everywhere else a fan or friend runs into Sanchez. Or Addy, for that matter.

Driving toward the hospital, Addy is tempted to lift her hands off the steering wheel to see if the car will go there on its own from memory. Hell should know where she is going, Lucky should know where she is going, someone besides Sanchez should know what is going on, but Addy is suddenly too exhausted to lift the cell phone off the car seat and dial a number. She is too tired to do anything but steer and her tiredness is all she thinks about as she drives to the hospital, gets out of her car, walks toward the Outpatient door and then just stands there with her hand on the door.

Tiredness.

Solitude.

Time alone.

A stretch of quiet.

These four thoughts seep from someplace deep inside her mind and intoxicate her. She is drunk on these thoughts and for a moment considers turning away from the hospital because there is nothing wrong with her, nothing at all. Nothing that time alone, sleep, a few weeks of nonaccessible space, and the shrinking well of responsibility opening up into a garden of delicious "me" choices wouldn't cure.

But then her heart thumps wildly. This recent addition to her bodily functions was at the beginning so strange and frightening when it occurred for the first time several weeks ago, right after Lucky hurt his back, it took Addy's breath away and when she lightly pressed her fingers near her heart she could hear the rumba of excess pounding. The "spell," as she was calling it, came now so often that she was no longer frightened but considered it the first beckoning finger of menopause tinted with a bit of stress and maybe the frightful unspoken notion that her entire goddamn life was about to go into freefall and change.

She goes inside. Hand on heart, bracing for the needles, for the treadmill, for whatever in the hell else Sanchez has ordered for her and before she can get to the desk she has to sit down once, lower her head, take a few yoga breaths and drink a glass of water which also allows her to say her name to the receptionist and to call the school to let them know she has had a tiny emergency and will not be back at the end of her lunch break.

She may as well have alerted the entire United States Navy, because her phone starts ringing halfway through her admissions routine.

And Addy lies.

"Lucky is coming," she tells her teaching assistant, who is perfectly capable of finishing the three hours of class even if it is almost the last day of school. "Just something routine, really."

Jeezus, Addy, maybe you can steal some narcotics while you are here.

Maybe they can do a quick open-heart surgery.

Maybe you can crawl out of the lobby, through the parking lot, and back to your car and no one will notice.

Maybe a wild turkey giving birth to an eagle will fly out of your left nostril.

Maybe when the shit hits the fan it will smell like sage and musk.

It will be a very long time before Addy remembers anything that happens during the next three hours. She will talk and be funny and two former students will come hug her and she'll grab a bagel and a piece of fruit in the cafeteria and she will finish her tests and then take a wad of paper with her as she walks like a normal person back to her car which she will start and carefully drive the few blocks back to the office of Sanchez. She will float into the office and pass no one in the waiting room because it is now past 7 p.m. and it is only Sanchez who is still there with her head bent over piles of files and a look on her face when she looks up and sees Addy that Addy instantly interprets to mean, **Holy crap—you are in trouble, Lipton.**

"Sit," Sanchez orders.

She is drinking wine. There is a bottle on her desk and a box of crackers and a hunk of cheese that she is biting off as she goes along.

"Do you live here?" Addy hears herself blurt out.

"Upstairs and, yes, this is dinner. I'd offer you some but you have high blood pressure."

"I am **not** going to quit drinking," Addy snarls.

"Addy, Addy, Addy," Sanchez says, spinning around in her chair so she can prop up her feet. She reaches for her wineglass

"I was married once for about fifteen minutes," Sanchez shares. "He didn't get me. Loved my body, apparently. Loved to tell people he was marrying a doctor. But me? Nope. Didn't get my passion. Didn't understand the fact that I was in this doctor business because it was a calling, a gift from the universe, and not a way for me to buy him toys and so we could build a big house."

"I didn't know that," Addy says, forgetting for a few minutes what she thinks they are supposed to be talking about.

"And I found out marriage is damn hard

work, at least for most people, and I didn't
think it should be that way," the doctor confesses. "Is this too unprofessional for you?"

Addy laughs so hard she snorts.

"Hell no, Sanchez, you are so human,
that's why there is a line at your door.
Talking with another woman like this is not
unprofessional, it's called having a conversation. Besides, it's the damn men who made
up all the rules anyway," Addy says. "What
could be more intimate than looking inside
another person's body or trusting someone
to look inside of yours?"

"Not much. But I can usually tell which
patients I'd rather just be sitting behind the
desk to talk with because they dislike personal
contact. But then I don't do that either."

Addy latches onto the marriage theme.
She asks Sanchez if she would ever marry
again.

The good doctor laughs, pours some
more wine, and drops her feet to the floor.

"What I was starting to tell you is that
now I have a girlfriend, partner, whatever in
the hell you want to call her, and I wish I
would have thought of this sooner."

"Are you telling me that if I become a lesbian everything will be better?"

Sanchez snorts, too, and wine actually comes out of her left nostril.

"Christ, Lipton, did I also tell you I flunked Psychology 101? No, that is not what I am trying to tell you."

"Try harder then, unless your girlfriend has a sister you want me to meet."

"Hey, I do remember that laughter and a good sense of humor can help almost anything, so you have something there."

"Sounds ominous," Addy says. "Cough it up, sister."

No heart attack on the horizon.

Stress test was gallant and good.

Blood work—so-so.

Addy needs to start on some medication and get rid of the stress in her life and read eighteen pamphlets on women and heart problems and it's fabulous she's already exercising, but the drinking needs to slow down, and did she mention that she needs to get rid of the stress?

Which dances them back to the marriage slice of the conversation.

"Addy, the reason you came in to see me," Sanchez says, "is because you wanted a referral to work through some of your marriage issues."

"That was so long ago I barely remember it."

"My practice is mostly women, you know that, and many of them are unhappy and taking care of everyone else but themselves," Sanchez continues. "That's what you do right after you take your first pill and wash it down with water and not wine. Take care of yourself. Well, you can have some wine, but taper off just a bit."

"I know I should cut back a bit on the drinking but sometimes a few glasses of wine are the best medicine."

"No kidding, Addy, but we have to get you through this window, which I suspect is partially due to your unhappiness and probably due to all these other issues, especially your marriage. And you need to address those issues."

"So I need to see the shrink, take my pills, do a little personal AA. Did you get me this shrink's phone number?"

Sanchez puts down her glass of wine, grabs her chair by the handles, and scoots it right in front of Addy.

"Here's the thing, Addy," Sanchez says, holding on to Addy's hands. "I've already called him, his name's Dr. Tecal Mensky. I was going to clear the path for you, but you won't be able to see him, so I'm going to have to call someone else in the morning for you."

"What? Doesn't this Mensky like middle-aged women with high blood pressure who fantasize about driving their cars through garage doors?"

"Take a breath here, Addy."

"Take a breath? What the hell is the problem? Why won't this shrink see me? He's just run off with three patients at one time? My insurance expired? He's a fake? What?"

"Addy, Dr. Mensky can't see you because he is already seeing Lucky."

The blow strikes Addy just below the top of her throat and sucks the air right out of her windpipe, her lungs, and her stomach. It sends a zap of adrenaline right through her heart that actually makes her shirt rise off her chest.

"You didn't know, did you?" Sanchez asks.

Addy shakes her head. Speaking is out of the question.

"This is probably a good thing. It means Lucky is worried, too, which is a good thing, but the bad thing is that you are not speaking to each other," Sanchez adds.

Now, the good doctor adds, might be a good time to have a little bit of wine. Or in your case, Addy, to just drink some right out of the bottle.

EIGHTEEN
What I should have said to Addy · · ·

I'm not happy either, Addy. This time, this wound to my heart and my back, it has given me one good thing so far—time to think.

And I really need to think, Addy.

How easy would that have been to say before the shit hit the fan?

You'd think real easy, but no, I didn't say a damn word. Maybe it's because if I said it I knew everything would change. So as much as I wanted that—I couldn't say it.

I just couldn't.

NINETEEN
The art of conversation . . .

The predictable moment arrives with such a silent beginning that there is no reason for Lucky or Addy to prepare for battle. Three days have passed in rapid succession. School has ended, which is usually cause for at least one wild night of celebration on the cul-de-sac, but Addy has been hiding out at Hell's, in her classroom, at the First National, at the library, and at every coffee shop within a twenty-mile radius.

Lucky has immersed himself so deeply in his list project for Dr. T and with helping with the wine selections for the Fall Community Festival that he has been oblivious to the existence of his wife, the passing of time, the sometimes receding ache that climbs from the back of his knee around his thigh and up the center of his back where it nestles like a wild porcupine against his spine and renders him temporarily insane with agony.

"It will eventually go away," beautiful Dr. Patty has explained more than once. "Sometimes your body remembers pain, Lucky. Sometimes you must simply change position. It is a process of healing, Lucky. The process might seem long but it's necessary and it will work, Lucky, as long as you work too."

"I'm working," Lucky tells himself constantly. "Working on me."

Which is exactly what he is doing the moment he literally bumps into Addy in the kitchen when he comes in from his seemingly continuous nomadic walks, cooking lessons, doctor appointments, cigar-smoking rituals, and list-making at Bob One's. Addy is standing in front of the refrigerator with her hand on her heart trying to hold it in place, trying to regulate the wild thumping, the pounding that feels like the roll of a Tongan drum that is boiling in the pit of her stomach and climbing its way up her own spinal cord.

She hears Lucky coming in through The Kingdom of Krap and she knows it is time. Lucky does not know she has been to the hospital. He does not know that his wife has placed him in a basket, tied it to a long rope, and flung him out over a cliff where that movement launches the echo of dangerous wild waves crashing against boulders the size of Toledo out into the wide universe.

Lucky sees her frozen left hand pressing against her chest, eyes roving the nearly empty shelves of a refrigerator that was once so filled with food, life, drinks, and containers with mismatched lids that standing in front of the cooling machine could cause permanent damage when the door opened.

Empty now.

Fucking empty.

"Addy."

"Lucky."

Their eyes meet and dance like knives sliding so close that to blink, to breathe, would be to open a wound as long as the length of an entire body. It is a moment as cold as February when the Pennsylvania windows freeze shut, the brave winter birds huddle in Addy's pine tree, covering each other with wings that turn them all into one giant mass of feathers, and when to experience walking through the ice-carpeted landscape of life is to risk everything.

Everything.

Addy blinks first and she is only calm enough to think that it is her anger, her sense of loss, the bile from her rising emotions, that allows her to do it.

"Lucky, we should talk," she says, pushing the refrigerator door closed and then crossing her arms in the classic defiant, up-yours stance that is an obvious gesture of defense, but what is really, for Addy, a simple way to hold herself so she does not fall over.

"We should," Lucky agrees, wanting desperately to add, **But we don't**.

"Look, Lucky, I'm sorry about your back and everything that has happened, you know that, but we can't go on like this, we cannot live as if we don't know each other,"

Addy begins, not knowing what she will say next, what she wants, where and when she will stop.

"I know."

"I'm a mess inside, Lucky, and I'm not sure of things I used to be sure of and, well, shit, Lucky, I know you are seeing a therapist."

Lucky looks down, pulls his eyes away from Addy, rotates his neck in a circle and then looks past her when he speaks.

"I should have told you but . . . Well, I didn't and maybe that's part of the problem."

"Are you happy, Lucky?" Addy asks him abruptly, trying hard not to be furious and failing miserably.

"I thought I was happy. But maybe I never really thought about it enough."

Addy feels something rolling toward her, toward Lucky, that is much, much larger than an oversized bowling ball.

"Addy, you look like you are going to explode, you are all red, are you okay?"

What happens next is a heat-seeking missile of explosion. The blast is a tangle of dead

vines, roughage from shreds of loss, the tearing out of veins and a rupture of scars that
have grown thick with age until the throb-
bing weight of unhappiness bursts them
into a thousand pieces.

"I. Am. Not. Fucking. Okay. Lucky."
Addy begins halfway between loud talking
and yelling. "My blood pressure is through
the roof and I'm on medication and I have
to change how I live and what I do and
where I go and what I keep bottled up inside. I am angry and depressed. I feel as if
years have passed through me while I was
waiting for a bus to paradise that never came
because I was holding the wrong ticket. I am
a mess and I am exhausted and I am sick of
your whining and your boyfriends and your
bowling balls and the goddamn garage that
looks like a disaster zone . . ."

Lucky takes each accusation like a practice boxer, shifting from foot to foot with
every sentence, each word, as Addy's cannon
of complaints fires again and again.

"I hate this house and the way Mitchell
takes advantage of us and the fact that I am
bouncing on the edge of menopause, hear

that word, Lucky—**menopause!**—and I am digging mighty deep, Lucky, to try and salvage something these days, anything, a tiny piece of what we are supposed to have to be considered partners and in a real relationship. A relationship that we once had but seem to have thrown away."

Lucky stops moving when Addy stops talking. He has no idea what to say. He is desperately fighting an urge to simply turn and walk away and why he cannot do that will be a question that settles inside of him like a wedge of titanium.

"I don't know what to say," Lucky finally says. "I didn't plan any of this."

"What do you want to do, Lucky?"

The question.

The pause.

The refrigerator grinding to a halt quickly with nothing to keep cold.

The dishes from days past moldering in the sink.

The whisper of summer blocked by the cold force of the fierce Lipton energy.

And out of the corner of his eye the soft blue haze from Bob One's patio lights that are winking at Lucky, seducing him, calling him to a place that has recently calmed his heart.

"Take a break," he finally tells Addy.

"A break?"

"From each other, maybe."

"Is this what you've learned in therapy or what?"

"It is what I've learned from my heart. Which aches as much as yours."

Addy sucks in a wad of air, determined not to cry, not to waver, not to give in to something she has never ever felt before in her life.

"Maybe I should just move in with Bob One for a while. He's got room. I know you could move in with Hell but this would be easier for both of us," Lucky says, keeping his eye on the blue light of Bob's patio.

"That's it?"

"For starters, maybe."

"What about talking together, therapy, the two of us?" Addy asks.

"I don't think I can do it yet, Addy. I need . . ."

He stops fumbling for words. And suddenly Addy realizes she has never felt this angry, cannot remember ever wanting to hit her husband like this—hit him so that his head rolls back and he cries out in pain, shows some serious emotion, and hit him so that she can feel as if she has done something to make him pay attention the way she needs to have him pay attention. But instead she forces herself to be still, to lower her head, to talk softly.

"What do you need, Lucky?"

"I just need some time, space, something to see what I want, too."

It is, of course, the perfect thing to say, but it is not what Addy Lipton hears and she raises her head, pushes one hand against the refrigerator, and moves her lips in a tight line so that when she speaks again it is in a voice Lucky has never heard before.

Harsh.

Foreign.

Unforgiving.

Savage.

"Fine. I'm just going to leave for a few hours, Lucky. Take what you want, but do me one favor."

"What?"

"When you see me here or know I am here, please do not come over. Please. Leave me alone."

"Fine," Lucky says, raising his hands in a white-flag salute of surrender. "I can do that. That's fine."

Addy leaves without her purse, without raising her eyes, without bothering to put her sandals back on her feet and when she walks past the garage door she raises her right leg, does the backward side kick that she learned in self-defense class ten years ago, and puts a dent in the garage door three inches deep that sounds like an assassin's gun as it echoes around and around the cul-de-sac.

TWENTY
What I thought
Addy was thinking · · ·

I hate him.
I hate my life.
He makes me sick.
He is an insincere slob, male pig, selfish ass, is what she was thinking and she would be correct.
Sort of.

TWENTY-ONE
A smashing evening...

Lee, the resident Parker expert on divorce, bad relationships, men, how to file for a divorce, the glories of flirting, how to select the proper attorney, and why it's necessary to make the first move in legal matrimonial-related issues, has dragged Addy home from the Y and a particularly wild workout session that resulted in Hell planning a spontaneous reunion of her all-women cigar trip to Honduras for Friday evening.

"Sit," Lee orders as she rummages through a bookshelf in her living room and produces a book.

"A dictionary?" Addy asks, bewildered.

"Shhh," Lee admonishes, putting up her hand as if it is a stop sign. "Do you want a glass of wine or something? I've got some great samples that we might use this year in the Fall Festival."

Addy sighs so deeply the pages in the dictionary flutter.

"See that," Addy says, pointing to the pages. "That's just what my heart has been doing. I'm drinking water and tea these days until the storm passes."

Lee laughs and sets down the dictionary. "The storm, my darling friend, has just begun," she says, sitting down on the coffee table so that she is right between Addy's legs. "This isn't something that is going to go away by morning, you know, so stop worrying so much about your heart."

"Which side of my heart are you talking about?"

"Both sides, Addy. The one you need the medication for and the one that you are trying to put an emotional Band-Aid on," Lee explains.

"Look at me," Addy says. "I'm a well-educated, seemingly intelligent woman who has had the warning signs for a long time and I simply blew them away, ignored them, did not pay attention."

"And the difference between your short-ness of breath for that side of your heart and the way you ignored the shortness of breath on the other side of your heart is what again?"

"Shut up," Addy says with a half smile, knowing the answer could be spread like thin butter over years and years of schedules and meetings and soccer games and profes-sional commitments and child rearing and in-laws and bowling balls and sisters that eventually led to a sinkhole of emotional emptiness that holds the wedding vows, the pledge of love, and the mysterious connec-tions of commitment that add up to the one-plus-one-equals-one equation of life.

"Listen to this," Lee pleads. "Just listen for a second."

Lee runs her finger down the thin white pages of the dictionary that is as big as her entire lap. She stops at the word "separate." She says it out loud, "Sep-a-rate," pro-nouncing each syllable as if she were teaching an English class. Addy listens with both sides of her heart.

" 'To set or keep apart. Disconnect. Sever. To sort. To sever conjugal ties with. To become divided or detached. To cease to live together as a married couple. To go in different directions.' "

When Lee stops reading and looks up, Addy has her head tipped back on the sofa. She is not moving. Lee sets down the dictionary and places her hands on Addy's knees.

"Addy . . ."

"I'm trying really hard to make good use of this separation," she replies. "It's only been, what, a week and I'm going to therapy, I'm thinking about things, I am trying to stay away from the house because even a glimpse of him right now might push me over the edge, but Lee, you don't really **prepare** for a disaster like this. When you plunge—and we all do plunge, don't we, into a relationship?—you do not have to sign off on a 'What If I Screw Up' list that waltzes you through this, this pile of shit."

"I'm not an expert but I've been through

this a few times, sweetie. What you need to do now is just focus on you and not on Lucky or anyone or anything else."

You.

As in yourself.

Shut off the oxygen to the world.

To the mass of yelping "help me's."

To the son of Lucky.

To the leering looks of the Bowling Bobs.

To the posse of marauding men.

To the reflection of guilt you see in every mirror.

To the seduction of surrender.

So easy to say and to think, Addy knows, but moving forward, getting past the point of guilt and self-doubt and imagining that maybe you were headed in the right direction before all of this mess anyway is not so easy. Maybe it is also possible that, if you move too fast or too slow, you will be making the biggest mistake of your life.

Maybe or maybe not.

"Lee, how did you do it? And how in the hell did you do it more than once?"

"Damn," Lee says, smiling, "I was hoping you wouldn't ask that."

"You were not!"

"You're right. Actually, I have no idea what in the hell I am doing most of the time, especially when it comes to relationships. The first one was a no-brainer. I was too young, we had nothing in common except the fact that our body parts fit together, and the last one, and all the ones in between . . . you just **know**."

"Did you love them?"

"Sometimes painfully so," Lee admits. "And that part never goes away. Sometimes you can love someone so much, so much, and it doesn't matter, it just will not work and then the real hard part is trying to figure out what to do with that love. How do you go on? How do you turn a lover into just a love and still keep breathing? But really, that's not the issue here, is it?"

Lee refills her wineglass, pours one for Addy, says, "This is medicine," and launches into Separation 101 with her friend, her fellow Sweat-Her, a woman who looks as if she is hanging on by a thread so tiny it would take a lab microscope to spot it.

The trick, Lee says, is to try and disengage

for a time. Try not to think about what was, what might be, but what is now. For a woman, especially, that's hard to do, she says, because women are always so busy saving the world, the universe, the town, the state, the Pacific Ocean, the kids, the husband, the relatives, and every whale and endangered dolphin that ever floated on the face of the earth.

"Everyone keeps telling me the same things," Addy sighs. "Do something for yourself. Have some fun. But it's hard to do that when you feel so miserable, when you are riddled with self-doubt, when you still feel as if you want to drive the damn car through the garage door while going a hundred miles per hour."

"Maybe you need to write down a plan, you know, things that you want to do, especially the rest of the summer before time swallows you up and you are right back where you started in fall," Lee suggests. "You know: you have time, freedom, some emotional energy to burn. How do you want to burn it?"

"It's not like I wasn't free before, because

we were both pretty much doing what we
wanted to do," Addy admits. "That is the
whole point of this. Because I felt like I was
alone anyway."

"Well, now's the time, Addy. What do
you want to do besides figure out if you
want to stay married? Go to Paris? Learn to
knit? Clean out the garage—just kidding.
Start to jog? Find a new job? There has to be
things you've been thinking about."

Like sex with a stranger.

Like redoing the entire house.

Like training with one of those walking
groups to do a marathon.

Like hiring someone to clean.

Like being able to park the car in the
garage.

Like making people laugh really hard for
a long time.

Like staying up all night to talk with a
lover.

Like kicking the shit out of Lucky.

"For starters, why don't you come to the
Honduras reunion Friday night," Lee suggests. "You know all of the women who'll be
there. It's going to be fun."

The Honduras trip last year that Addy passed up because of the time, the money, the uncertainty of Mitchell's college applications, and about thirty-seven other items and people that took precedence over the one thing that Addy wanted to do so badly the soles of her feet hurt. Hurt like the time she wanted to go to Girl Scout camp for a week and her parents told her they could not afford it. Hurt like the day Mitchell left for college and she realized as much as she wanted him to go was as much as she would miss him. Hurt like the very moment she realized she was ready to ram her car into the garage door, out the back, around to the front, and right on down the road to Route 66.

The trip had been invitation-only, four days, and all women. They'd be jaunting from Pittsburgh via the cigar-filled humidor at the First National to Miami, then to Tegucigalpa, Honduras, where an exotic ride of cigar tasting, cigar-factory touring, tobacco fields exploration, native foods and discussion, and most likely some very wild times and lots of rum would create a never-before-seen Latin American sensation. This all hosted by Rocky Patel—one of the most respected names in the cigar world and a man who could sweep a dozen movie stars off their feet with the wave of one of his lively Sun Grown signature premium cigars and his dark sexy eyes.

"It's impossible!" Addy had cried to Hell, who said she would pay for Addy's plane ticket, offered to talk with the school principal to get her some time off, and did so much begging her knees hurt. "I can't go! It's the worst possible time for me and there isn't a damn thing I can do about it."

Maybe there was something to do about it but Addy didn't do it and she wouldn't let Hell do it and the sixteen women who went without her had so much fun, smoked so many cigars, got so little sleep, and made such wonderful intimate connections that they were glowing in the dark when they got back.

So Addy promises Lee she will go on Friday night and she will feed off the light these women emit and she promises to lighten up and to fall into a lovely routine of pleasure just for herself. And twenty minutes later, she's driving past Hell's house and beeping three times in their "Hello, I'm driving past" greeting, then she stops for groceries so she will stop eating out, and then turns into the cul-de-sac where she forces herself not to look at Bob One's house where Lucky is at the same moment forcing himself not to run to the front window to catch a glimpse of her as she gets out of the car, which she parks way too close to the garage door, and walks into the house with bags of food while glancing at the dent she had kicked into its metal face.

The untouched house is a silent statue that at first taunts Addy with not even the hum of appliances—everyone and every-thing, it seems, is holding its breath. The quiet is disconcerting to Addy who has lived with her ear half-cocked for the arrival of teenagers, the bowling team, the bowling ball artists, burly neighbors, Hell or any one of at least a dozen of her friends from school, the Y, or someone she has befriended from First National.

It has been a week, a mere week, and although friends like Lee have warned her of this, this choosing of sides, the people who don't know what to say, the ones who are torn and feel as if they have to choose between one or the other, she is astounded at how quickly it has happened.

There are no phone messages.

The mail is filled with 3,274 Citibank Visa applications and the only piece of personal mail is her second summer paycheck.

Not one note is pasted to the front screen door, which is actually still a storm door because she has been busy **separating,** and no one has attended to the house.

When she pulls open the refrigerator a nauseating smell, probably the last container of food—Chinese from when, shit, maybe late May—makes her gag.

There are at least fifteen daily newspapers thrown over the side door near The Kingdom of Krap and twice that many unread, folded neatly in a stack braced against the door leading to the patio where Addy used to smoke.

The thought of a cigarette almost paralyzes her. Addy slams the refrigerator, then decides the only way she can keep from smoking, drinking, raising her already high blood pressure is to open the door again, clean out the refrigerator, and jump into her life.

Jump.

Fast and hard.

Like a woman who is on fire.

Like a woman who is separated from her husband.

Like a woman who never stopped to just stop.

But first the Dixie Chicks.

"Oh my God," she says out loud. "When is the last time I filled the house with music, when did Lucky and I dance last in the dining room, where is **Taking the Long Way,** where the hell is Addy Lipton?"

Addy cannot stop. She races to her car to find the CD, runs back into the house and locates the CD player in the cabinet where she keeps dishes she has never used, never intends to use, and has been dying to throw away since the day she got them at her frigging wedding reception.

When the CD starts and the Chicks start

wailing and she leans over to push the buttons and hear "Not Ready to Make Nice,"
she cannot take her eyes and then her fingers
and then her hands off the dishes. The
damn, useless, dusty, **ugly** dishes. While the
Chicks roll, and their song bounces through
the kitchen, down the hall, past Lucky's new
bedroom, and up the stairs, Addy starts
throwing.

Her movements are graceful, calm, almost elegant, as she moves with the music,
dancing with herself, balancing objects from
elbow to wrist.

First come the saucers that never matched
anything anyway. She props open the back
door, the one leading to the backyard that
never got quite finished, where the barbecue
island sits that never got finished, close to
the fence that was supposed to be a lovely
rock wall that housed a small waterfall that
never made it out of the garden store. Then
five plates from some relative whom Addy
has never met; three serving trays from the
wedding that someone who had to have
been insane designed because they are black
and brown and look as if they have been per-

manently stained with gravy; an aluminum
tray that will never break but that sounds
like a shotgun when it bounces off the lone
stretch of bricks where the garbage can is
supposed to sit but since it blew away nothing has sat there; and finally an assortment
of dishes that one might use if there was ever
a dinner that included something besides
pizza, a turkey breast, pasta, or the cheesy
potatoes Addy has made so many times all
she has to do is touch the potatoes and they
jump into the bowl.

Yeah baby.

When Addy is done 4.8 minutes later, the
yard is littered with pieces of pottery, glass,
and plastic and she feels terrific, light, giddy.
She has not even thought of having a cigarette, and because this realization astonishes
her, it takes her a few seconds to realize the
phone is ringing.

"Yo," she says, breathless.

"Mom?"

"This is the mom."

"It's Mitchell. Are you okay?"

"Oh yes."

"Is Dad there?"

Addy has not called Mitchell to tell him
the news. Neither, apparently, has Lucky.

"No," she answers, steadying herself on
the counter.

"I've been trying to call."

"I know. Why didn't you try our cell
phones?"

"I wanted to catch you at home."

Addy's heart stops. "What is it? Are you
okay?"

There is a pause. Addy can hear her son
breathing, knows that he must be standing
with one foot up on the base of a chair,
which he loves to do when he talks on the
phone, and that his head is down so that his
hair covers his eyes. Addy can see him take
in a huge swallow of air and she holds her
breath waiting, waiting for what is coming
next.

"Mom, my birth mother called me. She
wants to see me. I'm going to meet her. I just
wanted you and Dad to know."

A bird the size of a small seagull has just
flown into Addy's mouth, worked its way
down her throat, sucking it totally dry, and

is backpedaling across the insides of her stomach. In a moment she will speak. She **will** speak.

"Mom?"

"Do you want this, Mitchell? Is this something you need now? Can you handle it?"

"We've talked about this, Mom, and I never tried to find her, but it's okay with me and I was thinking I'd have her come to the counseling office, meet me there, set something up. I'm not freaked or anything. I'm curious. I mean, you know, I want to know more. But it's okay. She probably needs this more than I do."

Addy has a name. That is all. The name of a young woman who had a baby and did not keep him and who saw Addy's photo and knew she was a teacher and never asked about Lucky but saw in Addy's eyes the heart of a mother and as she sits onto her kitchen floor, clutching the phone so hard her fingers hurt, Addy knows that there are so many endings right now, so many beginnings, that there is no place for a middle.

"Mitchell, do you need me?"

"I'll be okay, Mom. I just thought you should know."

"I'm here, Mitchell, always here for you, honey."

"Mom . . ."

"What, baby?"

"I love you."

"I love you too, Mitchell. So much. I do."

And then Addy hangs up and she cries until the shadows behind the house have covered up all the shattered pieces of plates and cups and saucers, any hint of the past, of before, and when she gets up she takes the container of spoiled Chinese food, walks it into the center of The Kingdom of Krap, sets it on top of a piece of wood that is half painted green and has beer caps nailed all over it, opens the top, walks back into the house, and starts the Dixie Chicks all over again.

TWENTY-TWO
Espionage on Lipton Lane · · ·

The spying starts immediately.

Lucky wants Bob One to find out what is happening next door.

Addy wants Hell to run interference and to let Lucky know about Mitchell and his birth mother.

Hell, of course, is game for anything.

Bob One, of course, wants the entire world to be happy.

Addy has refused to pick up the shards of the past in the backyard, and The Kingdom of Krap smells like its name. Mitchell continues to be fine and his parents continue to be somewhat agitated, confused, secretive, weary, wary, and alternately happy and despondent.

Word of the Lipton separation has spread throughout Parker like a medieval plague that is passed from nose to lip to mind with the simple in- and outtake of breath. People know. Dogs know. The neighbors know. Grocery-store baggers know. Secrets in Parker are as visible as a pregnant movie star.

And Lucky and Addy are definitely on stage.

And doing their best to hide—especially from each other.

"Can't you just go over there and see how he is and tell him about Mitchell," Addy begs from her kitchen table as Hell thumps her fingers like she's keeping time to a precise song. "He needs to know about this birth-mother mess and I am not ready to see or talk to him."

"Addy, Addy, Addy, I detect a tone of caring in your lovely voice."

"Well, I don't **not** care about him, I just can't stand to look at him, be in the same room with him, talk to him, or think about him for more than twenty-five seconds. But he deserves to know about Mitchell."

"What's it worth to you?"

Addy has a tiny bomb to drop and the second her sister smiles, Hell knows that something is not only up but halfway into orbit.

"I'm coming to the Honduras reunion," Addy says. "And I was thinking, if you still need someone in your roving shift at First National, I'm going to take it."

"What?"

"I need to be distracted and away from this and I know how to handle things at the bar anyway, so it makes sense. Besides, I love the place, love the people who come in. I've been thinking that you should maybe have more entertainment and maybe I can work on that, too."

"Well, hell's bells, you want me to strip or anything when I am over there? Addy, you have totally saved my rear end. Are you serious?"

Totally serious.

Totally ready for something new.

Totally unwilling to stay locked inside of a house which reeks of The Kingdom of Krap seepage and dozens of years of memories.

Totally not ready to do anything hard like forge a life plan that needs following like a map to a country retreat lest you lose your way—again.

And totally dying to find out what is going on at Bob One's.

Hell bounces off her chair, flies next door, and before Addy can take the coffee cups off the table she sees Hell jogging—not walking, jogging—back through the yard.

"What?" Addy demands.

"Lucky asked me to get him a couple of things and you are never going to believe it—"

"What?"

"Lucky grew a beard and those two, Lucky and Bob One, are over there **baking**."

"What?"

"Addy, you are saying 'what' all of the time."

"Well, listen to what you are saying! What the hell does Lucky need? Did you tell him about Mitchell? Baking? What are they baking?"

Hell ignores the questions and asks her if she knows where Lucky keeps his notebook.

"What notebook?"

"It's blue, looks like a book, he says it might be in his new bedroom."

Hell finds it, tucks it under her arm, bends down and grabs a torte pan out of the bottom of Addy's oven, and is about to leave again when Addy blocks her way.

"It's a lemon torte," Hell tells her. "They're baking a lemon torte. I'm going to hang over there and get as much information as I can. Looks like the two of them are going steady."

"Baking? What's in the notebook?"

"He didn't say. Do you want to peek?"

"Of course I want to peek but I'm not going to. I didn't know he had something like that. It looks like a regular book. What do you think is inside?"

"They're waiting," Hell reminds her.

"Go."

"Don't wait up," Hell jokes as she jogs back to Bob One's.

What the hell, Hell . . .

Addy leans against the back door as Hell disappears into Bob One's house and contemplates everything that has just happened in the last, what—ten minutes? If I do not start jogging myself, she thinks, I am going to miss the parade and everything else that comes after it. Lucky with a beard? A beard, maybe, to replace what he has lost from the top of his head, from the receding hairline that has climbed back from his once wavy dark locks to a frenzied-looking crop of bushiness that Addy has tried to get him to shave bald for several years.

Good for him, but the baking has her mystified. This from a man who has a hard time carrying pork chops from the kitchen to the backyard. A torte? Are they doing crack over there?

Throwing up her hands, Addy walks through the house to assess the damage done from weeks of neglect. Lucky's new room is littered with newspapers, glasses with bendable straws, two pairs of blue hospital pants that he stole, and dirty sheets, and there is dust on every other thing in the room, indicating a good seven to eight weeks of hibernation-from-cleaning madness.

Every other room looks the same. To Addy it is as if The Kingdom of Krap is slowly taking over the house. Bathroom garbage cans filled to the brim, dirty towels piled almost to the windowsills, shower curtains that should have been thrown away months ago, the hall moldings tinged gray from shoe exhaust, windows with dust tags that could breed an entire new species of spiders—and this only from the first few rooms.

Up in her bedroom Addy cannot help herself and she peers out the side window to see if there is any action in Bob One's backyard. Nothing. The boys must still have their buns in the oven. Addy leans her cheek against the window, closes her eyes and then opens them and spins around, imagining what the bedroom would look like if she remodeled it like she has been talking about for the past five years. She wants to raise the ceiling, knock out the wall to the small room that's supposed to be an office but that has been used as a recycling plaza for used soccer equipment and clothing for the past fifteen years.

She'd make a master suite. Make that a goddess suite. Huge bathtub. Skylights.

Floor-to ceiling windows. Funky modern furniture. And then she'd do one room after another.

Maybe.

And who would live with her in the new house?

Shuffling through the bedroom, Addy paces off the square footage, grabs a notebook from the bedside table, kicks a pile of her clothes to the side, and strips off the smoky sheets on the way back downstairs.

The laundry room, the spare bedroom, kitchen, dining room, and the small porch that leads into the backyard are all a crying, dirty shame and suddenly Addy does not really give a damn. She stuffs her sheets into the washing machine and sits down with her tablet at the kitchen table after she grabs a calculator.

The numbers of hours are astounding. Hundreds and hundreds of hours spent cleaning and picking up and organizing.

"My God," she says out loud, "I could have written a novel, knitted slippers for every orphanage in North America, finished my Ph.D., or drunk more."

The phone call takes less time than it did for her to strip the sheets and throw them into the washing machine.

"I'm interested in something major immediately and then maybe something minor every week or every other week after that," Addy says to the very merry Merry Maid. "No, give me an estimate now . . . three bedrooms, office, kitchen, dining room, two full bathrooms, small porch, and it's not filthy here, but it needs like several injections of Botox."

There's a moment of silent figuring while Addy taps her fingers on the table and watches the crumbs from about fourteen meals dance all over the place.

"I can do that," Addy finally says, knowing exactly what is in the savings account and what she will need to cover bills for the summer. "The sooner the better. Tomorrow? Are you kidding? I'll be here."

Addy looks at her watch. Cool. It only took ten minutes to do a major housecleaning. Next she calls the teenage Zeland kid from across the street and signs him up for a summer and fall of yard work with specific instructions to weed, mow, trim, and be on call if she needs any heavy lifting—especially on garbage day.

During the next hour she sketches out her dream goddess suite and halfway through the design picks up the phone again, calls three painters and asks for an exterior estimate. The house color needs to change, something bright, maybe three colors bright. Before nightfall it's possible that Addy Lipton could have her entire home rearranged, painted, cleaned, and ready for phase two of its life.

This flurry of activity, she knows, will drive Lucky nuts and it will make her feel as if she's done something.

A few somethings.

Taken a step.

Moved in some kind of direction.

Started a plan.

And, of course, avoided the obvious.

"Me," Addy whispers. "Maybe even this is about me, something I need, something I should have done a long time ago."

Addy pauses to remember the times when she stayed up late to clean or cook or bake something that Mitchell needed for a class or for soccer or for one of a hundred other things that she does not remember at all fondly.

Lucky was there, surely, but in her mind she remembers usually being the last one up, the first one to get up to get the medicine in the middle of the night, the one to clean up, cook, organize everything from birthday parties to wedding anniversaries. And always, until she started working out again, being so damned tired.

A tired that seemed to weigh more and more every year. And a tired that in this truthful moment she realizes she used as a weapon. A weapon to say no when she thought she couldn't move, when the ache of school, Mitchell, Lucky and his boys, ailing parents, and a growing seed that she now recognizes as unhappiness nailed her in place.

Oh God.

Is there more to clear away? Anything else tied to my ankles, Addy answers herself, so that I can move about freely, bake my own goddamned torte although shaking up a Torte Martini is more like it, keep tearing apart all the layers of the what ifs, why nots, and maybes that have seemed—in spite of everything that is so good, so wonderful—to have slipped a rope around my heart, my own passions, the laughter I so need to keep me floating.

There is another list Addy Lipton needs to make if only she knew where to start, if only the laws of love were written in stone the way the laws of marriage are written in stone, if only she could clear away not just the dirt from the windows and walls of the house but from the huge sheet of tempered glass that has lodged itself around her heart.

When she gets up, when there are no more phone calls to make, Addy walks over to look at Bob One's house. Hell's Jeep is still in the driveway and it looks as if every light in the house is on over there. Addy walks outside to the Jeep. She fishes around inside the glove compartment until she finds a packet of flavored cigars and then she backsteps without looking up toward what by now must be a small neighborhood party.

It is not easy to think of herself. It is almost totally impossible, but Addy grabs a lighter off the counter, bypasses the water and tea and grabs a beer out of the refrigerator, picks up her notebook and goes out to the barbecue smoking station, stepping over the broken dishes and stopping once to see that a design from one of the plates now looks absolutely beautiful standing all alone against the edge of a pot of flowers from last year that are crying to be repotted.

It takes three beers and two cigars but Addy gets into a rhythm. She thinks about the lovely weeks of summer. She thinks about biking again like when she was in college and cranking forty miles in a day was like walking fast. She thinks about Hell's bar and telling jokes in front of an audience. And mixing drinks she's never tasted and national publicity and maybe standing in front of the microphone and not just behind the bar herself one day. She forces herself not to think about Lucky, about what he would want, what she would normally be doing in the summer hiatus and about what her life might look like if everything changed. Addy thinks about being seduced and flirting. She thinks about the sting of love when it first hits and how intoxicating it is every single time Hell begins yet another new affair, which she will watch from the sidelines.

And she wonders what might have happened in Costa Rica, in that oasis of paradise which has nothing to do with Parker, PA, but her mind will not reach that far. There is an ocean to cross, a marriage to finish dissecting, and the sudden and unmistakable sound of a wave crashing against every side of Addy Lipton's life.

TWENTY-THREE
The cigar kiss . . .

Joyce Linderman walks in twirling her slip on the end of her finger like a Frisbee.

Mary Gonzalez is wearing the red bandana she dipped in rum and sucked on during the bus ride back to the airport.

Cindy Buchron is carrying a volleyball like the one they used in their Cigar Pool Games Tournament.

Beth Kincade has a cigar behind each ear and one in her mouth.

Carrie Schwartz has made a hat out of Rocky Patel cigar boxes that fans out across her shoulders and has a plastic wineglass glued to the top.

And of course, bold Brenda Franklin comes to the Honduras reunion at The First

National Wine & Cigar Bar wearing nothing but the red bathing suit, duct-taped flip-
flops, and Minnie Mouse towel she wore for
hours and hours when she refused to leave
the swimming pool area to eat a meal or listen to a discussion about how weather af-
fects tobacco crops.

And these are just the first six of the fifteen women who arrive for a reunion, a
party, an event that has the potential to
break windows, records, and everything else
that stands in the way of a group of women
who **really** know how to have a good time
and live life large.

Hell has reserved the entire back room of
the bar and as politely as possible tried to
convince men not to linger and leave
quickly so the women can be almost as free
as they were on the cigar-tasting extravaganza that turned out to be much more than
just a quick trip to sample cigars a world
away in a country that several of them still
could not spell.

It's the feminine magic of openness and
acceptance, the roping together of lives that
are as different as a sweet cigar and an earthy,

dark, natural Robusto, the essence of laughter and letting go, the unavailability of cell phone and Internet connections in a third-world country, and the easy, loving way women can undress every part of themselves without blinking an eye.

And all this and more is what Addy missed because she believed she couldn't go, because the possible seemed impossible to her, because she had wedged herself so tightly into her own life that she couldn't raise her hand to even ask if she could leave the room for a moment to go to the bathroom.

"Damn it," she says the second she sees the women begin to arrive with their bawdy clothes, loud voices, elevated attitudes, and something she does not share with them—the experience of their trip. "Maybe I can live through it by simply listening."

Maybe.

Or maybe not.

Addy is tending bar because Ginger Carlson called in sick and Addy has strict instructions to pay attention to how much fun the women are having from her baby sister,

Hell the terrible. Hell, who ended up sneaking home from her counterintelligence visit to Bob One's so late that she never bothered to stop in and see her sister. Hell the awful, who reported the following day only that she had a good time, and that Bob One was apparently good for Lucky, and that Lucky was happy for Mitchell and would call him to check in.

The next day, there was Bob One knocking on the door with a piece of the damned torte which looked frigging perfect and Bobbie was being so nice that Addy itched to push his face into the cake.

"Just checking up on you," Bob said, leaning against the door and looking past her as a brigade of cleaners worked their way through the house like starving ants looking for crumbs. "What's going on?"

Spy, Addy thought. **You are a spy sent from Lucky and I'm not going to give you one clue.** And then she suddenly wondered if she looked happy, perky, and ready to roll through the day without a man at her elbow.

"Just a few projects, Bob, that's all, and I'm fine but thanks for the offer," she answered vaguely. "I've got the yard covered. And everything else, too."

"Well, Addy, I'm your friend too, you know, and just because Lucky is bunking with me doesn't mean we can't stay friends, you and I. I just wanted you to know that."

Spy, Addy kept thinking, **they are all so nice until you wake up with a knife against your throat or a garage full of shit**.

And how interesting that all the boys from Lucky's gang were having a night at Johnson's Bowling Palace, almost directly across the street, the same night as the reunion. Addy can actually lean over the side of the bar and see Lucky, limping less, with new shorts on, that new little beard, and what appears to be a shaved head.

What is going on? What is coming off?

"I am saying 'what' too much," she finally admits, working hard to focus on Honduras and quickly leaning into the flow of female power that has rolled into the bar and seems to have captivated every single man and woman in the place.

The party begins with a slide show on the back wall while Addy hustles drinks and sips on her new drink of choice these days—water. Water and a side of atenolol for the blood pressure. A cigar now and then. No cigarettes—well, almost no cigarettes—and maybe tomorrow, the start of phase two of the exercise program, when the new bicycle arrives, and the eventual—hopefully, please God—droppage of twenty more pounds **and** her damned blood pressure level.

The night is a crash course in Bartending 101. Addy has worked the bar before, but not seriously, not like this, with first six, and then ten, and then fifteen women who drink rum as if it is water, and then a group of men, and more after that, and then the unexpected arrival of a group of teachers from school, and every member of the Sweat-Hers, who have been invited to the reunion along with all but it seems a dozen people in the entire town of Parker.

Everyone else is across the street at the bowling alley.

Addy temporarily forgets about this, and about Lucky, and about being separated, and about Mitchell, and everything else hard and lonely. To her astonishment, at this moment she feels as close to sane as she has felt in months. Addy follows the lead of bartender Greg and lifts her eyes in between drinks and talking and laughing, to watch the photographs that Hell has turned into a slide show that starts out instructive and turns into a hilarious demonstration of what happens when women travel together and do not care about anything but having a fine and wild time.

"Tobacco fields. . . ." Hell narrates, flicking first through the arrival at Tegucigalpa airport, then the bus ride and the beginning of a three-day cigar adventure. "Drying the tobacco . . . this is the first cigar factory, here's our first taste of one of Rocky's vintage blends that has just been rolled and there, oh, there is, who is that? Jean with her blouse pulled over her head on the way home, and oh yes, there are three other people dancing on the bus as we are trying to pass some horses and donkeys on the side of the road, and . . ."

The reunion has filled up the bar with smoke and Addy finally gives in, lights up something brown that appears to be a cigar

that Hell has sitting by the cash register just
as a man sidles up to the bar, looks into her
eyes as if he has a right to do that, and orders
a tap beer, "The darkest one you have," and
asks what she is smoking.

"A cigar. I think."

"I love to see a woman smoking a cigar."

"If that's all it takes to make you happy,
then turn around, buster. This joint is loaded
to the gills with cigar-smoking babes."

"I'm selective about who I watch smoking
a cigar," the beer drinker tells her. "My name
is Ron and you are?"

"Addy, and I must say that's a lovely
pickup line. If you'd like me to blow smoke
in your face there's a ten-dollar charge for
that."

"You're funny."

"You should see my sister Boris."

Ron snorts.

"I love that in a man. Public snorting."

"I charge ten bucks for that," he retorts,
still laughing. "I guess that makes us even,
Addy."

Addy has not flirted in so long it takes her
two refills of Ron's beer to realize that is ex-

actly what is happening. When it hits her, she has her back turned to Ron and imagines he is looking at her ass as she scoots around the bar in a skirt, a white tank top, blue vest, and a pair of lovely Teva flip-flops that give her arches perfect support.

She freezes.

Flirting? **Oh my gawd.**

Ron, to his eternal credit, is fun, sort of nice-looking in that guy-who-works-out, gray-haired, nice-dresser, educated kind of way. Addy can feel the blood pressure medication take a break as her heart thumps against her rib cage and her knees go weak and just as she tries to take a breath Mr. Nice Ron asks if he can buy her a drink.

"I've been drinking water but I hate to be a cheap date," she manages to say. "I've been good all night. I should have some of that wild rum all of my friends are drinking."

"My pleasure," Ron says, extending his hand toward all the bottles that are lined up.

A possible mistake.

A misleading gesture.

A turn toward hell.

A moment of pure abandon.

A remembered spark of attraction.

A gutsy middle-aged bartender letting go of a very long rope.

Or simply—danger ahead.

The rum zips through the lining of her stomach and dances into Addy's blood-stream as if she is mainlining the stuff. She pauses to shake her head, closes her eyes, and when she looks up, Ronnie is smiling as if he's just seen the end of a terrific movie.

"What?" she gasps.

"That was good, huh?"

"It's like drinking a knife, for God's sake. Am I supposed to buy you a drink now? This is my first full-night shift and my bar-tending etiquette is not what it should be."

Ron is so nice he says no and then he moves over three seats so he can be at the end of the bar where Hell is constantly drop-ping off empty glasses for her to fill up again and where he tells Addy everything but his shoe size and where she nods her head, then rises to focus on ice cubes and liquor, all the while remembering how damn much fun it is to flirt.

And beyond that The First National

Wine & Cigar Bar is as wild as it's ever going to get.

Or maybe not.

In spite of the state-of-the-art ventilators and a few open windows toward the back, the bar looks like an old-time saloon, with cigar smoke hanging like billowy muslin curtains as Hell's women begin feeling the mighty effects of their drinks, large doses of laughter, and the sometimes heady push of cigar smoke filtered through mouths that rarely seem to close for longer than a few seconds.

The music is what does it. Bold Brenda steps out of her towel long enough to put a brassy folk tape into the CD player and within seconds the few brave men who remain in the bar, and almost all the women, are on their feet whooping it up as if they are dancing at the gorgeous edge of some shrub-covered foothills not so far from the Nicaraguan border while military guards are firing blanks at their feet.

Hell has totally surrendered to the evening and that means she's turned over the keys to Greg, asked Addy to help him if he needs it, and grabbed two bottles of rum which she is pouring into the glasses of the Sweat-Hers—who are acting as if they have just recently immigrated from Honduras—and all of the women from the trip.

Addy wants earplugs. The bar was not designed to embrace the crackling bass of the CD player and the noise of at least twenty women who love to hear themselves screaming and who have totally parked the few inhibitions they possess between them, mixed with the loud laughs of the small group of men who are dumb as ducks and do not realize they could be tossed out at any minute.

And there sits devoted Ron. His eyes following Addy as she slips from behind the bar out to the tables to pick up glasses, stops for a swig out of Hell's bottle, empties a good dozen ashtrays, and then goes back behind the bar.

"Are you married?" Ron boldly asks.

"What?"

"You have on a ring. I don't want to keep flirting if you are a happy and well-kept woman."

Addy thinks quickly about the dictionary

lesson with Lee. She thinks about the word she has not yet been able to say out loud. She thinks about Lucky's bald head shining like a new penny when the streetlight in front of the bowling alley hit it and how for hours now she has not thought of him once. She thinks about how Ron must be looking at the legs she has been exercising for six months and how she bravely put on a skirt and how she feels almost sexy knowing that someone, anyone, a man who could probably date the moon, is having a conversation with her that is the most intimate discussion she has had with a man in years.

"I'm separated."

"You okay about that?"

Addy smiles. She smiles because she said it aloud for the first time, because she is okay for this moment, and because feeling sexy has seemed to slow down her rocketing heart.

"Yes," she tells Ron. "I'm okay."

And then the chain dance of the year starts throwing their conversation into something that will be remembered in Parker, PA, for so many years that even the greatest high school

prank of the century—live pigs in the court-
yard and an entire Volkswagen sitting sideways between the two concrete pillars—will
become a blurred memory.

It's Malibu Heidi on a table with a bread
basket on her head, a Rocky Patel vintage
Euro in her mouth, and with what is the second greatest idea of her life, the first being a
lovely name change.

"Hey, let's rumba!" she yells. "Follow me!"

Addy is mesmerized as she watches
Malibu jump down from the table and order
the woman next to her to put her hands on
her waist. Within three minutes, every single
man and woman in the bar is doing a la-
de-da-de-da-da dance through the First
National until Malibu reaches the front
door, turns to Hell, who nods her head, and
then proceeds without any caution whatso-
ever into the street, which in Parker, PA, is a
definite paradise for those searching for
quiet, calm, and suddenly an occasional vision of a herd of women and six brave and
nonthinking men gone wild.

The dance moves to the street and Ron,

who has been a restrained saint all evening, grabs Addy by the wrist, and Addy looks at Greg the Great who winks and nods yes, and then Ron twirls her to the back of the line and they join a wild chain gang of rum-drinking cigar-smoking men and women who swirl through the street and would stop traffic if there was any to stop.

His hands on her waist.

The movement of freedom.

Separated.

The golden rum of life flowing toward the heart of everything.

Music to die for, a cascade of levity, life, love.

The song of freedom pounding like a drum.

Addy turns to smile, to live, to laugh and Ron lifts his hands for just a second, then another, and runs his fingers over the soft folds of her face and he kisses her lips so softly it is as if a breeze has planted a layer of light just below Addy's nose.

She is startled, pleased, ripped with rum, and as she starts to laugh, to acknowledge the kiss, she sees Lucky walking toward the end of the line with the other bowling freaks.

Addy sees Lucky looking at her as if he has just witnessed the dropping of the first atomic bomb, the moon landing, the assassination of a Kennedy, the election of someone named Bush, all rolled into one instant of time.

She pauses her heart. She freezes the kiss in her mind, the feel of the warm fingers, the rush of the blood from her heart, to her lips, to her chest, to the folds of the most intimate, most private, most neglected parts of her body.

Then she stumbles out of the line, first moving her fingers across Ron's face and saying "Thank you," and then jumping out of line so she can finish her night's work—the garden of dirty rum glasses and overflowing ashtrays, and when she turns to watch as the line tangos itself down the street, there is Lucky.

"Lucky."

"Addy."

"Are you okay?"

"Physically."

"Oh."

"You?"

"Physically—mostly."

"Oh. Addy, will you have coffee with me?"

Addy hesitates, not knowing if she really wants to have coffee, a conversation, and an ounce of time with Lucky.

"If it's decaf and not at Bob's."

"Tomorrow?"

"Sure."

"Down at that place, you know, where we used to go."

"I know."

"Ten?"

"Okay."

"Addy?"

"What, Lucky?"

"You look great."

Addy says nothing else but when she walks back into the bar and looks behind her she swears to God what she sees is a line of friendly female humanity that could push her over with a mere whisper.

A breath.

A small breeze that offers a glimpse of a possible future.

Anything to escape the pounding she feels from the basement of her guilty heart.

TWENTY-FOUR
What I should have said to Addy · · ·

I saw you kiss him.

I saw you flirting.

I saw you through the window tending bar.

I saw you having fun . . . without me.

But Lucky does not speak. Lucky bites a hole in his lip and tongue to match the hole that is burrowing through his heart.

I am not so lucky lately.

TWENTY-FIVE
A heartbreaking dose of decaf . . .

Lucky is waiting for her.

Addy can see him in the back booth, watching the door, slowly moving his coffee cup to his lips and then back down to the table where he balances a spoon in between his fingers and thumb like a small boy who might be holding a favorite blanket or stuffed doggie. She is exhausted from thinking, from a long phone conversation to her therapist, from the weight of the kiss, from the tangled mass of indecision that seems to have lodged itself sideways in her throat.

And there sits Lucky Lipton, her husband, and Addy is trying to figure out how to open the door, get out of the car, and walk into the coffee shop.

Lucky is trying to keep from tipping the table over with his jumping legs. He's trying to stay calm, to remember not to be pushy, to ask some simple questions, to let her know about his conversation with Mitchell, to try and weave a small opening back into the life of his wife, Addy, and to try not to cry.

"It's okay to cry, to let your heart open again," Dr. T told him during his own emergency, "help me" phone call.

"I don't want to scare her away. I feel like I need to be strong. Act cool, you know."

"Lucky, could it be that acting cool and distant got you into this place?"

"I suppose."

"Lucky, women crave intimacy and so do men, but somehow, because of some rewiring just before we all sprang up here, or because of testosterone, or because we are just dumb asses sometimes, us men often cover up the most important part of who we are."

"What if I lose her? What if she's already dating that man I saw her kiss? What if she just continues to hate me?"

"Lucky, take a breath. Slow down. Something like this that has broken does not get fixed in a few weeks. This is about you, too. You are in as much pain as Addy is. Put on some slippers when you have coffee. Walk softly. Tell her something that is in your heart."

Something in your heart.

Lucky has been chewing on what to say and how to say it since he slid into the booth thirty minutes early. He thinks he has it. He decides it needs to be simple but the moment Addy appears in the door, smiles at him, and walks over to the table he feels as if the four cups of coffee he has consumed are going to climb right back out of his throat and land on the table.

He cannot even get up.

"Hi."

"Hi."

Lucky motions for the waitress. Addy slides into the booth. She needs coffee like she needs to be slapped with a razor.

"I better just have a cup of tea," she tells the waitress. "Green, please."

"Anything to eat?" Lucky asks.

"No, I'm fine."

Lucky stops breathing and then pushes his hands down on top of the table and tells Addy he thought it would be a good idea if they just talked a bit, about what they are doing, about Mitchell, about how long this might go on. Once he starts talking he cannot stop.

Lucky has been going to therapy.

Lucky has been thinking.

Lucky needs to know she is okay.

Lucky has told Mitchell about them.

"What?"

"I talked to him, I know you did too, about his meeting with the birth mother next month, and then I just told him."

"Why did you do that? He's got enough on his plate."

"Jeezus, Addy, he's our son. He should know we are separated, what's happening, and he's not dumb, he'd figure it out."

Addy doesn't even know why she didn't want Mitchell to know. Embarrassed? A failure? Cautious? Frightened? But suddenly she wants to throw her cup of tea into Lucky's face. Where the hell does this anger come from?

Lucky lets go. He puts his hands back on his lap and then to keep himself still he grips the edge of the booth. He's watched Addy turn red and just like that he can tell she's pissed at him again.

"How long do you want to keep doing this?" he finally asks.

"What?" she says, realizing as the word slips from her mouth that she really does say "what" all of the time.

"This passive-aggressive dance. This anger, this distance."

Lucky is about to keep going and then remembers that he has not shared something that is in his heart. Well, except the interesting observation about how when Addy sees him she gets pissed off.

"This stuff doesn't just get fixed in a month, Lucky."

"You sound like my therapist."

"Listen to us, Lucky. We can't even talk for ten minutes. You are angry too. I know you saw that man kiss me. It was innocent. I was having fun, which is something that has moved way to the top of my list."

"Well, good for you. Kissing is fun. Jumping around the street is fun. Is living alone fun, Addy? Is that what you want?"

What Addy wants is to lean across the table and slap Lucky on the face, just like a movie she suddenly remembers, **The War of the Roses,** which she is going to stop and rent on the way the hell out of the coffee shop.

"Yes. I want to live alone."

"For how long?"

"Maybe forever."

Lucky thinks he will be lucky if he makes it to the bathroom in time. He thinks maybe his luck has run out. He thinks he is in much deeper shit than he imagined oh, say, forty-five minutes ago.

"Addy," he starts, on the verge of tears, "I know I've made mistakes. But I never stopped loving you. I never did."

"Love isn't always enough, Lucky."

"Are you that miserable? Was it that horrible?"

Addy drops her head and remembers the

idea of love at sixteen. The idea of someone with all his hair, great calves, a wicked laugh, a string of adventures, and a romantic heart. Where does that go? Why does it go? Does it have to go? Lucky, for sure, has been constant, a wonderful father, but his edge as a lover is as dull as every knife in the house.

"I haven't been happy like I think I should be happy in a long time," she answers, "and I do not want you to think that it's just you, Lucky. It's me, too."

Well, there's a crumb, Lucky thinks, letting one hand slide free from the booth death grip.

"Did you hear me say I love you?"

Addy raises her head and looks right into Lucky's tear-rimmed brown eyes and knows for certain that there are few kinder men in the world. Goofball that he is, Lucky could never even kill a spider, could barely raise his voice when Mitchell was a shit, occasionally even remembered to do something nice instead of just being nice. But nice is not enough. "I heard you, Lucky."

"Would you go to see someone with me so we can talk this out with a referee?"

Well, yes, that would be the second step toward divorce, Addy knows from the friends she has seen scurry through this very same discourse and dance. The joke around the lunch table at school always goes, "Oh, they're in counseling? That means, what, an extra two months before one of them files?" And it was almost always true.

Almost.

Always.

True.

"I don't know, Lucky. I've barely started my own painful walk through all of this shit. It seems like it wouldn't be fair."

"You are saying no."

"Yes, I am saying no."

"Addy, are you going to divorce me?"

"I thought maybe you'd be the one to make the first move."

Lucky is astounded. She's **thought** about it. Damn it. She has. Sweat is trickling down his back. He wishes he was drinking something much stronger than coffee. He wishes he could push his cup an inch to the right, touch a magic button, and that would fix everything. He wishes it was five years ago so whatever he did or was doing wrong he could rearrange right from the start or the middle or closer to what seems to be the end.

"Me?"

"Look at you, Lucky. You've gained weight, you play with old car parts. When was the last time you whistled like you used to, for God's sake? Be honest with yourself. Something has slipped away."

"That doesn't mean it can't come back. It's not that far away, is it?"

"I don't know."

"I so wanted to take you to Costa Rica, Addy. I thought it might have been the paradise we needed. I'm so sorry."

Addy suddenly wants to be anywhere but in the coffee shop talking about divorce attorneys and a make-believe paradise that does not exist anywhere she looks or lives.

"Lucky, your back therapy from the injury," she says quickly. "How is it all going?"

"I'll get there. I may go into work for an hour or so but then again, I may just, you know, stay on disability and try and fix myself up and figure out how to have a conversation with you that doesn't piss you off."

"Is all this okay with Bob?" Addy asks, totally ignoring Lucky's quest for a glimmer of hope, an incentive to keep breathing.

"He's wonderful, but Addy, you and I haven't gone anywhere with this conversation about 'us.' "

Addy laughs, which surprises and then angers Lucky.

"You're laughing?"

"We've gone really far, Lucky, it's just that we may have different road maps. That's all."

If Lucky had Sylvester Stallone's phone number he'd call him immediately to get some help getting back his Addy. This has not gone the way Lucky Lipton has hoped. "So now what?"

"More space. More personal therapy . . ."

"More kissing," he says snidely, cutting her off.

"It was innocent," Addy says, getting up. "And it was also none of your damn business."

"We're still married."

"Not really," Addy says, turning to leave as Lucky's lower jaw falls within an inch of his chest.

TWENTY-SIX
Long-lost greetings from the trail of life . . .

It takes Addy a week to realize that the broken dishes on the back patio are missing. She's taken a major cigarette backslide and has even occasionally reverted to sitting inside the grove of pine trees again where she's finished off the Dunhills and is now halfway through a pack of Camel filters. She tells herself that the smoking gives her a ledge of comfort, a moment when she doesn't have to worry about a mess of Bobs, Lucky, or any other damned neighborhood spy who may be looking at her through binoculars.

And they are all looking.

Between Hell and Bob One, it took less than a day for news of the coffeehouse fight, the utterance of the word "divorce," and the harsh reality of a marriage gone stale to make its way around Parker. This vicious and most sought-after rumor instantly surpasses the rumor of separation and throws a whole new beam of light on the Lipton marriage laboratory.

"Paradise, my ass," Addy told Hell when she recounted the coffeehouse conversation and Lucky's desire for them to find **it, it** meaning paradise in Central America. "Paradise should be here, it should be every day."

"Addy, you are so angry. Can't you give Lucky a small break?"

"I didn't hit him."

Issues, Hell told her, seem to be keeping you tied in place and then Hell asked her to describe what her life might be like if Lucky was the man Addy wanted him to be. What would that look like? What would Lucky look like? What in the hell would she actually do with him if he actually turned into Prince Charming?

Addy avoided the questions, said, "People don't change," and then ran to her backyard pine tree where she has just smoked three Camels, tried hard to envision what Lucky might look like as a prince, and then worked to imagine what the new Lucky, lucky man of her dreams, would be like—if that could, would, might ever be possible.

He would be kind.

He would be nice.

He would be romantic.

He would laugh a lot.

He would dance at midnight in the middle of winter on the front lawn.

He would surprise her.

He would clean out the goddamn garage.

He would take care of himself.

He would know without asking.

He would put something lovely under her pillow.

He would plan romantic adventures, walk her to the park, sing under the window.

And that's just for starters, Addy decides, on her last puff.

And then she gets up, puts her three cigarette butts into her pocket, walks toward the house, and pauses on the patio, where it finally dawns on her that someone or something has picked up the broken dishes, plates, and cups. What else has Addy missed? What else?

Hell says she does not know where the broken dishes are. Malibu and Lee, who have been standing guard at her kitchen table way too often, do not know. That leaves the Bobs, the lawn boy, or any one of the bowling marauders who may have been sent over to make certain Addy is not kissing strangers or changing the sheets more than twice a week following a wild night of uninhibited sex. If only.

"I'll be glad to go on another spying trip," Hell says from her cell phone. "Bob One ordered some special cigars that just came in and I was going to drop them off anyway so I can snoop around. Want me to?"

"Do it," Addy orders. "I'm going for a bike ride so I can get rid of this anger and so I don't hurt anyone."

"Are you, like, trying out for a marathon? All you seem to be doing is working out, biking, selling rum at the bar, and shouting these days, and now that I know you smoke, I know you are smoking too. Knock it off.

The smoking crosses out the exercising and messes up the high blood pressure even more than it is already messed up."

"I think I'm regressing, Hell. I may be boxing myself into another corner. I was thinking we should do an overnight road trip or something."

"You mean just get in the Jeep and head out like we used to before you screwed up your life by getting married? When do you work next?"

"What's today?"

"See, you've totally lost your reality focus. It's Tuesday."

"I don't work until Friday."

"Let's go today."

"What?"

"Spontaneity, baby. It's the middle of the week. Greg can handle things. We'll go one night. Drive with the top down. Sing dirty songs. Whistle at men. Go for your bike ride and then I'll pick you up after I spy on the boys."

"Okay . . . I think."

"You've been thinking too much. That's just one of your problems."

"Up yours."

Addy gets so excited she can barely ride two miles without turning around and cranking it back to the cul-de-sac so she can get ready. Then she remembers that part of the deal about spontaneous trips, back in the old days anyway, was that you could only take one very tiny and very quickly packed bag. A toothbrush, maybe or underwear if you feel like wearing any, an old T-shirt to sleep in, a bathing suit, and—of course—a cooler with beer, wine, water, and some snacks just in case of a sudden need to pull over or a long nap in the car because of no vacancy signs, is required.

Playing the game, Addy searches for her long-abandoned hiking fanny pack, the very one she used with Hell all the years before she was married, during college, for quick weekend trips, and for every single thing, it seems, since Mitchell and Lucky and this endless conveyor belt of life grabbed her by the throat. She gallops through the recently cleaned and superbly organized house, opening cardboard boxes and remembering everything from wild camping trips with

Hell's boyfriends to random Jeep excursions that took them up the East Coast, into New York City and once, back in the good old days, the drive in the old blue sedan to Milwaukee, Wisconsin, so that Hell could taste a bratwurst and tour an old-time brewery to see if she could find Laverne and Shirley.

The memory of wild fun stings Addy as she realizes, following the dismantling of three closets, that the fanny pack is most likely in The Kingdom of Krap.

Shit.

Addy tiptoes to the side kitchen door and sniffs. She sniffs for a good minute because what she smells is nothing.

Where is the shit?

Before she pulls open the door Addy grabs a dishtowel off the refrigerator door, places it over her nose, and then boldly pushes open the door with her right foot.

Still nothing.

She takes a step forward, breathing cautiously through the towel. She is amazed to see that someone has removed the rotten vegetable fried rice. It is nowhere in sight and neither are several washing machines. Has the bowling ball pile diminished dramatically?

What is going on?

Maybe the garage is eating itself. Maybe there's a krap thief who is stalking neighborhoods. Maybe the junk has melted and slid under the door and right into the garbage man's hands.

Maybe it's Lucky.

Damn it.

Sneaking in when he sees the car gone.

Cleaning up a trail of mistakes.

Regrouping so he can find a new home for the krap.

Apologizing by way of a dustpan.

When Addy moves around toward the side of the garage door, she also notices that someone has pushed out her dent. Not. She leans way over, places all of her weight on her right leg so that she looks like a wild-eyed boxer, and kicks it back to where it was the night she walked out on Lucky, only this time the dent goes in the opposite direction. Addy has to stop herself from kicking the entire door out past the far side of Manhattan.

Addy finds the fanny pack tucked inside of an old and terribly thin blue foam camping mattress that she decides is probably why her left hip will hurt her the rest of her life. Desperate to get out of The Kingdom of Krap, she races into the kitchen, where she throws the pack on the table, pours herself a very tall glass of water, sits down and bends over to see if the zipper still opens in spite of its rusty exterior.

Good God in heaven. When did she use this pack last? On a grade school outing with Mitchell? A camping trip before that with Lucky? A million years ago? During a shopping trip in 1995? When she last hit the road with Hell? Before the alleged birth of Jesus?

The zipper slides open without hesitation and when Addy reaches her hand inside she quickly pulls it back out. The almost broken-down blue fanny pack has a whole life to live and to tell. This trip down memory lane is not written on the assignment cards. It is not part of the road trip. It is not something Hell has written down on her list of things to do and love and accomplish and exhume and it is definitely not something Addy can stop herself from experiencing.

There is first a red-stained wine cork still attached to a tiny backpacking bottle opener. Addy pulls off the cork and smells it. The ancient earthy mix of old tannins, musty cracked crevices, the slice of a long forgotten taste of wine slips her into a kind of trance. Her fingers go back into the pack. They pull out wooden matches, a wad of tissue, a handful of rocks from the last lake on the last hike, and then there is a tiny green notebook with a slim pencil tucked inside of its metal binding like a caterpillar taking a nap.

The notebook.

Addy runs it between her fingers, closes her eyes, and tries to remember how it started, when it started, why it stopped. It was Lucky, she thinks, pawing through the shadows that linger in all the passageways of her own dusty memory banks. Lucky who thought it was a grand idea to carry it with them in case they wanted to write a note, a lusty thought, the first line of a poem. And so they had. Possible baby names. An island they wanted to see. What they might be doing in twenty years. Directions to the next campground. What they would look like as an old man and woman. A recipe from the back of the soup can.

Addy opens the notebook slowly, terrified of what she might see, how she might feel. She thumbs through pages of her handwriting, Lucky's handwriting, a scribbled page from Hell, and toward the back rediscovers little notes from Mitchell.

MOMMY, ARE YOU SURE I AM ADOPTED?

STOP FOR CANDY.

BUY MITCHELL A FAST BLUE CAR.

WHY IS IT SO QUIET JUST BEFORE THE SUN SETS???

A diary of years, thoughts, a puzzle of possible lost lives and the very last damn entry. A love poem from Lucky Lipton.

This morning a sliver of lost light
moved through the bushes
Found your face . . . lovely, light, calm
And I kissed you
With my heart

With my life
With a promise of forever
Addy, you are my love

Her stomach rises to her throat and Addy snaps the small book shut. She drops it on the table and she vividly remembers that camping trip. Five years ago Mitchell had just finished junior high, and they did what she is about to do with Hell—threw bags into the car within a thirty-minute time limit, laughing, Mitchell grabbing the fishing gear, which was actually all in one place before the garage turned into The Kingdom of Krap, and off they went before Now, before everything slipped south, before the spontaneity, the fun, all things worth writing about seemed to vanish like the stinking food from the middle of Lucky's hellhole.

Addy cannot hold on to the green notebook or any thoughts of joy, or even the slightest memory of something fine, sweet, and wonderful from her married past. It is as if her mind and heart have created their own anti-virus, spam-eating filters and nothing she can see, nothing she does, nothing she feels from the bits and pieces of the past can stay lodged within her tender parts.

She gets up just as she hears cars, several cars, maybe a truck, and then more cars driving into the cul-de-sac which, of course, ends at Bob One's house, and by the time she looks out the side window there are at least six cars parked in Bob's driveway, around the edge of the circular drive and up to the beginning of her property. She recognizes almost all of the vehicles. Guys. Men. Lucky's posse. The gang.

Now what, she thinks, as she hears Hell's Jeep roar into her driveway. She slips the green notebook from the past into the tiny drawer in the cabinet by the front door, under the mittens and winter scarves that no one has touched or used in a very long time.

TWENTY-SEVEN
Betrayal on Underwear Lane · · ·

"Where are the broken dishes?"

"What in the hell are you talking about?"

"You know, the dishes and plates and platters I threw all over the back porch. They are gone. Where are they?"

"I'm not sure."

Hell is lying. Addy has always been able to tell when Hell is lying because she tips her head first left, and then right, and then she takes in a huge wad of air that she must think is like holy water or a dispensation from the pope and every saint from Santa Fe to Rome.

"You liar."

"Why would I lie? I said I'm not sure."

"But you know something?"

Hell is considering turning the Jeep around, slowing a bit as she comes into the cul-de-sac, and then shoving her lovely sister out of the car and onto her own front lawn. They have been driving back toward Parker and have taken an intriguing side road, a missing sign, a tin barrel tipped on its side with gravel spilling out across the road, a row of trees bending toward the sun and a really curious-looking set of men's briefs nailed to a dead tree stump that caught Addy's eye as they crossed over the intersection and then Hell suddenly turned down the irresistible road.

Hell has never hit her sister, except for the three thousand times when they were growing up and once when Hell accidentally knocked her in the face with a beer can during a college visit. She's seen Addy through the adoption and the testing and counseling and heartache that came before it. Addy slept in Hell's arms the night their mother died and every night for two weeks after that. Addy came to her each and every time Hell ran from the altar. Hell has told Addy almost—**almost**—everything and she's watched way too silently as Addy's marriage to Lucky has hit the biggest brick wall she has ever seen in her life.

And.

And this is the first time Hell has not totally, truly, for sure liked her sister. Her kindred spirit. The one person in the world she can trust. The woman who is always there for her, who never judged, who helps her pick up the pieces so perfectly it's a wonder she ever bothers to get up in the morning or worry about anything.

"Shut the fuck up, Addy."

"What did you say?"

Hell brakes so hard Addy hits the window. She turns off the Jeep, opens the door, and starts walking up the underwear road.

"What the hell?" Addy yells.

Hell stops, turns slowly, her fingers balled into fists. She's as angry as Addy has ever seen her and Addy shrinks back into her seat, she cannot stop looking at her sister, her Hell, and she is scared.

Hell slowly uncoils her fists. She walks to the side of the gravel road, sits on a rock, and thinks about the last twenty-four hours. The

way she avoided Addy's quiz about the cars
parked at Bob One's, how easy it was to de-
flect questions, how quickly she could avoid
answers by stepping an inch to the right, and
then to the left, and then back around behind the next set of questions. How easy it
was to hit the road, get lost, spend the night
at a forty-dollar roadside hotel watching two
Katharine Hepburn movies while drinking
wine, eating an entire box of crackers, two
apples, a wedge of cheese. Sleeping with all
the windows wide open while she listened to
her sister's breath slow from its fast-beating
tempo to a smooth, sweet, and finally re-
laxed rhythm.

Shit.

Double shit.

Damn it.

Hell gets up. She walks back slowly to tell
her that she has lied—sort of. That she
knows more—sort of. That a very large part
of her is in despair because of this marriage
mess and she's terrified that her only sister,
the left half of her heart, her emotional heroine, may be making the worst mistake of her
life.

"What are you saying?" Addy questions as they both sit in the tall weeds on Underwear Lane like deer that are pausing before a wild gallop through the summer fields.

"I've been talking to Bob One and we've been meeting and discussing you and Lucky, and when we left yesterday all of Lucky's pals were meeting with him to try and help him win you back," Hell blurts out.

Addy gasps. Is this a betrayal? She feels as if she's been hit by falling debris from a large cargo jet. Has her sister defected? What in the holy hell has been going on with Hell? And what about her own secret . . . should she tell Hell?

Then Hell says, spilling her guts out onto the gravel: "I kind of like Bob One."

The wind picks up, trees shake, somewhere in the world babies are wailing, people are tumbling off bicycles, there's a house fire, and some stupid fools are falling in love. Addy thinks that if Hell says one more thing, reveals another secret, moves, or tries to look into her eyes, she is going to lie down and never ever get up, breathe, walk, talk, or move again for the rest of her life.

"Well, Jesus, Hell, have you slept with him? When has all of this been going on? I feel like you just kicked me upside the head."

"It's not what you think, baby."

"What is it?"

"I went to spy on Lucky, and for God's sake the man started to cry, and Bob One and I got him settled down and then we talked and then I met Bob for coffee and we kept talking and it started to just be about you and Lucky and then I just looked at Bob, you know, **looked** at him, and realized what a great guy he's turned into."

"Well, he was a complete asshole before he got divorced."

"I suppose a part of every man stays asshole-ish," Hell agreed mildly, "but look what he's done. He's totally changed his life. He's fun to be around and we've been talking about everything from philosophy to the texture of tobacco in Cuban cigars—"

"Stop it, Hell, you are making me sick. Why didn't you tell me? I feel used and dirty."

"I didn't tell you because I'm trying to help you. Lucky still loves you, Addy, he's trying to figure out what to do, how to get back what you both had and that's what all those guys were going over there to help him do. I shouldn't even be telling you this . . . I'm kind of in a mess now, aren't I?"

Addy suddenly feels exhausted. The last twenty-four hours have been erased in a flurry of confessions that have left her winded, wounded, and wrestling with everything she feels, everything she may or may not want.

"Hell, I called an attorney."

The wind stops and suddenly the air becomes as thin as a December morning on top of Mount Everest. Hell turns slowly, she is instantly in the middle of a movie, suddenly breathless, suddenly wishing that she had a magic key she could turn to change the world, the direction of the conversation, Addy's heart.

"Oh, Addy . . . no."

"I'm going to file. Hell, I'm exhausted. I don't think I can love him the way I once loved him again. I don't think so."

"He's trying, you know, he's working on so many things at once."

"Hell, you are supposed to be on **my** side."

"What do you **want,** Addy? Do you even know what you want? I'm trying to help you. I spied on him. I told you about that and should I have told you about Bob? Maybe. But that was for me and I see things differently sometimes than you do. This is not all Lucky's fault. He—"

"I know that," Addy says, cutting her off. "I'm no poster child for a perfect marriage. I know it's not just his fault it all melted away. But a part of me blames him. A part of me sees him slipping into the same place so many other men slip into and it's been a relief to have him gone. A relief."

"No therapy together? Just a divorce? That's it?"

"I think so."

Hell latches onto the word "think" like a starving dog. **Think** means it's possible the marriage will not keep folding in half until the two pieces permanently separate. **Think** means that Addy is speaking without having already connected final thoughts in her totally bewildered mind. **Think** means that she can still sneak around, fill in some of the blanks for Lucky, see luscious Bob, and practice flirting and keep lying to her beloved and acutely confused big sister who has been acting like a horse's ass. A lovely horse's ass, with reason to be furious and reason to want to start over and be alone, but a horse's ass nonetheless.

"Well then, you may want to reconsider hating me for trying to keep you together with the man you were crazy about the day you married him," Hell boldly says. "And . . ."

"And what?" Addy snaps as if the words were flying scissors aimed at Hell's throat.

"And, I know for a fact that when we get back there is going to be a planning session going on for a neighborhood barbecue in the middle of the cul-de-sac that is meant to lure you into the street, into some conversations, and into the outstretched arms of Lucky Lipton, who is at this very moment undergoing a romantic infusion of ideas and suggestions and everything else his posse can pull out of its own limited resources."

Addy laughs.

She really laughs.

She laughs so loudly that nesting birds rise right out of their grassy cocoons as if they have been electrocuted and then sit slowly back down again.

Addy laughs because in her mind she sees Lucky seated in a straight-back chair with a Celtic kilt, shaved legs, manicured toe- and fingernails, a trimmed beard, waxed eyebrows, one hand on a book of poetry and the other on a fine bottle of red wine while he listens to some sexy blues music and gets ready to pluck rose petals so he can lay a trail to the newly decorated bedroom.

She tells this to Hell who writes it all down in her mind so she can remember to tell Bob One, who will tell Lucky, who will then—with a bit of practice and fortitude— be able to do one or more of those things to satisfy Addy's apparent craving for romance, lust, and seduction.

Hell laughs too, but she laughs because she is scared shitless that her only sister, her beloved sister, her terribly sad and distraught sister, may never speak to her again when Addy realizes, which she eventually will, that her baby sister Hell, the golden, wild apple of her life, has turned into a double spy, a traitor who has now told her everything.

Well, almost everything.

Sort of.

Kind of but not really.

TWENTY-EIGHT
What I thought Addy was thinking · · ·

The Jeep pulls out and Addy looks back, I know she looks back, and Hell is driving fast and Addy is thinking that she never wants to come back to this place.

She wants to drive herself into a new life and she thinks I am not up to it. I am the old life and not the new life.

Addy is thinking that I don't care she is taking off like the old days.

I think that is what Addy is thinking but I am hoping I am wrong.

TWENTY-NINE
The therapeutic nature
of angry art . . .

Addy discovers the birdbath four days after the ill-fated trip with Hell and just after she slips into her spandex and slightly frayed workout shorts and leans over to pick up her tennis shoes. She is preparing to ride her bike to the Y for her workout session—a session with the Sweat-Hers that most likely will turn into yet another discussion on defining Plan B, Plan B being whatever the women come up with to either support the proposed divorce or get Addy and Lucky back together.

Addy would rather be drowned in the hot tub or pummeled to death with a barbell during the weight-lifting sessions where she has steadfastly refused to speak out loud, to talk about what she might be planning to do or when she might be planning to do it. The Sweat-Hers, her so-called friends, usually continue on speaking as if she has left the building.

"Forget it," she said when Hell told the entire class that Addy had contacted an attorney. "It's my divorce, not your divorce. And I haven't filed papers yet and I know you all love me and care about me, but you are not helping with this constant marriage discussion."

Such anger, they hissed.

Such a sassy mouth.

Such a low attitude.

Such a negative response.

Such ungratefulness.

Such narrow vision.

And still they did not stop. Addy even considered dropping out of the class, but then she looked at her thighs that still needed a good three thousand miles of work, and the bottom part of her arms that swayed, not a lot, but enough to make her think of the old choral director from high school, and thought about how absolutely shitty she feels when she misses working out more than three days in a row, and how her friends were really just trying to help and there she was putting on her shorts that made everything in between the thighs and arms look worse than it actually was, sausage-like, Malibu always says, hoisting up her own shorts like some dude named Vinnie.

Why it took her all those days to discover the birdbath was not really a mystery to Addy. She had simply not bothered to look out the window or to go into the backyard or to have a smoke since she came back from her road trip with Hell. She'd smoked but it was a very tiny cigar and it was at the First National where she had been working daily because of some summer virus that was jumping from bartender to waitress faster than Hell could fill out the schedule sheet.

"What the heck?"

Addy saw something shimmering when the light moved through the trees. It was several feet tall and looked as if it had dropped from the inside of a UFO. She managed to get one shoe on before she couldn't resist it anymore. She walked outside limping with the other shoe in her hand.

A birdbath?

A statue?

A statue birdbath?

Addy dropped her red Adidas shoe and knelt in front of the statue. She took off her glasses and ran her hands along the sides, up onto the lip, and around the center of the bowl. It looked like a birdbath. A one-of-a-kind birdbath. A birdbath that had been strung together with something that looked like a washing machine agitator hooked together with intertwined strands of wire that were covered in pieces of broken dishes, cups, platters, and saucers. The same dishes, cups, platters, and saucers that Addy had flung out the back door and stepped on and over for several weeks before all those pieces of pottery, china, and glass mysteriously vanished.

Addy ran her hands over the pieces, which were edged together so skillfully that the entire surface was as smooth as her own skin. The damn wedding gifts she'd shattered all over her lawn looked fabulous as a birdbath. It was beautiful, and of course, Lucky had done it.

"Crap."

Addy walked around it three times until she noticed the initials, **L.L.,** handwritten along the side edge so that one of the pieces of pottery looked like a tiny flower. She finally sat down, without taking her eyes off of it, put her shoe on, and then, shaken by the fabulous gift, walked over to the smoking tree where she fumbled for her metal box. That's when she discovered something else, which prompted a lively personal conversation with herself.

"Is this an ashtray?"

"It's an ashtray."

"If Hell told him about this tree I'll kill her. That's it."

"If Hell didn't tell him, I have to find someone else to kill."

Addy yanked her cell phone from her T-shirt pocket and speed-dialed Bob One while she lit up a cigarette and turned the ashtray over in her hand. It was so odd that it was uniquely beautiful, which pissed her

off even more. Lucky had used the few broken edges that he must have hand-picked
from the backyard and laid them around
what she guessed was half of the old license
plate from her first car. A 1965 Volkswagen
that she had painted lime green and driven
for seven years. While that thought was in
her mind and the cigarette was in her mouth,
Lucky picked up the phone.

"Lucky?"

"Addy."

"Who the hell told you about my smoking tree?"

"It wasn't Hell, so back off before you
even say it."

"Who?"

"I saw you smoking back there about
three months ago. I sort of knew it all along
anyway. One day I went back there, found
the cigarettes—oh, hell, Addy, I don't care if
you smoke."

"Damn it, Lucky."

"What?"

"This is **my** place. For **me**. You know, like
your Kingdom of Krap. I feel **violated**."

"So this means you are still angry?"

"I'm everything, Lucky, including angry."

"But do you like the ashtray? The bird-bath?"

"They are both beautiful."

Lucky sighs big and before he can say another word Addy hangs up.

She smokes until the cigarette is so close to the filter her finger is singed. She never thinks that Lucky might be watching her, hoping for a polite wave, a smile toward the back window, a positive smoke signal. Lucky would be happy if she flipped him off. Anything to acknowledge his existence beyond a harsh word.

Addy just sits and smokes but what Lucky doesn't see is that she cannot bring herself to use the ashtray, not because Lucky made it, but because she thinks it's not really an ashtray but an impressive work of art.

She rolls the words "work of art" around inside of her mouth and then says them softly, out loud, turning the ashtray in a complete circle and then holding it toward the light so she can see how all the pieces fit together. What has Lucky been up to over there at Bob's? And why can she not bring herself to be at least a little bit polite or even civil to him? **What in the hell is wrong with me, and my damn high blood pressure, and is this anger that makes me want to scream and shout?**

Except Addy likes the powerful feeling the swell of anger gives her and this realization prompts her to gently set down the ashtray and make an emergency phone call to her counselor, who, of course, is busy for the next six hours. Addy puts away her cigarettes and turns once to look at Lucky's gifts before she gallops toward her bicycle, and toward the Sweat-Hers, who are eagerly waiting for her just as much as she is eagerly waiting for them so she can drop a bomb that is much larger than the boundaries of Parker, PA.

THIRTY
The spy who came clean in the hot tub . . .

It's Malibu's fabulous idea, they all finally agree, and Addy thinks they have created a monster by agreeing to support Heidi's make-believe name change, which has resulted in something that could also change the way the earth is tilted.

And possibly the rest of Addy Lipton's life.

The women have just lived through a mandatory weigh-in that is supposed to propel them into signing on for another session of the Sweat-Hers, into a round of personal and group satisfaction, into the joyous arms of the gratifying aches of hard work, real sweat, and painful muscle extensions.

"Consider it a mental diploma," the tiny

and very buff trainer told them as she forced them one at a time onto the scale. "Remember that lots of your fat has turned into muscle, feel it, grip your arms, and don't be disappointed if the weight loss isn't as great as you think it should be, because, dear Sweat-Hers, you look **fabulous**."

"Fabulous, my ass," Addy grumbled just loud enough for Hell to hear her.

"Addy, you are a pain in the ass," Hell said. "Have you bothered to look at yourself lately? You have muscle definition for the first time since ninth grade. And the little ass you keep talking about is no longer riddled with dimples."

This as Addy stepped onto the scale for the first time in a month and discovered that she had lost six more pounds, bringing her total weight loss since she started the class to a bountiful eighteen pounds.

"Holy cow," she exclaimed.

"See," Hell said, leaning over to look at the numbers. "You are so cranky these days and look, look at what is happening. Your body, and apparently the life you once knew, is disappearing before your very eyes."

Addy wanted to smack her. She wondered if the weight loss and muscle tone hadn't woken up a nest of hibernating testosterone. She's wanted to smack things, lash out, break dishes, and scream at something or someone every fifteen seconds. This she confesses to her lighter-than-ever pals as they all slip into the woman-sized hot tub.

"I'm sure your counselor tells you this anger is normal," Lee tells Addy. "It sure as hell was for me each and every time I went through a separation or a divorce."

"Well, Addy, it's not like you have just one little thing like a marriage falling apart to deal with," Debra adds. "Lucky hurt his back, Mitchell is connecting with his birth mother, and your heart is fluttering. It's a lot, hon."

Addy takes a deep breath and tries to form a polite thought before she speaks but the mere act of speaking without fire rolling off her tongue seems impossible.

"Look, I have just frigging had it and you might as well know that I am going ahead with the divorce and yes, yes, I am angry," Addy snarls at her friends. "I am angry and I wish to hell you would all stop trying to talk me out of it."

The silence that follows could be used as a new military weapon that might drive people crazy. There is only the constant gurgle of water bubbling around breasts and shoulders and necks and against the sides of the extremely large hot tub and only the small sound of the tip of a ripple from the wave of Debra's hand hitting the plastic filter. Now all of the Sweat-Hers are taking a deep breath and moving their eyes east to west to see if anyone has a clue what to say next.

The idea comes from Malibu who leans forward, puts the inside of her hand against Addy's face as if she is feeling for a high fever and says, "Well, okay then, Addy, let's just take it from there."

But it's Hell who finally manages to say, "Holy shit, sister. Holy shit. Really? You signed the papers? Oh my God. Really? You are going to **divorce** Lucky?"

There is a small slice of Addy that still feels a twinge of compassion, especially for her beloved, if overbearing, wild-ass sister, but it is not large enough for her to think that Hell, or anyone in the entire world, might have her—Addy's—best interests at heart. Addy is Helen of Troy, a female CIA operative, a trained killer, Mata Hari, Cleopatra. She seems to possess the magnified power of five thousand women in the throes of menopause.

Addy turns slowly toward her sister and the energy in her eyes is blinding, horrid, and just an inch on the back side of evil.

"Really, I am really filing papers. And they are being delivered in about an hour over to your boyfriend's house where Lucky now lives, and I have this powerful sense that this is what I should be doing," Addy not so much says as spews. "This is about me and not about what you think I should do or try. Let me be, for the love of God, please let me be."

"Boyfriend?" bellows Lee, bewildered. "What boyfriend?"

"Tell her, Hell," Addy demands. "You seem to be the relationship advisor these days. Tell her about your new boy-friend."

"You are possessed," Hell says instead. "Addy, here we are, your best friends in the whole world, just having a conversation. And you're acting as if we have just tried to slip poison into the bathwater here. Lighten up. You are not very attractive right now."

"What boyfriend?" Lee asks again as if Hell has not even spoken. "Hell? Are you seeing someone?"

"Seeing someone?" Hell responds. "If you think hanging out with Bob One to spy on him for Addy and discovering he is a nice guy and will help me with the Fall Festival is seeing someone, then yes, I am seeing some-one."

"You think he's nice and attractive and you've been out with him," Addy snarls.

Hell does what any sister would do. She gently moves her hands under the water, forms a small cup by placing them together, and—just as Addy is about to say something else stupid, selfish, inane, and insulting— uses her hand cup to dash water right into Addy's very surprised face.

"What the hell . . ." Addy sputters as she forms her own cup to douse Hell and within seconds there is a naked water fight that if recorded on film, could not only result in several lawsuits, but could also be used for blackmailing purposes for the rest of the century.

Hell and Addy are standing upright in the hot tub and are flinging water at each other with their cupped hands. Malibu and Debra have each hopped out of the huge tub and are straddled on each side of it lobbing cups of water at each other and Hell and Addy are using tiny paper cups they hastily pulled out of the water dispenser. Mighty Lee is still sitting inside of the hot tub, she has not moved, and throws water first at the dueling sisters, then at Malibu and Debra, and then into her own face.

The water fight does not end when there is a loud bang on the door and the workout room attendant yells, "Hey, is everyone okay in there? What are you women doing?"

"Water aerobics!" yells Lee, who starts laughing and then quickly adds, "We're fine, really, just finishing our workout."

"Here's a workout," Addy yells, dropping herself into the tub with her arms clenched in a mini-cannonball-like form that throws a waterfall onto Lee.

This only makes Lee laugh harder and it's the kind of laugh that you beg for on a depressing winter day when the sky is dark, it's colder than hell, and you need a reason to smile. It's a laugh that makes everyone want to laugh and that's exactly what they all start to do.

They laugh.

The Sweat-Hers **laugh**.

Then Addy throws up her arms and yells, "I surrender!"

Malibu and Debra hop back into the center of watery hell, the real Hell sits down, and the women laugh together uncontrollably until Addy finds the courage to say she is sorry. She finds it in a place lodged below the spot where her heart used to lie, next to her fond memory bank, across the street from her bin of forgiveness and just down the aisle from her stacks of guilt, wrath, jealousy, and the little tin of insanity that has lost its lid.

"What?" Hell asks. "Did you just say you are sorry?"

"I am," Addy confesses. "I really am sorry I have been an ass. I am **not** sorry that Lucky will be getting the divorce papers any moment, but I am sorry I turned on all of you. Really. I am sorry."

"Honey," Lee says softly, "don't think twice about it. I know what you feel like and you feel like shit. You look pretty hot, especially all wet like that, but really, there isn't a woman in this tub who wouldn't help you and support you. It's okay."

"It is," both Debra and Malibu say at the same time.

Addy looks up at Hell and says, "I'm especially sorry about how I have treated you, Hell. You have been supportive throughout this roller-coaster ride and listen—if you think Bob is hot, go for it. I feel like I don't even know what I am saying half the time."

"Addy, Addy, Addy." Hell shakes her head. "This is why I am still single. Relationships are too much work. Let's just get through this. Let's figure out what to do next. If this is what you want, if you are sure, then you know I am there and—as if you don't know this already—so are they."

All the heads in the hot tub bob up and down and Addy says, "Now what?"

Hell closes her eyes and wishes for a moment that she could slip under the water, out the drainpipe, through the sewers, where she figures she belongs right about now, and into her own bathtub where she would lie in tepid water without a beverage as her penance for being a double spy.

A sort of double spy.

A sister who cares.

A sister-in-law who cares.

A bumbling fool.

A hormonal idiot who was temporarily lured into a masculine web by her own frailties.

A best friend almost gone bad.

"Okay," Hell starts sputtering as she begins, because she has no idea what she is about to say. "I guess I know more than I have let on, because I've been hanging out over there and because Bob does have a crush on me and because I thought I was being a savvy spy for my sister here."

And then Hell confesses.

"They have this plan," she says. "And they, before you ask, are the Bobs, the rest of the neighborhood guys, the pals from

Lucky's job. And honestly, Addy, I thought I was helping. I talked to them about what women want and why we think most of them are assholes and how selfish they always seem to be and why we are not really that turned on by things like washing-machine parts and old bowling balls."

"Are they really that dumb?" Debra asks, and before she can take a breath her friends all say "Yes" at the same moment.

So, Hell, so what the hell are they doing? The Sweat-Hers want to know.

Planning and scheming and trying to figure out how Lucky can win back Addy's heart, Hell tells them.

Like how?

It's the barbecue. The neighborhood barbecue, Hell confesses. Lucky's tribe has organized the cul-de-sac event as more of a crusade than an evening of fun with friends and neighbors. The men are dressing up. The men are cooking gourmet foods. The men have hired someone to play music. The men have so many plans that Hell covers her head, shakes it up and down and back and forth, and cannot remember everything.

"He loves you, Addy," Hell says, raising her eyes. "But clearly you are ready to move on. So what do we do now?"

Malibu Heidi jumps to her feet, forgetting for a moment that she is naked, and raises her hands and this is where the fabulous idea is born. Malibu says it is time to fight fire with fire. Malibu says it is time to gather Addy's own tribe even closer. Malibu says it is time to pull out all the stops and to make their own plans for barbecue night and every night after so that the boys will know that trying is good but trying too late is not so good.

"Are you in?" Malibu asks, dropping back into the blanket of water.

There is no hesitation. Hands go into the air, there are war whoops, splashing feet, two wild birdcalls, and the not-so-quiet rumblings of the hearts of women warriors revving up as they prepare for battle.

THIRTY-ONE
What I should have said to Addy · · ·

But I still love you is what I should have said.

Standing there like a dumbass with the divorce papers in my hands I should have walked over there even though I am in a stupid male coma, knocked on the front door of my own house, and just said, "But I still love you."

THIRTY-TWO
An astonishing event in the middle of the street . . .

Addy is certain Mitchell has been drinking cheap beer or some really bad two-buck chuck when he calls her. She knows this because she knows Mitchell. She knows how he taps his left fingers when he is on the phone and how he talks slowly after he has had more than two alcoholic beverages. Addy knows that he has assimilated many of Lucky's lovely habits and that it is often hard for her son to say what he really thinks and feels when he is in a normal state. Normal being sober and not under any kind of duress, stress, or in unfamiliar territory.

So when the phone rings as she is trying to assemble something to wear that is sexy and wild and hot and tempting for the cul-

de-sac party of the year and she hears
Mitchell slip a few vowels, and there is no
finger-tapping, Addy drops everything to sit
and focus on the conversation.

"So I was just thinking about you, Mom,
and you know Dad called me, and I just
thought we should talk," Mitchell says.

"Are you okay about the separation?"
Addy asks, sitting on the edge of her bed,
left hand gripping her left thigh, heart
pounding fast enough to propel a small six-
seat airplane.

"Well, shit, oops, sorry, Mom, is any kid
okay when they hear about stuff like this?"

Mitchell pauses and Addy thinks she is
supposed to say something but then she realizes that Mitchell probably just needed to
refill his glass or take a swig out of the bottle.

"You know," he continues, "in high
school it's like, 'Can I get some poor girl to
go to homecoming with me—will I make
the soccer team, will I ever really need to
shave'—and it wasn't like I was watching
and thinking that you and Dad might be
happy or anything."

Addy rises a bit so she can look into the

mirror by the dresser so she knows she is still alive and really having this conversation. She thinks, once she realizes she is not dead, that it is now her turn to say something. But she is wrong again.

Mitchell keeps talking as if he can't remember he is having a conversation with someone besides himself.

"But then I started thinking about it and I was thinking about how you and Dad sort of live separate lives and how he hangs in the garage and stuff and has his friends and you love your job and your sister and stuff and I was thinking that maybe that's just what happens and maybe it's okay as long as you guys can still be civil and not like assholes, oops again, sorry, Mom, like all the other people and then Dad has been sick and stuff . . ."

Mitchell trails off and Addy wonders if he has not now wandered to Africa or off the coast of Australia but she waits anyway because she has already tried to speak twice and there is a huge pause. She can see him sitting there, eyes closed, his big feet flopping around, and now she wonders if she can really speak.

"So . . ." Mitchell says, letting out a wad of air.

"So what?" Addy manages to whisper.

"So, what I really wanted to say was first of all that you should not be worried about this birth-mother thing, that you are my mother and stuff and that you and Dad have both been, like, the greatest parents." Mitchell is on a roll. Addy is hoping he is home and will not drive or walk or move after the call. "She might have, like, hatched me out but you are my mom and, hey, Mom, guess what?"

"What, honey?"

"I'm drinking red wine."

Addy drops her head into her left hand and imagines this too. Imagines her boy drinking out of a nice wineglass, or a jelly jar, or his Wisconsin Badgers coffee cup, and she smiles wide, really wide, to keep herself from crying.

"Are you okay, honey?"

"Oh, yeah, Mom. I am in the dorm and

alone and I can't go anywhere, believe me. I probably can barely walk, but I just had to say this. I had to."

"Thank you, Mitchell."

"Mom, I really hope it doesn't happen. I hope you don't get divorced."

"Mitchell . . ." Addy manages to get out his name and cannot say another word.

"But, Mom, Mom, if it does, just be happy. I'll take care of Dad and it will all be okay and oh, holy shit, Mom, wait . . . okay, Mom, I have to go, this really cute girl from down the hall has more wine and I have to go."

"Mitchell! Mitchell, wait . . ."

But he is gone.

He is a man.

Mitchell has a life.

A heart.

A soul the color of maturing, sun-ripening berries.

A possible girlfriend.

Glasses of wine.

Mitchell James Lipton is a son who has apparently just passed through the pain-in-the-ass phase of his young adult life and into a sheltered cove of rest and warmth and light and understanding, and Addy, the mother of this boy-man wonder, is now wondering herself.

She knows that the red wine helped fuel the call but she also knows that the words he said were most likely formed over and over again inside his lively brain until he found the courage via his wine to say them. But he did say them and she heard them and Addy Lipton wonders about timing.

Mitchell could have called last night or tomorrow or next month but he chose this moment when Addy is about to put on her lift-them-high bra, throw a low-cut sleeveless black camisole over the top of that, yank up her very hot, tight-fitting white clamdiggers, and stride into the cul-de-sac barbecue in her new neighborhood-seductress disguise that includes a ton of lost weight, newfound freedom, and the desire to make every man holding a hamburger bun **want** her.

Addy knows that if she were into horoscopes, a card-reading kind of woman, that she would sit for a very long time to try and figure out why this moment, why her son picked this unpredictable, astonishing, wonderful, confusing, revealing moment to call her. But Addy continues to be a do-it-or-die woman—at least recently—a woman who thinks there is something to stars aligning and hawks flying into her backyard to speak, and the power of a mess of silver bracelets dangling from both wrists, but a woman who also believes that stuff just happens.

People get hit by cars.

Men die on the way to their own weddings.

Birds fly wildly because they can.

Storms hit the same house six times just because.

This one lives and that one dies for no particular reason.

Men and women fall in and out of love.

And a son can call home because of the wine, the woman, or the song, or just because it was the only free moment he had and not because his separated parents are about to attend a neighborhood hoo-ha, divided in half by his side–her side. Mitchell doesn't know it's going to be a boys-against-the-girls night to cascade through the ages.

Mitchell just called.

That is what Addy latches onto as she hears tables being dragged into the street, aluminum lawn chairs clanking across thighs, cars braking at the throat of the circle drive and both her front and back doorbells ringing at the same time. Addy stops in front of her bedroom mirror before she heads for the doors. She pushes her fingers against the sides of her eyes to wipe away her tears, smacks her lips to set her lipstick, pushes up her breasts another inch and then releases them so her cleavage shows just a tiny bit more, looks herself in the eye and says out loud, "You can do this, Lipton." And then she breathes very deeply, following the exact instructions from her acupuncturist.

Hell is at the front door looking like a hooker. She has on red shorts, a black lace bra that is clearly visible under a tight black tank top, a pair of dark shoes with heels so thin and long they could be used as weapons, and not another thing.

"Are those hot pants?" Addy asks, staring at her sister's thighs.

"Anything is hot when I wear it, baby," Hell says, landing one arm up against the side of the doorframe and throwing back her head.

"Well, Jesus, Hell, you are, like, a step beyond sexy."

"I think that's a compliment and I also think there are a mess of women standing in your backyard."

When Addy pulls open the back door with Hell at her shoulder she sees a blur of color and is attacked by a scent that reminds her of her mother's Avon parties and a now-deceased aunt who not so much wore as bathed in exotic perfumes.

"Girlfriends!" Addy shouts as the Sweat-Hers, four of the wild cigar-smoking women from Honduras, and Carla and Mimi from school sort of fall into her house. "Why the back door?"

"Did you look out the window?" Carla asks.

"No, I was on the phone with Mitchell when the doorbells, both of them, rang. What is it?"

"Look!" everyone commands at once.

Addy moves past the women and back to the front of the house where she moves against the wall like a cat who has just spied a wild bird and then leans in to look out of the big picture window. She can feel the women pressing in around her and she suddenly starts to laugh because she imagines they all look hilarious and pretty damn ridiculous even if they do smell good.

"Holy hell," Addy says, peering out.

The men, the competition, the boys, the bowling jocks, are all dressed in tuxedos. A large truck has backed up to the center of the cul-de-sac and the men are helping to unload cartons of what must be food, cases of what must be wine, boxes that must be filled with flowers, and an assortment of wrapped packages that could be anything from spare washing-machine parts to unexpected gifts from Treasure Island.

"Wow," Hell breathes.

"What is going on?" Addy asks.

"Well, you got the invitation, didn't you?" Debra asks.

"I haven't opened my mail in about a week," Addy admits, quickly rifling through a mountain of mail that is on the table near the window.

The handwritten invitation almost jumps into her hand. It's purple, with a wax seal, and her name is written on it in copper ink. When she opens the envelope, tiny pieces of silver, gold, and blue paper fall from the envelope and onto her freshly painted toes. Addy pulls out a piece of paper, runs her fingers over the embossed letters, and feels the breath of several women on the back of her neck.

The cul-de-sac barbecue is in our hands.

Come but bring nothing.

Drinks, dinner, and a lovely set of summer stars are all on us.

No RSVP is necessary but it is our sincere hope that you will join us for this wonderful evening.

Sincerely,
The Men from the Cul-de-Sac
and Beyond

Addy looks up slowly, wonders for a second how long her potato salad will keep, and then asks the women who are huddled around her if they know where their husbands are. To a woman, they say their husbands disappeared in the early part of the afternoon, leaving notes saying they would meet them at the barbecue.

"Holy shit," Hell seethes. "We have been outmaneuvered. The men are onto us. They are going to throw some kind of a big-ass, wild-ass, cul-de-sac party. And all we thought about was looking sexy."

"Hey," Beth from Honduras almost shouts, "I spent an hour trying to look like this. I feel sexy. I'm hungry. I can flirt. I say, so what?"

"You look fabulous," Lee assures her. "We all look fabulous. I think we should play the bluff."

"Play the bluff?" Malibu asks.

"Yes, play the bluff. Fly into their party. Act like we expected it. Eat, drink, and be merry. Flirt as if we are on fire. Let's enjoy this and then we can figure out what to do after the party. They are **men** for crying out loud. Do you really think they can make us do backflips because of a tuxedo and some cheese curds?"

"Oh God," Cindy from Honduras moans. "I can barely stand when I see a man in a tuxedo."

"Snap out of it," Hell shouts. "This isn't about you. It's about Addy and Lucky and their divorce. It's about showing solidarity."

"That doesn't mean we can't have fun," Cindy fires back.

"She's right, Hell," Addy admits. "This isn't going to be easy for me but I don't expect you all to sit around on your hands. This might be a historic night. Men in tuxedos serving us dinner in the cul-de-sac. And who knows what else they have planned?"

"Well," Heidi says, "you've made up your mind, Addy, the papers are filed, it's sort of up to Lucky now to make the next move, so I say we just go out and flirt, and be sexy, and do what we had planned anyway."

"It would be a shame to waste all this makeup and I hired a babysitter who plans on spending the night," Debra announces.

"I vote we go act like movie stars. But we stay close to Addy, we keep our eyes on Lucky, and we think all night long about what we are going to do next."

They agree and then they boldly walk from the Lipton house, past the dented garage door, past Lucky's Folly, down the middle of the driveway, and into the cul-de-sac that has been swiftly transformed during their conversation into an outdoor cabaret where men in tuxedos stand ready to pour wine, a jazz quartet has started to sing in the Zelands' driveway, and where astonishment seems to be the accepted attire for the evening.

THIRTY-THREE
A confession of a lifetime . . .

Bob One and Lucky are perched on the front step of Bob One's house, smugly looking over the front bush and into the heart of the cul-de-sac where just two days ago they changed the course of history in a town that once prided itself on celebrating ninety-nine percent of all simple and complex occasions by having a requisite chicken-and-hot-dog-and-hamburger cookout in a backyard. The glow from the cul-de-sac barbecue-à-go-go has cascaded throughout Parker and turned Lucky and Bob into temporary celebrities.

"It was a brilliant idea to call the newspaper," Bob One congratulates Lucky, who can actually sit on the step for almost twenty minutes without too much pain.

"Do you think she's pissed?"

"Addy seems to be pissed all of the time, so what difference does it make if seeing herself on the front page of the **Parker Pioneer** dancing with her estranged husband made it worse for a few seconds?"

Lucky shifts his left hip, eases out his leg, and wonders if he maybe went too far. He wonders if the band, the five-course meal that he helped cook, the multitude of wine selections—none of which Addy tried because of her overactive heart—the flowers, the linen tablecloths, the dancing, and his one sort-of-nice-but-not-really-nice conversation with Addy was just a bit over the top.

"Stop worrying, Lucky," Bob admonishes him. "What we did was really very nice and the women deserve it. And I don't know how you feel but I kind of had the time of my life."

"Well, shit, Bob, you kissed my sister-in-law, of course you had the time of your life. I had no idea you had the hots for her."

"Oh, Lucky, we've been flirting like crazy since the day you moved in here a few weeks ago. My God, those shorts she had on, did you see those things?"

Lucky drops his head into his hands and runs his fingers across the top of his bald head. The bald head that he now shaves every morning just before he spends at least fifteen minutes meditating, followed by some reading, stretching, then a daily walk that has now increased to three miles.

"Bob, listen, you are helping me so much. I have no idea what I would be doing or where I would be living without you but this Hell-and-Bob thing is like, well, wow, Bob, it's kinda spooky considering my romantic situation. Do you know what I mean?"

Bob turns slowly and raises his eyebrows. Then he says, "Give me a break, Lucky."

Give me a break because it's been a very long time since Bob One felt his heart move.

Give me a break because Bob One finally feels as if he has something to offer a woman, especially a woman of substance like Hell.

Give me a break because it's obvious Hell makes him happy.

Give me a break because Bob One is much further down the road than Lucky

Lipton is and jealousy is an evil, sad, and very horrid thing.

And Lucky knows. Lucky knows so much more than he knew just weeks before when he was humming through life by more or less just breathing and occasionally moving his limbs to get where he needed to go. He knows that he still loves Addy and that he will do anything, become anything, try anything to get her back. He knows Bob One is the best friend he ever had and that without him he might at this very moment be lying facedown in the gutter that circles the now infamous cul-de-sac. He knows that the changes in his world, his life, in his heart, have just started and that the end of the road is nonexistent. The road does not stop.

And Lucky knows the sadness of loss and of regret and of always settling.

Settling.

Always accepting the comfortable furniture of life.

Always taking for granted.

Always easing back instead of running forward.

Always lying low instead of looking ahead.

Always remembering instead of dreaming.

Always treading water on an endless, clear, beautiful lake.

Always thinking you should do something important and remarkable and then falling asleep at the wheel instead.

"I'm sorry, Bob," Lucky finally admits. "I have been selfish long enough. I realize this and I'm changing but I don't know if Addy can see it. I don't know if she wants to see it."

"Jeesh, Lucky, you can't give up now, for crying out loud. You have to stay on this. Be consistent. How's your list of desires coming along? And what's next? What do you have planned next?"

Lucky raises his head, looks at the now empty concrete cul-de-sac as if he's waiting for a mirage to become real. He shakes his head, says, "What is next?" out loud. "What?"

"You answer that, big guy," Bob says.

What is next could mean what Lucky's

life might have been like if he hadn't screwed up his back and his relationship. What is next could be every possibility in the book, every dream, anything he wants . . . or not. It could be a divorce or a very long separation or it could mean reconciliation.

"I don't think standing still is a very good idea," Lucky says. "I think that I have to push myself, push Addy, say what I want, keep going to all these damn therapy sessions, stay positive, and did I say keep moving?But can I confess something first?"

"Are you going back to that gay thing again? I love you too, Lucky."

"Well, wow, I don't think I've ever told a man I love him, and what a shame that is, but I love you too, Bob. I really do love you."

The sun does not crash into the earth or implode after the word "love" is shared between Lucky and Bob, and both men pause to let the love settle in, to create a shared smile, to lean into each other just another inch.

"Women are so much smarter than we are," Bob admits. "If we would just watch them and listen and see how they bond and connect with each other and how easy it is for them to be emotional we would never have been in this damn mess to begin with."

Lucky laughs, forgetting for a moment what he was really going to tell Bob. He thinks about how he actually believed he was okay before his world exploded. He thought he was warm and tender and kind and yet when he thinks back he sees how he was wrong.

Lucky stopped being romantic and started looking at Addy as someone to take for granted.

Lucky started to gain weight and laughed it off.

Lucky stopped thinking about his real dreams and settled.

Lucky stopped looking at the woman he loves with delight and passion.

Lucky started letting everything go—himself, his job, his relationship, his sports, his ideas of future glory.

Lucky stopped living and was cruising, surviving, breathing on empty.

"Bob, I do love you and if I was gay you'd be my man but what I wanted to say was that even without this back injury, without not going to Costa Rica so Addy could catch a glimpse of paradise, without Addy backing away, we would have been in trouble," Lucky confesses.

"This much in trouble?"

"Yes."

"Wow, Lucky, that's big trouble."

"And I'll be really honest with you, Bob. I've looked around these past couple weeks. I've looked at other women. I tried to imagine myself with them, tried to think of someone that I could love like I love Addy. I cannot do it. I just cannot do it."

Bob turns slowly and he puts his right arm around Lucky, drawing him close against his chest, and then he reaches around in front of Lucky and gives him a huge, tender bear hug.

"So?" Bob prods. "Now what?"

"Can you help me, Bob? I am a klutz about this shit and I think now that it was a flipping miracle that Addy ever fell in love with me. I may have lost her for good, Bob, but I have a couple of ideas. I was wondering if you would still help me."

Because, Lucky thinks, I am already new and changed and changing and wherever this goes and whatever happens it is making me a better man, a better person, a better father, a better husband.

And I love Addy, he adds.

I love her so.

THIRTY-FOUR
Hell's high water . . .

Addy is sitting on top of Hell's bar, feet crossed, papers spread out in front of her in a long line that looks like a procession that ends at the huge silver coffeepot that is never empty and never turned off at the far end of a bar that was hand-carved by a couple of German immigrants who realized that a bar was a necessity of life. They built and opened the bar before they'd built homes or schools or a church.

Sister Hell is sitting at the last barstool with her right shoulder nudged up against the coffeepot and she's taking notes as Addy blazes through one paper after another, scooping them up when she is finished, and then scooting forward as if she's auditioning for a part in a circus.

The First National Wine & Cigar Bar business plan is having an autopsy. Addy has started with the original business plan, plowed through tax records, receipts, incoming and outgoing vouchers, overhead, and the mortgage plan, and her accountant-like financial eye has created a small tornado every morning for a week.

The very long and interesting week since the cul-de-sac dancearama barbecue event of the summer and probably the decade.

The week when Addy set a new record for not speaking to her sister—34.3 hours.

The week when Addy caught herself looking out the window to catch a glimpse of Lucky.

The week when she had absolutely nothing to drink that had alcohol in it, smoked only two cigarettes, and worked out so much she got shin splints.

The week when Mitchell called her three days in a row just to say hi and to ask if she was doing okay.

The week when Addy's therapist gave her

some anger exercises and told her it might be a good idea to look into her own mirror and open her eyes really, really wide.

And when she did that, when Addy Lipton looked into the mirror, it wasn't Lucky that she saw, it was **herself**. Addy saw her red-eyed, tired-of-complaining, sad, cranky, hurt, bitter, totally unattractive self and she immediately went to sit under the tree where she had her two pitiful cigarettes that tasted not like any she had ever remembered smoking and slapped herself upside the head by gently hitting it against the scratchy bark of her smoking tree.

Then she crawled out from under the tree, stripped off her clothes, put on her jogging bra, running shoes, and baggy shorts, because she is not a fan of anything that grabs her thighs tighter than her own skin, and took off walking faster than most people jog.

Addy walked for three hours, breathing out the bad or in the good or some version of what her therapist told her to do, and the entire time she thought about Lucky, who must have lost over thirty pounds, in his studly tuxedo smelling of musk and pine, walking with only a slight limp, dancing slowly, mostly from the knees down but dancing nonetheless, and doing everything he could not to irritate her, say something that had anything to do with the D word, or act as if he wanted to discuss anything legal and binding.

"Have you heard from Mitchell?" he asked politely.

"Yes, he seems to be fine," Addy replied, also politely.

"Everything okay at the house?"

"Yes, it's fine."

"I'm still getting my checks, so let me know if you need anything."

"Just the usual. Thanks for depositing the money every week."

"How's your heart?"

That question almost did it. **My heart,** Addy wanted to yell, **my heart is in a bag behind the refrigerator, you dumbass, where do you think my heart is?**

But Lucky meant the high blood pressure, the stress, the **everything** that was making Addy's heart take a step backwards.

"I'm on top of it," she told him. "Thanks for asking."

And that was it. That and one short dance and then Addy was left to watch him out of the corner of her eye for the next four hours as he delivered drinks, occasionally sat down to rest his back, talked to every woman, appeared to be trying hard to flirt, and just looked over at her now and then to smile and nod his head as if to ask if she was having a good time.

Of course there was the Bob One and Hell kiss that was witnessed by the entire cul-de-sac population, the Sweat-Hers, the Honduras babes, husbands, a few extra friends, and probably a spy satellite from some dating service based in Los Angeles.

The kiss made Addy furious.

"Why?" Hell wanted to know when Addy threw the keys to the Jeep in her face and told her to drive home.

"Well, Jeezus, we were supposed to be sexy and try to seduce them and I guess I figured that meant just tempting and taunting, not actually doing."

"Get over yourself, Addy," Hell seethed.

"The kiss just happened. Bob has been nothing but kind to you and me and to Lucky. Not that any of **that** matters to you."

And that was the beginning of a twenty-minute kitchen argument that ended in Hell backing out the door because she was afraid her sister might jump on her and gouge her eyes out if she turned them away from her. It was also the beginning of the standoff which ended when Addy completed her marathon walk, realized that she needed to clean up her own Kingdom of Krap, called Hell to apologize, and then distracted herself by deciding to redo Hell's business plan, beef up the marketing, and give the bar a makeover that she hoped would parallel her own.

"Hey, don't throw a pen into my eye, but any word from Lucky on the divorce stuff?" Hell asks, while pouring herself another cup of coffee.

"No," Addy shoots back without freaking out. "My lawyer called him and he asked for some time and I said that was fine."

Hell looks startled. "You seem so calm, honey. Are you on drugs?"

"Up yours."

"That's my old Addy."

"Just thinking a lot. The house painters start today. I had a weird desire to hop in the car and go see Mitchell in Madison, but he needs his space and I'm just giving some of that to myself and to Lucky too."

"You sound way too calm. Did you tell Lucky you were painting the house three different colors?"

"Left him a message. Maybe I'll just paint my half and leave his the way it is."

"That's the sister I know and love. Don't get all mushy now and forget that you are getting divorced, completely changing your life, and becoming manager of a bar in Parker, PA."

"It's a far cry from Costa Rica and I am not, let me repeat that **not,** wanting to be the manager of that bar. I'd say it's more like the facilitator of a close-to-major face-lift. So knock it off."

The facts of life for Hell are simple. The bar is making money but not a lot of money. And the business climate in Parker, what with the burbs exploding, is about to bust open, so it's time to create some magic, make some changes, spruce up the joint, and Addy, who is changing everything from the color of her house to her marital status, has offered to crank out a plan for the new and improved First National Wine & Cigar Bar.

Addy's plan started with a wide idea that included closing the joint for a month, which has now been scaled down to a major look at the books, closing for three days in midweek to put in new carpeting, paint the walls, haul in new furniture, and—gasp— build a stage at the far end of the building so Hell can bring in live music on a regular basis and something else, something new like poetry readings, and maybe a stand-up comedian.

Hell laughed at that idea at first.

"That's what I wanted," Addy told her. "A laugh. People love comedy. Think of my life, most lives, how funny is that? We all need to laugh more, Hell. It's a wonderful escape, just like wine and cigars, and Hell, no one else will do this, I'm almost certain no one else is thinking of it and if those new places open out by the mall you will have beat them at their own game."

"Serious?" Hell asked.

"The potential is unreal. We could get the big names that cruise through Pittsburgh. They're here anyway. And one more thing."

"One more thing," Hell repeats as if she is a mesmerized puppet.

"Can you handle one more thing from me?"

"Well, jeez, Addy, let's see, smoking, the divorce, hating me, shutting me out for, like, how many hours was that? What is it now? Do you want to tap-dance across the bar on Thursday nights?"

"Sort of," Addy said without hesitation.

Hell paled just a bit which is a big deal for a woman who was one of the first streakers at her university, smoked dope in the principal's car when he was at an all-staff meeting, and had the guts to open a bar that sells cigars in a town where big news means someone from Parker did something really cool someplace else.

"I want to try and do stand-up comedy."

Hell looked at her sister with her head

first tilted left and then right. And for a moment she very nearly decided that maybe Addy had been adopted and her birth parents really were circus workers or people who lived at the edge of town in a bus that they had dragged from the dump one spring morning when it had snowed unexpectedly.

"You want to do what?"

"So a guy walks into a bar," Addy jokes. "I'm serious, Hell. I have always wanted to go to this drama school in Pittsburgh where they work with you and help you write jokes and throw you on stage and I **really** want to do this."

"You are not **that** funny," Hell points out.

"But I **feel** funny. And I have a file of jokes tucked away somewhere but obviously it's the delivery I need a little help with."

The two sisters talk after this for a very, very long time about who they are and where they might like to go and do and be and Hell confesses that she does not want to miss the relationship boat and she has been thinking lately that maybe she should open another business someplace else and change her life, move maybe, travel—and the sisters talk beyond where they have ever talked until Hell agrees to let Addy do what she calls the "Early Phase One Makeover" of the bar which has brought them to that very place to take one last look at the books before they call painters, carpenters, and the one comedian they both know to kick-start this part of their journey.

Addy is bumping along on top of the bar, throwing out figures, asking Hell to write them down in this column and that column and as she creeps closer to the coffeepot the extreme bar makeover looks more and more exciting to her. The investment in the changes could, should, would more than pay themselves off and if Addy decides to keep working part-time, which she has come to love, Hell could actually start taking more time off to date.

Or travel.

Or leave.

Or start over.

And Addy feels her heart leap toward some unseen underground tunnel. She puts the stack of papers behind her, pushes over a couple of ashtrays, and lies down on top of the bar so that her head is just a few inches away from her sister.

"I couldn't take it," Addy admits.

"Take what?"

"You leaving. It would break my heart, Hell. It's too much. You can never leave me."

Hell puts her fingers on Addy's face and moves them back into her sister's hair where they rest like the fingers of a large comb and then begin moving slowly, twirling like she used to twirl her hair when they were little girls and fell asleep in the same bed.

"Oh, sweetheart, I'm not going anywhere. And if I do I'll take you or Bob with me."

Addy rises up a little and acts as if she is going to spit in her face but instead plants a big wet kiss on her lips.

"You can love Bob if you want to, I guess, if you have to. But no sex, or overnight trips, or anything like that. Do you hear me?"

"It's too late," Hell tells her.

"What?" Addy squeals. "You had **sex**? With my neighbor?"

Hell starts to laugh, says, "Got you," and then promises her sister, her friend, her other self, the only person in her entire life who really knows her, that she will never leave her. And that Addy's own run for the border, her pending divorce, the upheaval that has turned the entire town around has made her think, too.

"It's sort of like changing the answers on a test," Hell explains. "Your first instinct is usually right but then you second-guess yourself, you see that someone else has a different answer, and you want to change yours. That's what you're doing to a lot of us, Addy. The Sweat-Hers, your neighbors, friends from school—you're making us think about where we are, where we are going, and, well, whether or not we are as happy as we could be."

"I didn't think about that. It's mostly been Lucky, you know, but this thinking everyone is doing, is it okay, Hell?"

Better than okay, Hell says, jumping up onto the bar and curling against her sister, just as they used to curl together when Addy would jump down from the top bunk after the lights were out so her sister would not be afraid in the dark.

And the Sinkman sisters lie there on the First National bar, promising each other that they will always hold on tight, always be there, always say what is most important, what is true, no matter where the change takes them, no matter where the positions of love throw them, no matter how hard they fail or fall or fly.

"Even if my jokes are bad?" Addy asks.

Even **when** the jokes are bad, Hell promises, just as the beer truck pulls into the back parking lot and the deliveryman is astonished to find two women lying on top of a bar in the middle of the day in Parker, PA—the last place on earth he expected to see such a thing.

And just as the sisters-a-go-go decide it's time to huddle with the other women warriors and throw some ice cubes on the testosterone pot that has been simmering since the tuxedo street dance.

"Make war, not love," they both say at once as the beer man drops an entire case of Miller Lite on his own two feet.

THIRTY-FIVE
What I thought Addy was thinking · · ·

I did not plan for Addy to see me walking with Kathy Zelm. But there we were, two co-workers, heads hunched together, trotting through the park so we could talk a little bit and I could get my exercise and there was Addy zooming past and catching my eye just as I slipped my arm around Kathy's shoulders.

It was innocent. But, sweet hell, I am sure Addy was thinking that I am dating, and that I have already moved on and am about to have my attorney call her but she would be wrong.

It was just a walk.

But probably not to Addy.

THIRTY-SIX
Underwear miracles on a Thursday evening . . .

The painters have circled the Lipton house with scaffolding, stacks of paint cans, and enough ladders to form into a bridge halfway across Parker. Addy loves the deep pink, dark blue, and tan colors that have started to make the house glow but she is not happy about the faces of the male painters who keep appearing in her windows at inappropriate moments or with the alliance the painters have set up with Bob One, Bob Two, Lucky, and every other man within a three-block radius who apparently has a paintbrush fetish.

She is also wondering if the one-week paint job will stretch into two weeks and then into three and she's heard so many painting horror stories that she is thinking of lying in the bushes during the day to keep the male gawkers, especially Lucky, off the property with a garden hose. Addy is almost afraid to leave her own home.

This is how the next phase of the Lipton War of the Roses is hatched. The Sweat-Hers decide to have a lingerie party at Addy's house to keep her spirits up, to spend an evening telling their versions of Marriage and Divorce Horror Stories and to make every man in their lives jealous. They have all left huge notes pasted to refrigerators, close to the telephone, and on their significant others' cell phones to remind them that this is the night, the big, lusty, and very lovely night when Addy's blinds will be down, when the painters will leave early, when no men will be allowed within fifty yards of the house, when no calls will be sent or received between the hours of 7 p.m. and who knows when—if ever.

The insanely jealous men who have tried to think of a way to install cameras inside of the Lipton house have been persuaded by Lucky to back off. And to his own amazement Lucky comes up with an idea that he thinks will stun the garter belts off of every single one of their women.

"Let's all go to that fancy underwear place up at the mall, have someone do one of those personal-shopper nights with us, and we'll each pick out something for the women in our lives and when they get home we can shock them all with silk," he told them after bowling night while they were all huddled around the tiny bar that was attached to the shoe rental cabinet.

"You mean **if** they come home," Bob Two said mournfully. "Ever since you and Addy split up it's been like hell around Parker. I just look at my wife and she's all over my back. For crying out loud, Addy will probably have you assassinated if you give her underwear."

"None of us are perfect," Bob One shared. "Maybe this is good for all of us."

"Listen to Mr. Therapy," said Barry from Cooper. "Maybe what these women really need to think about is what their lives would be like if we weren't around."

There was a moment of stunned silence

unknown in Parker bowling land history. No one talked or moved and even the men bowling on the lane closest to the bar who had been on and off listening to the conversation froze, holding their bowling balls as if they had just received news that bowling had been outlawed and the first man who moved would be taken away in handcuffs, without a beloved round ball.

The women **were** thinking.

They were thinking hard and laughing harder.

They were drawing huge marks around their lives and using a fluorescent orange marker to outline what they wanted changed.

They were working late.

They were playing with their friends almost every day.

They were calling old pals from college.

They were supporting Addy and dismissing Lucky.

And yes—they were definitely thinking about what their lives would be like if their men, husbands, lovers, neighbors, and every single member of Lucky's posse were not around.

To a man, they instantly committed to the Thursday-night underwear run. They agreed to allow Dr. Tecal to visit with them afterwards to talk about relationships and the differences between men and women and they planned to have this lovely session at the First National because they could and because they knew it would drive the women crazy when they found out about it.

So while the men were shopping for underwear, they would have been astounded to learn that the women were already trying it on, playing with it, imagining new lives, feeling sexy and alive and not thinking for one second what the men on the other side of town might be doing.

Addy and Hell had enlisted the services of Sharon Malatsky, a former teacher, who was making a fortune selling lingerie and bedroom accoutrements from the back seat of the van in which she traveled from town to city throughout Pennsylvania delighting women with articles of clothing that were made to fit and enhance every single female body type in the universe.

Sharon's approach was time-tested and

simple—loosen the girls up with margaritas and then bring out the goods. Smart Sharon had also arranged to get some of the clothing sizes and the exact shapes of the women who would be attending the Lipton lingerie extravaganza so that the attendees would actually become the models and the clothing would be perfect.

And it was as close to perfect as a male-bashing underwear-and-tequila party in the middle of the week can be.

The underwear—bras, panties, and an assortment of camisoles, slips, and sleek tummy tuckers and exotic or classically simple nighties—was about one hundred miles beyond beautiful and when Malibu waltzed in from the bathroom wearing a long, black, low-cut nightgown with slits that ran from the bottom of the seams just below her more than ample breasts and straight down to the floor, the women were enchanted and just a little pissed.

"What happened to our underwear?" they all seemed to ask at once. "Why did we go from being seductive and feeling sexy and buying yards of lace to wear under our clothes to embracing cotton underwear that won't give us yeast infections? When did we stop caring about our cleavage? Why did we give up silk?"

The questions precede a flurry of purchasing activity that is then followed by Hell demanding a fashion show.

"Everyone take off your clothes, put on what you bought, and let's have a little parade around the house," she orders, throwing her top and bra into a pile and stripping naked in less than five seconds.

"Don't look," half of them shout as they start snapping on sexy garter belts, lacy bras, and nightgowns.

Addy, who has been sipping on tepid water, saddles up inside of her new matching bra and panties—color: dark blue; fit: very tight—on her slimmed-down hips and breasts. Feeling: voluptuous, wild, hot, and so sexy she is wondering if she can walk without moaning.

But she does and Malibu, Hell, Addy, Lee, Debra, three elementary-school teachers, and Dee Zeland from across the street begin a sort of refined bunny-hop parade/

modeling display that starts in the living room, wanders through the top half of the house where there is a brief stop to look at Addy's house-remodeling plans, back down-stairs where there is a not-so-brief stop at the tequila bottle, and then moves toward the kitchen and then, and then Dee, who is go-ing first and looking lovely in a soft, deep red satin nightgown that is just long enough to cover her butt crack, opens the garage door.

Dee opens the garage door, flips on the light, and steps into something that was once The Kingdom of Krap but is now just an empty garage. An empty clean garage with a freshly sealed floor, strips of wood on the walls that usually precede drywall, and not one other goddamned thing. There are no bowling balls, the Chevy is gone, there is not one coat hanger or screwdriver in sight. The garage is so excruciatingly clean it could be used as an operating room.

Addy takes in a breath and then lets it out so fast her new bra almost falls off.

"Holy shit."

"Addy?" Hell asks.

"The Kingdom of Krap has vanished,"
Addy responds as she begins walking around
the spacious, clean, and oh-so-empty garage.
"It's all gone. What the hell."

"What does this mean?" Lee asks.

"It means Lucky is getting the hell out
of here, that is what it means!" shouts Dee.
"This is not Lucky's garage anymore. It
is not."

"What did it look like before?" asks
Honduras Joyce.

"It was a shithole," Hell tells her. "Lucky
put junk in here, everything from dead
washing machines to crap he found on the
side of the road. It was sort of a holding pen
for everything he wanted to do but never
did."

The women walk around in circles as
Addy thinks about what it all means. The
empty garage is surely a sign that Lucky is
out and gone, ready to accept the divorce,
move on, set her free. This should be good
news but the empty garage feels instead like
a surprise kick in the stomach. The krap is
gone. Lucky is gone. The marriage is gone
and isn't that what you wanted, Addy?

Addy looks up to see that all her underwear-clad friends are looking at her.

"Well . . . ?" she asks as a question and because she has no idea what else to say.

"Cause for celebration, is what I say," Hell decrees. "Does anyone know where the men are tonight?"

"Out someplace drinking or acting stupid," Debra confides. "Probably downtown. Nowhere around here, that's for sure. Why?"

"I say we forge ahead. I say we leave on our new lingerie and burn those torches in the backyard and tell our stories and let me light up a very fine, feminine cigar aptly named Deliverance," Hell decides.

Sharon, the lingerie queen, has decided to stay and as the women high-five, Sharon slips into a see-through barely there bathrobe that plunges to the very tips of her nipples so she can show off a black bra that is a perfect match for the black panties that ride like a proud homecoming queen below it. No one wants to miss what might, could, and will possibly happen next.

"No one will see us?" Honduras Brenda asks tentatively.

"God, I hope someone sees us," Lee laughs. "I haven't felt this sexy in fifteen years. I may drive to work with this on tomorrow morning."

Laughter leads them all into the backyard where chairs are circled for the storytelling, a variety of drinks, chocolates and tortes and cheesecakes that are to die for make their way from the kitchen table to the rickety picnic table, and the delighted divas adjust slip straps, push-up bras and hemlines as if they are about to hit the runway instead of the muted shadows in a Parker, PA, backyard during a hot summer weeknight.

The male trashing starts out only after every woman has a cup of rich, dark coffee and a cigar if they choose, and at least three pieces of something usually forbidden. A cigar called Deliverance, Hell explains, that has a very old wrapper and was designed by the wife of an infamous Honduran cigar maker when she got sick of being a part of the business but really not a part of the business. One day, Hell explained, when the men were at yet another "men only" meeting, this woman stormed into the cigar factory, grabbed all the women rollers, who knew just as much if not more than the men rollers, and within an hour had a cigar designed and rolled that has become the number one bestseller for the company.

And that starts off the bashing.

The stories roll in like wild spring storms. Honest, empowering tales of male abandonment, deceit, sexual exploitation, inhumane behavior, and raunchiness.

An ex-brother-in-law who slept with his fiancée's sister and impregnated her the night before his wedding.

The lover who lied about his first wife, the second, the third, and the one he happened to be married to at the time he was trying to set an infidelity record.

The boyfriend who sent a plane ticket for the weekend getaway and never showed up.

The jackass who showed up one night on the doorstep because someone else threw him out and gee hadn't they hit it off once and couldn't he just move in anyway.

The husband who justified his affair by saying his wife's breast cancer had turned him off.

And finally all the husbands and present lovers who forget, who take for granted, who think that perhaps cleaning out The Kingdom of Krap when no one is looking is the answer to everything.

And then the brave and suddenly tiny voice of Lingerie Sharon piped up, saying what ended up to be a very loud **but**. **But** women let it happen. Things happen. Sure, some men are assholes **but** if we walk into it again and again, if we want to be seduced every Friday night, if even when we turn fifty or sixty or seventy or eighty and can no longer bend forward without a slight groan, if even then we want to know he is attracted to us, wants to touch us, loves us—we maybe have to ask for it, work for it just a little bit and help out these poor bastards who have no idea what they are doing.

Some heads nod yes but not Addy's head.

"What if you are too tired?" Addy asks. "What if every dream you have ever held in your hand has been carted off with the krap in the Kingdom? What if the spark has diminished and you are so exhausted that feeling anything is about as likely as bending over again without getting hitched up on your own stomach?"

"But you can bend over now, Addy," Malibu says. "You look fabulous. Which shows me that anything is possible."

"Yes," Addy admits, shifting forward so that the light from the torch bounces off her new bra. "But some people fall out of love. And of course that means they can fall back into love, but crawling to that place can suffocate a woman. It can. It can also make her lame and terribly sad."

So the women toast the breaking point. They celebrate the courage to change. The big step forward and the right of every woman to make her own decisions, plan her own seduction or escape. And then Hell rigs up her camera on top of a pile of the would-be barbecue bricks, turns on the floodlight, and captures a brilliant moment when all the women she loves are gathered in their silky new underwear in her sister's backyard to talk about what bastards men are and to savor the joy of feminine bonding.

As at her beloved bar, Lucky and all the boys are sitting in a circle with gorgeously wrapped boxes from the underwear store under each chair, holding hands, and taking turns sharing one or two or three things they could have done, should do, will do as soon as possible to make sure their relationship flowers again and does not ever, ever flounder.

THIRTY-SEVEN
Wedding bell blues . . .

An announcement for Parker's fourth annual Fall Festival, to be held during the third weekend in September, pops onto Addy's radar screen on the second day of August and sends her into a first-rate tailspin of reality. There were only a handful of weeks left before school would start, before everything would change yet again, before she would be thrown into necessary routines, before she would have to relinquish her hold on Hell's bar and her wild summer female harem.

There has been absolutely nothing routine about the summer except Addy's devotion to the Sweat-Hers class and her single-minded notion that any day now Lucky would be ready to enter into divorce settlement negotiations. He just needed to decide which damn attorney he would be using—as if there were three thousand to choose from in Parker.

"I'm making some calls, Addy," he told her, which was true because he made calls all the time.

"I'm thinking about what I want," which was also true, because if anyone in Parker was thinking about what he wanted 24/7, it was Lucky Lipton.

"I'm certain we can get through this with only a few more bumps," he added, knowing that Addy might not be happy at all with the bumps he was envisioning.

Her upcoming divorce was what Addy held on to in the days following the underwear miracles. The days when women who had been at Addy's house would pass each other in cars and at the grocery store and downtown and wink and then flash the edge of a bra strap or the hem of a fine lacy camisole in passing. The days when the women were stunned to find brightly wrapped boxes under their pillows and then the next day on the passenger seat of the car and then the day after that inside the microwave oven, like Easter eggs hidden all over Parker.

Addy found one such box wrapped inside of a larger box that was sitting on the doorstep when she came home from yet another long day of sort-of-lovingly slaving over the books and beer kegs at the First National.

She swept the box up off the steps, thinking that she had probably preordered a Christmas gift, something for Mitchell's fall birthday or, heaven forbid, just yet another box of textbook samples.

But no.

Not.

Hardly.

It was a sweet set of cotton panties. The seven pairs were the colors of the rainbow and each one had the name of a day hand embroidered along the seam of the crotch. Addy picked up bright blue **Wednesday** and started to laugh. She was suddenly a young girl again, an almost-woman.

"I had no idea they still made these," she said out loud.

And the card, of course, was from Lucky Lipton.

You had these on that first time and
I have never forgotten it. I never
will. Never.

With love,
Lucky

As all the women in Parker, including
Hell, were looking under bushes, inside of
freezers, and in empty garbage cans for a
week hoping to find another luscious gar-
ment, Addy decided not to say anything of
the one gift she'd received. She washed her
new panties and began wearing them because, truth be told, she needed new panties.

And something else.

Something small.

Something interesting.

Something unexpected.

Something unexplainable.

Addy sort of, kind of, maybe started
watching for Lucky out of the front window
each time she heard a car heading through
the cul-de-sac. She wasn't home a lot but
enough to know when Lucky liked to walk
or when he might be heading off to therapy,
and she started looking for him. She didn't

realize this until the day Ron called her. Ron, the man from the bar, the stranger she had kissed, the competition who had made Lucky insanely jealous. Ron called and asked her if she wanted to have coffee with him.

Addy hesitated.

A date, she thought. Holy shit. A date, after all these years. With someone, a man, for whom I will have showered and picked over my clothes and put on too much perfume and pushed up my breasts in front of the mirror, and made certain all my straps do not show and then tried hard to remember what it is one does on a date.

A date with a man who is not Lucky. Not that Lucky and I have had dates for a long time—more like meetings and engagements and appointments.

No dates.

Just stuff.

Addy said yes. Yes to a date for coffee in ten days which gave her exactly 9.5 days to change her mind, and less time than that to send her female posse on Ron's trail to find out if he was an ax murderer, had robbed a

bank, been a cruel husband, or done anything remotely revolting like sneeze in public, which would of course give Addy a
reason to break the date.

The date with a man who was not Lucky
that had made her realize she was looking at
Lucky when he was not looking at her. The
date that made her wonder if Lucky was dating that woman she had seen him with in
the park. The date that made her wonder
over and over again what in the hell he had
done with all the krap from his kingdom.

No one in Parker knew or no one was
talking. Hell had said she'd tried to get a detailed Lucky update on one of her own trai-
torous dates with Bob One, but Bob One
had made it clear he was a blank page when
it came to Lucky now. All he would reveal
was that Lucky was making some physical
progress and spending lots of time ponder-
ing his future **possibilities**.

"What the hell does that mean?" Addy
asked her sister.

"Let's see, a 'possibility' can be anything—
a dream, a job, a return to work, a vocation

for the priesthood, a new puppy, for crissake, Addy," Hell told her. "How would I know?"

"Didn't Bob say anything?"

"Why do you care?"

"I'm not sure."

"Worried Lucky might be moving a pace ahead of you?"

"He's **lame,** Hell. How could he?"

"I don't know. Underwear on the porch. An empty garage. That birdbath. The woman at the park. Should I keep going?"

That's when Addy realized she was watching for Lucky. She tried hard to stop and she did a little bit, but not totally, and then the Fall Festival announcement showed up and reminded her that her summer of freedom was coming to an end and Addy suddenly grew wings as if she were about to lay an egg. Nesting time in Parker. Nesting time for teachers who have to get back to the salt mines for all the minds in the community. Nesting time to wrap up the plans for Hell's bar because construction is under way and the grand reopening is less than a week away.

So Addy is nesting and making lists and

trying to remember everything she has not done in a summer that has not been like any summer she has ever experienced and all this while she occasionally lifts her head when she is pawing her way through her lists because she thinks she hears Lucky or Mitchell coming in and then realizes that neither one of them is coming home to stay. The boys are definitely gone.

But hardly forgotten.

In three days Addy has cleaned the top half of the house—major, serious cleaning, not like the bimonthly cleaning she has come to cherish from her very merry maids. She has washed the windows, written up a new series of directions for the yard boy, rearranged Lucky's downstairs bedroom, and disposed of all the medical supplies. Addy, like many women, thinks of housework not as a chore but as a link to the past, to all the women—grandmothers, mothers, aunts, sisters, and cousins—who did most of the real work.

The real work of raising up the babies and sewing up the seams of life and sweeping away the dirt that everyone dragged in on their heels and hearts and tongues from the world beyond so that no one would stumble. The real work and all the while imagining what it might be like now, now when women like Addy have choices, can leave a marriage, stay in a marriage, realize a place of professional magic that the grandmothers could only dream of. And for as long as Addy has done this work—the cleaning and organizing—she has loved it when she has had the time to do it properly. She has loved it and thought each time of all those women and of the tiny fingers of her great-grandmother who told her once that she had wanted to do something with numbers.

"Numbers?" Addy remembers asking her.

"Oh, my sweet Adeline, yes, numbers," her great-grandmother told her with her eyes closed as she nimbly worked her hands from one side of the sink to the next. "I add them and play games with them in my mind and when I pick up the books from the libraries with the thoughts of the great number scholars, everything I read is so simple to me and yet I had no choice. No choice."

"You will have a choice," her great-grand-mother told her more than once.

You will have a choice, Addy.

Addy thinks of choices as she moves through the lower bathroom, which is almost spotless, what with the absence of the two men who used to use it, exhausts herself in the kitchen and dining room, which has been the scene of dozens of late-night Sweat-Hers meetings, coffee-laced male-bashing sessions, exhaustive planning for the bar's grand reopening, crying over spilt milk, high blood pressure, and lost marriages. Where the women of Parker drew lines in the sand that have now turned into war trenches.

Losing herself in cleaning, Addy ends her assault in the back den where the big-screen television has sat in hibernation since Lucky left. For a long time the den was **the** room, with boys piled to the top of the highest doorjamb watching football games, eating everything but the coffee table, and sleeping everywhere but on top of the light fixtures. And now the room and the television are silent and Addy wonders as she sorts through old magazines, dusts, and vacuums under the couch if it might be ridiculous to even keep the house that she has been remodeling on those scraps of paper that now line the walls in her bedroom.

Silly to keep empty rooms of memories.

Silly to think she can keep it all up on her own.

Silly to think that the house will ever be anything but quiet again.

Silly to think that the silence will not occasionally drive her mad and make her drift to the window to see if she can spot Lucky.

And when she sits on the couch to ponder this thought and to catch her breath, her eyes drift throughout the room and she thinks about what she will give away. Lucky can have the damn big television, this couch, darn it—he can have the whole room because it was a rare evening or Sunday afternoon when Addy sat on anything, paused long enough to sit there with the boys, and she wonders if that wasn't wrong. Had she missed something important? Would it have been so hard to watch an entire football game, eat the pizza she had just made, or sit in the corner reading while the two men in her life worked on breaking the springs under the couch every time there was a touchdown?

Maybe, she thinks. But maybe not. Maybe the father and son needed the time together. Maybe she needed the time alone. Maybe she should just get her ass off the couch and finish the house so she can get back to the bar and see if the stage is being built in the correct spot.

That is when she sees it.

Addy cannot stop herself. Her hand reaches to the pile of books under the coffee table and she pulls it out. It is on the bottom where it belongs. On the bottom where it has sat unopened for so many years she cannot remember the last time she looked at it. The wedding album.

When it lands on her lap Addy touches the satin edges, moves her fingers across the gold lettering on the top, **Addy & Lucky— Our Day of Love.** Her heart quickens and Addy is suddenly flushed and can feel a small trickle of sweat begin moving across the back of her neck, under her arms, along the insides of her knees. Under the names there are two gold wedding bands linked together and when she moves her fingers over the circles she can feel the embossing and remember how she loved to look at the book in the months after her marriage and how she made it a tradition to have their wedding attendants over for years on the anniversary of the day they were married so they could look at the photographs together and celebrate.

Celebrate what?

Addy tries to remember. She tries to think about being happy and moving through her days without worry and with the knowledge that everything around her was solid and would last forever. When she opens the album and sees this man and this woman kissing, two people she once knew so intimately, so well, so perfectly, she cannot stop herself. In one swift movement she picks up the wedding book, and she holds it against her chest and feels a tidal wave of grief as powerful as any she has ever known.

Her sorrow is a flood of feelings and memories that trail through a book she dare not open any further. The wedding, the honeymoon, the weeks after when she could barely stand to be apart from Lucky. The notes he left her on the kitchen table because he always went to work before she did. The way he would sneak into the bathroom at Cooper Auto and call her on his lunch break, the times she would rush home and make his favorite dinner, light candles, wait at the door in a sexy nightgown.

The weight on Addy's heart is suddenly so piercing she has to put down the book and bend over for a second to keep from falling over. The sensation of loss, of something sliding away from her, is so immense Addy feels as if she is going to faint.

Addy cries. She cries from a place that is a deep and very long river that started a long time ago as the spring heart of a young girl who wanted to love, wanted to be loved, wanted a man to sweep her off her feet and sing under her window. The spring grew and the boys came and then the men and then she felt the waterfall of love on the day when she met Lucky and for the first time she'd felt that river—that rush of blind, total love—that kept her floating for so long, so damn long now.

Until now.

Until last week.

Until a month ago.

Until last year.

Until she feared she was a breath away from drowning.

Until the idea of paradise became something so far away it seemed impossible to ever touch again.

The book is wedged between her legs and her chest and even in this tight space Addy can feel something fly out of her heart. She can feel the wild wings of something moving fast and brushing hard against her chest so that she cannot breathe, cannot move, cannot imagine surviving beyond this moment. Addy cries for so long that there is a cascade of tears running down both sides of the wedding book. It is her river finding a new course, she imagines, the wellspring is drying up. Something is ending that started such a very long time ago.

Or maybe it is also the beginning of everything.

When she is exhausted from crying, so exhausted that she simply cannot cry anymore, Addy sets the wedding book on the floor and gently slides it backwards under the couch—out of sight, hidden, lost under the springs that sag from the weight of all those years, all those times she didn't join Lucky and Mitchell to watch TV and eat pizza.

Just as she stands, as she discovers that she is still alive, that her heart is slowing, that she can walk, her cell phone rings.

It is Mitchell, the boy-man, who is in Wisconsin foraging for food and still flirting with the girl down the hall, acing his psychology test and nervously asking his mother if everything is okay and then not waiting for a reply but saying there is something else.

Something bigger than Addy's river of loss.

Something that sends Addy to her knees. Something else that feels like a whip cracking along the sides of what is left of her heart.

Something that turns the aching, sore, lonely river inside of Addy Lipton into a deep and very thirsty and very small creek.

THIRTY-EIGHT
Heartaches times three · · ·

The day of the meeting it starts to rain before the newspaper hits the doorstep at 5:15
a.m. and Addy thinks this is an omen for
what is to come. Sleep-deprived, and feeling
hungover because of it, Addy finally turns
on the coffeepot at 7:15, opens the front
door, bends down to pick up the newspaper,
and gets a head full of rain from the hole in
the gutter that the painters warned her
about.

"Shit," she says as she shakes her head like
a wet dog just as Hell's Jeep spins into the
driveway so fast Addy jumps back inside of
the house because she is afraid she might
get hit.

"Honey!" Hell shouts, leaping from the Jeep before it stops.

"Hell," Addy mouths quietly. "Here you are."

"Here I am," Hell agrees, walking forward through the rain with her arms spread as wide as the front door. "Come here, baby."

Addy falls into her sister and they talk about the meeting. The meeting with Mitchell's birth mother.

The visit that is to occur in just a few hours between Lucky and Addy and the woman who gave them the gift of Mitchell.

The gift of a son who has asked them to meet with her prior to his own meeting with her, because the woman wants it, the woman needs it, and could you please, Mom, and have Dad be there too, please, Mom? Could you please because she has something to say to you, questions to ask, a story to tell, and please?

Please, Mom, will you and Dad meet with Melissa? Her name is Melissa, Mom. Please?

Of course.

Yes.

Certainly.

Okay.

Sure.

And this is the meeting day. Melissa is probably just miles away, driving toward Addy and Lucky before she heads up toward the college in Wisconsin, before she meets the son she gave away, before Addy finds the courage to tell her son's birth mother she changed so many hearts and lives.

Addy and Hell sit and talk and drink two pots of coffee before Hell jumps up and orders her sister to shower, focus, meditate, be open, relax.

"She gave you one gift. Maybe you can look at this visit as another gift," Hell assures her sister.

"The timing sucks."

"Honey, Lucky will be fine being here and dealing with this. And so will you. You have to admit he has been a terrific father and it was big of you to have the meeting here. Let go of the divorce for a moment. This meeting is all about Mitchell, about how he came to be in your life, about something he needs very much right now."

"How did you get so damn smart?" Addy asks, hugging her sister again.

"Call me the minute everyone leaves."

Addy throws Hell a kiss as the door closes. Then she heads to the shower and the mirror next to it that is unforgiving, a liar, a reflective piece of junk that she should have thrown on top of Lucky's pile of krap before he turned the garage into an operating room.

Leaning into the mirror, Addy balances herself on her elbows and peers into her red eyes, and then lunges forward standing on the tips of her toes, raises her right hand to trace the lines that run from the corner of her right eye and disappear into the dark strands of her recently dyed gray hair. She moves her hand to her chin and pulls at the loose skin, runs her hand down her neck, which has not so recently developed lines that sometimes look like slash marks from the Halloween stalker. She tries to remember what she looked like when Mitchell was a baby.

Addy has joked for years that she only looks good when she tips her head back so far that her lines and creases disappear just moments before she falls on her own rear end. But she is not an unattractive woman, she is now almost as thin as she was when Mitchell was born into her life, her laugh lines are sexy reminders that she has lived and laughed and her skin is soft, clear, luminous. What she remembers this day as she looks into the mirror is not how she looked then, but the lump in the pit of her stomach when she and Lucky drove over to Pittsburgh to pick up Mitchell. She remembers doubting how she would feel, if she would know what to do, how to hold him, what to say. And she remembers that overwhelming feeling like nothing she had ever imagined or dreamed that weakened her knees when Mitchell was first placed into her arms, when he smiled, and when he then tried to pull her lower lip off with his amazingly strong and awesomely beautiful tiny fingers.

And now this.

This meeting with the woman who gave

up her baby, who gave her Mitchell, who changed her life in such a way that everything else, every day, every minute, every second changed from that moment forward.

Addy looks very hard at her reflection in the mirror. And then she says, "Yes."

Yes, I can do this.

She showers, dresses in something that she knows makes her feel and look lovely, puts on makeup for the first time in weeks, starts a fresh pot of coffee, places sweet rolls and fresh fruit on a plate as if she is about to meet someone she has known for a very long time. Moments before she knows Lucky will knock on his own front door, she walks into the backyard. She steps close to her smoking tree, leans her face into its branches, and she asks every goddess she has ever felt close to for help. The Goddess of Mothers and the Goddess of Marriage, the Goddess of Love, the Goddess of Forgiveness. The Goddess of Understanding, the Goddess Who Helps Mothers Understand Their Sons, the Goddess Who Does Not Want You to Start Smoking Again, the Goddess of Weight Loss who has a half-sister who is the Goddess of

Menopause, and the Goddess of Diseases of the Heart and the relative newcomer deity, the Goddess of a Happy Divorce.

Addy loves her pine tree and she asks it for whatever she needs to get through the next few hours. She takes one pine needle and puts it in her mouth so she can taste the rich tang of life that always springs from the needles when she bites into them. The bite is a soft slap to her senses, a reminder of something bitter, something delicious, something that is totally possible.

And then she hears Lucky knock on the door, spits out the needle, straightens and walks back through the house where Lucky is dancing from one foot to the next as if he has to go to the bathroom.

"Lucky, come in," she says, realizing how silly it seems to be welcoming Lucky into a home that he partially owns.

"You look nice," Lucky says slowly.

"You too. New jacket?"

"It's Bob's. I've come down two entire clothes sizes. I am not done so I hate to buy anything new."

"Come in. I made coffee. We should talk before she gets here."

Surprisingly, it is Lucky who talks while Addy listens. He sits down at the table, pours some coffee, does not touch the pastries, and tells Addy he has been reading on the Internet about mothers like Melissa who just want to know that their babies are okay, that they made the right decision, that the family understands why it happened and how it really was for the best.

She knows about us too, Lucky tells Addy. Mitchell told her that you have filed for divorce and that he wants us both to just be happy.

"They have been e-mailing for quite a while," Lucky tells her.

Addy is at first so astounded by everything that is coming out of Lucky's mouth that she forgets to respond.

"Addy?"

"How long?" she manages to ask.

"Over a year, I guess. Mitchell didn't tell me everything but I am hoping we can make this as comfortable as possible for her. It must be really something for her to be doing this."

Where is Lucky? Addy wonders as she looks at the man seated in front of her with his lovely trimmed beard, shaved head, crisp white shirt covered by a light blue linen sports jacket and slip-on leather sandals that she is certain she spied in a waiting-room men's magazine. Where is the big man who left his underwear in the same spot every night for ten years and thought pepperoni was its own food group? The man who fell in the driveway on the way to Paradise?

"Are you scared?" Addy manages to ask this stranger.

"Yes, I'm scared, but maybe more so for her," Lucky answers. "She was brave to do what she did, Addy, and she must have something she feels she has to say to us. But I'm scared about a lot of things these days."

Addy is so astounded by this confession that she cannot speak.

Lucky moves his hand just a little bit and Addy thinks he must be trying hard not to touch her. She pulls her arms off the table and asks him if they should sit at the table or go into the den.

"This is nice," he says just as they hear a car, **her** car, pull around the cul-de-sac and park in front of the house.

Addy takes in a breath. She imagines what Melissa must be going through as she sits in her quiet car, looking at the freshly painted house, the summer flowers, the yard where her son must have thrown footballs and played with his friends. What must this feel like? What must be in Melissa's heart?

And then there is a soft knock on the door and there she is. Melissa who says hello and smiles and stuns Addy with her eyes— Mitchell's eyes—the way she leans left into the door—like Mitchell—the color of her skin, the curl in her hair that looks like it has just escaped from a small tornado—like Mitchell's. Oh, sweet Jesus. Addy wants to take this woman into her arms, she wants to feel her heart beating against her own, she wants to run her fingers through her hair, and kiss her and tell her that everything is okay.

Which is exactly what she does.

Addy walks forward and she takes Melissa into her arms and Melissa instantly wraps her arms around Addy and begins to sob with such vigor that Addy wonders if they might both topple over. But then Lucky steps behind her and she knows that, even with his bad back, he will catch them. He will catch both of them.

And the three of them stand there for a very long time until Melissa pulls back and Lucky hands her a napkin from the table to dry her wet eyes and then they bypass the kitchen table and go straight into the den where they can sit closer, where the echoes from all the years when Mitchell was living there seem louder.

"I knew you would be like this," is the first thing Melissa tells them.

Lucky has brought Melissa a glass of water and grabbed a box of tissues on the way down the hall and they wait to hear Melissa's story.

Lucky sits next to Addy on the couch after he pulls a chair close to Addy for Melissa so that the two women can hold hands, so that Melissa does not feel as if she is alone, so that the light from the window behind her can warm her back, so that he can be as close to Addy as possible.

Melissa tells her story quickly. She has stopped crying and she has taken both of Addy's hands into hers and she begins by talking about her own family and how much she loves them and how she had a fairly normal childhood and how she got pregnant the very first time she had sex with a man—a boy really.

A boy from high school who was sixteen, too, and who was a gifted student, a bit of a geek, Melissa admits, who went on to college and on to an advanced degree and to a career in medical research, psychology.

"Psychology," Addy finally says. "Mitchell is majoring in psychology, he loves it, he wants to do research."

"I know," Melissa admits. "He told me."

Melissa goes on to tell them how she left school in the middle of her junior year to go to a private religious home in **Nebraska,** a word she pronounces as if it will cause her to become ill if she keeps the syllables in her mouth too long. She tells them her parents had arranged for her to come back to Pittsburgh and have the baby at a private hospital so that the adoption transfer could take place as quickly as possible.

"I couldn't be a mother. I was so young," Melissa confesses. "And I want to be honest with you both. I want to tell you that for a very long time I hated the baby that was inside of me and I wanted to die and I wanted him to die because of what happened to my life."

Addy only holds Melissa's hand tighter.

"I thought that because of those feelings something would be wrong with him, that he would be somehow damaged, and that is why I never wanted to see him or hear anything about him after he was born," she tells them. "I stayed in the hospital overnight, never looked at him, and then I walked away."

"But you saw my photo," Addy remembers to say, crying along with Melissa. "You saw what I looked like and you said it would be okay."

Melissa shakes her head and the tears start again.

"You looked so kind and I thought you were beautiful and I imagined all the while, every year, every month, every second, that you lived in a house just like this and that you had a front yard and that Mitchell was happy and loved and given things that a girl—really, I was just a girl—could never give him."

And then.

Then two years ago Melissa married at the age of thirty-three and on a visit to the gynecologist she discovered that her horrid monthly periods were caused by a severe and chronic case of endometriosis that had swallowed up her uterus and was working its way to other parts of her body. She learned that she needed to have a hysterectomy as soon as possible and that is when she started to look for Mitchell.

"I'm sorry," Melissa says through tears that stream down her face. "I just had to find out—had to know—if Mitchell survived all this. I hope this hasn't hurt you, hasn't caused you any pain or anything. Mitchell has told me that he had a wonderful childhood and that he loves you both so very, very much."

When Addy turns to look at Lucky his face is as wet as a soggy washcloth. He is looking at Melissa and shaking his head and he says, "It's okay, Melissa, it's okay. Really."

Addy turns back to Melissa. She tells her that Mitchell is now a man and that there is room in his life for two mothers and that whatever relationship he and Melissa forge, wherever it takes them, whatever happens is fine with her.

It is fine.

And then without thinking, without bothering to look again at Lucky, she instinctively reaches for his hand and laces her fingers inside of his and when the warmth from him climbs up into her hand and beyond her wrist she feels as if it is finally time to stop crying and to get out the baby pictures.

THIRTY-NINE
What I should have said to Addy · · ·

I should have told Addy that she is a terrific mother and that Melissa would have chosen her even if she had first interviewed every woman on the face of the earth to be her son's mom.

I should have.

FORTY
Back to the reality of hating · · ·

The Sweat-Hers are devastated to learn that Addy has held Lucky's hand. Addy tells them the astonishing news at the beginning of class. This motivates every single Sweat-Her to do a personal best on the elliptical machine, the weights are increased on the stationary machines without one groan or swear word, and stretching goes on for an extra ten minutes.

"She was under duress," Hell tries to explain. "Face it. The birth mother shows up, Lucky was charming and barely recognizable. There was lots of crying going on. Give her a break."

"Well, it could be just an emotional, one-time relapse," Lee admits. "When I left my first husband I ran into him one night when I was downtown and we ended up rushing into the nearest hotel to do the nasty."

"You slut!" Malibu Heidi shouts as she is working her back muscles on the newest weight machine.

"It was just a simple, 'I need to get laid' thing and when I saw him on the street it was like all I could remember were the one or two good things about him that made me love him the first time."

"Does this mean you all forgive me for holding his hand?" Addy asks.

"No!" they all say almost at once in a single breath.

"But we are going to give you a chance to redeem yourself," Debra decides. "What do you think, girls? If we let Addy slip like this, pretty soon word will get around town. And before you know it we will be right back where we started."

Right back where we started.

The thought makes Addy just a bit nauseous and so she agrees that while her five-second hand-holding incident was not a mistake, but an emotionally induced instinctive response to a very tough situation, she still needs to be punished.

And she also continues to confess.

"There's also something else that is driving me mad and if you are going to punish me we might as well do it all at once," Addy shares.

"What could this possibly be?" Hell asks her. "Did you start smoking and drinking like a fish again?"

"It's worse than that."

"Holy cow," Debra shouts. "Should we all stop for a moment?"

"No," Addy says as she finishes a round of sit-ups on a machine that looks as if it belongs in a torture chamber.

Addy clears her throat. She tells her friends, her beloved Sweat-Hers, that when she first saw Lucky at the door radiating sturdiness in Bob One's jacket, with his sexy beard, and looking thin and speaking so softly, she felt something.

Every machine in the workout room screeches to a halt.

"Are you ovulating?" Malibu demands.

"Something? Like **what** something?" Hell

wants to know.

"It was like a little flutter that moved across the inside of my stomach," Addy answers. "It's been days since I've seen Lucky and, jeez, he never looked like that when he lived with me."

Lee gets up and walks to the middle of the mirror-filled room, puts her hands on her hips, and tells the Sweat-Hers this is nothing to worry about. Normal stuff, she explains. The man changes a little bit and the woman gets a scrap of hope to suck on and she thinks that maybe everything has changed and that a little romance fairy will sprinkle dust on everything in her life and there will be a sexy pair of underwear in the microwave every week for the rest of her sorry-ass life.

"It ain't gonna happen," Debra insists, when Lee finishes. "He's got a long way to go, baby. Addy, you cannot let this emotional riptide suck you out to sea. Snap out of it, woman."

"He was pretty damn nice," Addy continues to confess. "It was almost like being in the room with a handsome stranger."

"Well, there, that says it all," Debra continues, this time waving her hands. "He's a stranger, for God's sake, Addy! If you were not still legally attached to this man for so many years, would you even be thinking **twice** about him?"

Addy feels like she is in the middle of a sorority hazing. But she thinks about the question, she thinks about Melissa and what happened during the hours they spent together. She thinks about how Lucky was beyond nice, how she never expected that, how she has kept thinking about him the same way she has thought about him for a very long time and how maybe, just maybe, she hasn't always been fair to him.

"What are you thinking?" Hell asks as she senses something wild roving through her sister's mind like a ravenous animal who smells a hamburger someone threw out the window.

"I have been pretty mean to him."

All of the Sweat-Hers groan.

"Is this a total relapse?" Malibu wants to know. "If it is, I want my money back."

"It is not a relapse," Addy insists. "I'm just

thinking out loud. He has been a shit, and now he is more like a little turd. I guess that is what I am saying. That's all."

"Remember, honey, you have been under a lot of emotional stress, so let's not get carried away with being too nice, okay?"

This from Debra who has to be the person the word "nice" was invented to describe.

"Can a person be too nice?" Addy asks.

The laughter from the Sweat-Hers bounces around the room like one of the large balls that Hell is rolling on to strengthen her back muscles.

"Sure," Debra decides. "If your 'nice' means you are not honest about how you are really feeling. Don't you think that a lot of women are nice because, well, in spite of everything that has happened and societal changes, we still have this inbred sensation that we have to be kind and generous every flipping moment of our lives?"

"Well, honey, we don't all feel that way." Hell stands up with a swagger. "I **love** telling people off."

The conversation launches itself from

there so that the women quickly abandon their workout posts and end up standing in a circle. The discussion, Addy thinks thankfully, moves from her to the plight of women who have true and pure hearts but who also occasionally have had enough.

Enough.

Enough being in charge.

Enough caretaking.

Enough waiting.

Enough already with men behaving badly.

Enough with the bratty spoiled kids.

Enough with the demands of work and life and every other inch of the world.

Enough with trying to convince themselves that this is all there is.

Enough with the bitching about it and doing nothing.

As they talk it is as if a warm wind begins kicking up in the weight room. The steam from the women rises a bit, swirls around the room, fueled by their rapid-fire talking, by them taking ownership of their feelings, ownership of what happens next, for whom they should love and not love, fueled, too, by how absolutely wonderful it is for them to be together, to be united in the cause of all women kicking ass, spending more time on themselves, and laughing a hell of a lot more.

"Addy and Lucky can't get back together," Hell finally admits as the women begin fading from their circle and head back to the weight machines. "I'm already used to the idea of them never being a couple again, for crying out loud."

"Not just that," Debra says. "But this whole divorce thing has helped some of us kick it up a notch. I'm sick of making the damn dinner reservations, being the one who always has to find a babysitter, and washing the clothes he thinks he is taking me out in when it is me who is taking him out."

"Who said I was getting back together with Lucky?" Addy asks incredulously. She is the only one left standing who has not gone back to her machine and she suddenly feels invisible.

"First he looks good," Malibu says, "then you hold his hand. What's next? A kiss under the trees in Bob's backyard? What? What is happening in your lovely mind, Addy Lipton?"

"I have a date," Addy said, without moving.

The room stops again. The women run back to the circle they have just left.

"A date with Lucky?" three of them say at the exact same moment.

"No, it is not a date with Lucky."

"You little shit!" Hell shouts.

The women look at Hell, astounded that this is the first time she has heard about this monumental event.

"It's with Ron, the guy who I kissed in the street the night you all got ripped and made jackasses out of yourselves," Addy reveals. "We are just going to meet for breakfast. That's it."

"Wow," Lee says, beaming. "You put me to shame, girl. I always like to wait until the divorce is just a few steps further down the road before I start dating again."

"It's coffee," Addy protests, defending herself. "We are not going to elope or have sex in the car."

"How do you know?" Malibu wants to know.

"Because he's too short," Addy shoots back, cracking up at her own joke and definitely changing the mood of her weight-room inquisition.

Why the hell not, they all agree finally. But then they spend the next twenty minutes giving her dating advice which makes Addy double over with laughter again. Advice on dating from a group of women who just spent at least forty minutes complaining about the lack of such a thing in their own lives, she laughs. Preach to someone else, Addy says, hugging each one of them, thinking she is home free, eager now to hop back on the arm machines that will rattle her muscles in places they have never before been rattled.

But wait, Hell commands. Everyone come back here.

The punishment . . .

Addy hangs her head and pretends to slap the hand that held Lucky's hand. I will never do it again, she tells them. Please forgive me. But the women do not back off and they turn to look at Hell, raise their eyebrows in a very serious "Well, what are we going to do?" way, and wait.

"This is easy, Ms.-Bigshot-holding-hands-dating fool," says Hell, pointing a finger at her sister. "You will be the MC for the grand reopening night. You booked the band, you organized the whole thing, and in your sorry and sick mind you have this interesting idea that you are funny. Now you can show us."

"I'm not ready," Addy stutters, suddenly terrified. "I need to take the class."

"Oh, pish-posh, it's just us and the rest of the adult population of Parker and maybe a few hundred people from Pittsburgh and we'll all be drinking," Malibu Heidi says. "Don't worry, honey."

Don't worry. Right.

But what Addy worries about as she rides her muscles against the machine is how wonderful it felt to have Lucky right there, how warm his hand felt, how she wanted to lean into him even more.

Addy Lipton thinks this but she does not say it lest she end up singing in the band, bartending, and dancing with every single single man in Parker all at the same time as her punishment is extended beyond the simple, pure act of hand-holding by her so-called friends. But then the strangest thing happens as she pounds through her last set.

The new laughter queen thinks it just might be possible to do all of those things at the same time anyway, because suddenly anything seems possible.

Anything.

FORTY-ONE
Men behaving goodly . . .

There are moments in life, Lucky is thinking, that are not totally perfect. But they are so fine, beautiful, and full of possibilities that it is a wonder people do not explode from the pure energy of them.

Bob One is laughing at him as they sit in his kitchen and discuss their dress attire for the evening. The men are eating a light dinner and drinking an herbal tea loaded with vitamin B that will help prepare them for what will most likely be a wild evening at the grand reopening of The First National Wine & Cigar Bar. Bob is laughing because Lucky cannot get off the hand-holding thing.

They have talked about it incessantly for

days and Bob One has heard about Melissa and how great Addy looked in her tight white capris and how heartbreaking and yet wonderful the entire 3.8 hours of Melissa's visit were and how Lucky has such hope, such insane hope in his heart that Addy may be seeing that he is trying and changing in spite of all the literature and those damn talk shows that say people don't change, especially people who are men.

"Buddy," Bob One says, throwing a huge hunk of lemon into Lucky's herb tea. "Focus. We have to get dressed in like twenty minutes. Get over the hand thing. It was just the emotion of the moment. She filed for divorce. She does not strut down the cul-de-sac trying to seduce you. She has grabbed the reins of the house maintenance. Heck, she's done more in a couple of months than you have done in years."

"Dinner," Lucky groans, trying to change the subject. "You call this pile of green stuff dinner? I'm a frigging rabbit."

"And you have never looked better, Mr. Cottontail."

"Bob, you are killing me here. Sometimes I just need to eat something from a **mammal**."

Bob One spits a carrot across the table and cannot stop laughing. Lucky pounds him on the back and they digress from the initial discussion about what to wear to what it is exactly that women want.

And the conversation roars without a moment for a breath or a piece of celery throughout an entire pot of green tea.

What do women want?

Honesty.

No public burping or farting.

No farting or burping also within a five-hundred-yard radius of any living or dead person or animal, lest the animals know how to speak to women and will report their bad behavior.

Romance, women love that shit.

Space. Try and figure out when they do **not** want to see you.

More talking. Just say out loud what you are thinking—unless it is something really ignorant and too mannish.

Less controlling. They can do every goddamn thing we do, so ease up. If you see them lifting, pulling, ordering, whatever-ing—just back off.

Consideration. They had the babies, they do not have hard-ons but think about the other stuff you hate asking them about. Stop blaming everything on their periods.

Bob is ready to go on after this initial foray into female territory and Lucky moans that he cannot bear it. But Bob One puts up his hands as if Lucky may get up and charge him like a wild bull and he says there is one trait that he thinks men and women find universally appealing. And, no, it is not a nice ass.

But first, they digress while Lucky tries to imagine what it is that Bob will throw out as the most appealing female and male trait. They digress because they both painfully re-member at the same moment the secret and most intimidating meeting they had with Addy's friends just moments before the infa-mous cul-de-sac party. Hell and her band of merry maidens had walked arm in arm into Bob's backyard to confront them just before they went over to get Addy.

"What the hell are you going to do tonight?" Hell asked the men as the women stood behind her and all the men instantly wondered if the women had weapons.

"What do you mean?" Bob Two asked innocently. "It's just a little neighborhood party."

All the women noticed his smirk and they took a step forward. The men took a step backwards.

"**A neighborhood party** and you idiots are in tuxedos?" Hell snapped. "If you do anything to hurt or embarrass Addy, we will pretty much make you pay for it the rest of your lives."

The men were speechless. Which they realized much later is just what the women were hoping for.

Intimidation.

Making the first move.

Scaring the living hell out of them.

Getting the upper hand before the first beer was cracked.

Pushing dozens of fingers into a male chest to show who really has the power.

Spoiling the fun before it starts just to prove a point.

Bob One tried. He'd stepped forward, hoping that the magic he had created with Hell would save them all. He put his hands behind his back and rocked on his heels a little bit. Then he sucked in a wad of air the size of the watermelon he had just injected with vodka and he tried.

"It's just fun. And we wanted to treat you all and do something special," he sort of muttered. "We don't want to hurt anyone, Hell, especially Addy. You should know that."

His next thought, as Hell stepped forward and grabbed him by the neck right where he had **finally** tied his bow tie, was that he had no clue what this woman was thinking, what she ever thought, what he knew to be true, or what in the world they were doing with the barbecue.

While Hell gripped his neck all of the other women located their husbands, their men, looked them in the eye, grabbed them somewhere by a very short hair. Then they waited for Hell to finish.

"Just know that we are not stupid bimbos and that this is boys-against-the-girls and that we will do anything and everything to protect Addy," she said in a voice that reminded every single man of Xena, the not-so-princess-like warrior. "And boys—we know what's in the watermelon, we knew the first time you did it back in 1973."

To the astonishment of everyone, including himself, Lucky stepped forward at this very tense moment. He thrust both his hands into the air in the international "I surrender" stance and said that his intention was to serve and make women happy for the next five hours.

"Right," several of the women muttered.

"Serious," Lucky responded.

Hell glared at him. Then she took a step back and her warriors followed and then Hell said one more thing.

"Be sincere," she told Lucky.

And then the women turned and walked away.

"What just happened?" Lucky dared to whisper. The men looked as if they had all been hit simultaneously by the same stun gun.

"We were just totally intimidated," Bob One said. "They got us."

So when Bob finally tells Lucky what it is, what the most attractive feature in a man and woman might be, Lucky already knows.

"Intelligence," Bob tells Lucky. "I think that is what grabs most of us if you can clear away all the other debris and get to the heart of it all. I think that is what I truly find most attractive in Hell. She is one smart woman and she sure as hell, pardon the pun, proved that before the barbecue. The other stuff helps but really, Lucky, when you get through it all, someone who thinks for herself, someone who can make decisions, who is self-motivated, someone who is in touch with the world and life and feelings—that's the kind of woman you want to grow old with."

"Jesus," Lucky sighs, blotting out anything else he must have been about to add to their list. "How the hell did you figure all this out?"

Bob puts his head into his hands and looks into his tea, not for an astrological reading, but because the bottom of the cup is dark and empty like he sometimes felt. He tells this to Lucky. He tells Lucky how he had to ride the waves to the bottom of the ocean before he could come up for air and that he had lots of time alone after his divorce, months and months to think about it, and that Lucky's salvation, his ride to the dark side, was his own adventure, the one that dropped him on his own driveway.

"When everything is gone, you think about what is most important, what you miss the most, what few things you would want to have back. And what I ended up thinking about was not sex or security or having the wash done but it was all the conversations I had with Vicky when we were both still in love.

"Lucky, I hope that if what happened to us happens to someone else we know that you can be there for that guy or even for a woman, we could do this for a woman because we are so much smarter now, well, you are getting smarter but it's a journey, buddy," Bob One shares.

"I could. I would do what you are doing

for me," Lucky says, putting his hand on his friend's arm.

"Lucky, I would give so much to go back and to be able to have just one night where Vicky and I sat and talked, where we threw newspaper articles at each other, where we would read passages out loud from a book we were reading and, well, shit, that's all gone. Now all I can do is make it better the next time," Bob says, looking up.

Bob tells Lucky that he reached a point when he realized that Vicky was right to leave him, that she deserved better. Once he realized that his life was not over, that he could make a comeback, first for himself and then maybe someday with someone else, everything started changing.

"What I miss most are just those times when Addy and I talked, when we discussed things, when we were in the same room together and it was almost as if I could hear her thinking.

"But," Lucky is quick to add, "I guess I didn't really know what she was thinking. Not for the last few years anyway."

The two men talk then as if they have

been injected with truth serum, over their carrots and the whole-grain crackers that Bob uses instead of bread. While Bob boils water for one more pot of tea, they launch into sharing golden moments from their broken marriages. Discussions about the kids, walks during the first snowfall, the sounds a house makes when people you love live inside of it, the warm hand on a thigh, the patterns of life that fall into place when couples rely on each other for this thing and all the other hundreds of things after it.

And somewhere in there, Bob admits, is where the taking for granted springs up. Because men and yes, women too, lose their grip on that first blush of love. That "oh my God" phase of love that really does make people run toward each other in the street and do stupid things like trip over their own feet and sell the race car because she needs an engagement ring.

"Relationships take work. It's so easy to think of the work as—well, **work,**" Bob confides. "That's when everything starts to go to hell and that's why you and I are sitting here in our bathrobes like a couple of saps."

Lucky wants to believe that his months of angst, regret, and rebirth have not been for nothing. He wants to imagine that he can leap from his bathrobe into the clothes that Prince Charming wears without tripping over his own big feet.

"Do you think it's too late for me and Addy?"

Bob is silent for a moment. He was never very hopeful when this question was as persistent as a leg cramp in his own life. If there had been a window of opportunity, he'd blown it by lying on the couch like an old dog for months before he got up and cleaned himself off. He thinks about how Addy has already filed for divorce, how she's been out on the town, how she has already kissed another man, how she's quickly become so independent. Then he looks at Lucky, who has surely been transformed during the past few weeks. He's slimmed down, is making some huge life changes, changes that he does not even want to share with Addy yet, and he's doing all the right things—fast. And he answers Lucky: "It may be too late for you. Or maybe not. It's fifty-fifty either way."

And when Lucky closes his eyes and tries to mentally nudge the odds in his favor, when he tries to get back his lucky Lucky self, Bob adds, "There's one more thing, Lucky . . .

"You were on your way to paradise, Lucky, when all hell broke loose. But sometimes, paradise is not the kind of place you think it is. Sometimes it might not be a **place** at all."

FORTY-TWO
A brief truce for free beer . . .

Hell is shouting into her cell phone while she zigzags through her backyard as she tries to exhaust her little doggies before the big gig, the night that could determine her financial future, the hours before and during the grand reopening of The First National Wine & Cigar Bar, the event that seems to have ignited the interest of every man and woman living within and without the Parker, Pennsylvania, city limits.

The dogs know she is upset and they are jumping up and down in place to try and lick her face and calm her down. Addy, of course, is on the other end of Hell's phone.

She will **not** be riding to the bar with Hell but she will be coming a little bit later and this news has pushed Hell over to the ledge of her own usually very limited insecurities. She wants Addy to be with her, she needs Addy to be with her, why cannot Addy be with her right away? Why cannot Addy pick her up in twenty minutes on her way to the bar?

"Look," Addy says, pacing near the back door as she gazes at her smoking tree. "Everything is ready. The bar is stocked, the new floors are down, the carpet is in, the stage is perfect, the band is already set up, the table is all ready for the food we are having delivered. There is not one thing that is not ready."

Except me, Addy wants to say but does not, lest her usually self-assured and sort-of-calm sister fall to the ground and be licked to death by her own dogs.

"Why can't you come **now**?"

"I'm not ready, Hell. What is this all about? Why can't you go on ahead?"

"I'm just nervous, this is kind of a big deal," Hell explains. "And you did all of the work."

"It's not open heart surgery, sister. And

besides that, you are making me MC this damned thing just because I held Lucky's hand, so I have to get ready for that. I need a little bit more time."

Go, Addy finally says, threatening to hang up. So Hell has no choice but to go alone and then Addy quickly steps into her backyard, looks both ways as if someone very tall might be watching her over the bushes, and makes a mad dash for the smoking tree. There she crawls into her old smoking position, instinctively reaches for her weatherproof box, opens it slowly, and plucks a single cigarette from the container.

Addy puts the cigarette into her mouth but she does not light it. She sucks on it, inhales a faint hit of unlit tobacco. Just the simple physical act of inhaling and exhaling calms her wild, and more than slightly terrified heart. Addy smokes the entire cigarette without lighting it, and decides to smoke one more just the same way.

And Addy is scared. She's talking to herself. She is trying to think like a funny woman, she is wondering if she can pull it off, even for the few minutes she has to be on stage to introduce the band, the new building, Hell—the queen of the First National herself—and all the contractors who will be at the party to be thanked for their speedy and wonderful work.

The funny thing, Addy thinks, is that the whole thing really is funny because of everything that is going on in her life. "Let's see," she says out loud with an unlit cigarette hanging from her mouth as if she is a mobster on Main Street, "paradise lost, Lucky's Folly, broken and very sick hearts, divorce papers, birth-mother appearance—to name just a few"—and now she needs to get up on stage, as if she isn't already on stage with her every move in Parker, like she needs to have a garbage truck run over her.

But Addy gets up anyway because that is always what Addy Lipton has done. She tucks her cigarette box back where it belongs and walks into her house, where she gets dressed and then turns to look into the mirror and what she sees makes her laugh out loud.

"That's a good sign," Addy tells herself as

she calls her sister and asks her to meet her behind the bar in fifteen minutes.

"Why?"

"I have to pick something up quick and—well, Hell, you'll see when I get there."

"Jesus, Addy, the place is packed already. I am going to have to tap more beer at this rate."

"Are people buying drinks?"

"As if their throats are on fire. I am going to need your help when you are done with the introduction bit. Can you bartend?"

Addy laughs. "Of course. It will keep me from kissing strangers, and when they see me tonight there won't be a man in Parker who wants to kiss me."

"Addy . . ."

Addy cuts her off, shouts, "Ten minutes, back door," and leaves Hell to wonder until Addy maneuvers her way through town, makes her pickup, and then shows up at the back door of the First National.

And Hell takes one look at her sister, doubles over in laughter and cannot speak, cannot even breathe, which is something Addy tells her she has been waiting to see happen her entire life.

Addy Lipton is dressed in a full clown suit.

Big nose.

Big shoes.

Big red hair.

Big lips.

Big ears.

Big ass.

Big purple buttons.

And she is carrying a live poodle that is wearing a hat with a cigar sticking out from under the brim.

"You told me to be funny and what I said was I felt funny and so here it is, now I look funny too."

"The poodle?"

"It belongs to Malibu Heidi's mother and she's coming by to pick up the poor thing in exactly fifteen minutes which should be five minutes following my gig, Sister Smartass. Now go introduce me right away so that no one sees me before I walk onto the stage."

The introduction and Addy's grand comic debut bring Parker's cigar smokers and wine drinkers to their feet. The poodle starts to bark, Addy makes believe she is tripping over her own feet, and when she rolls onto the stage something wild and magical kicks out those bad-blood demons that are trapped inside of her artery pounders and replaces them with something that she will later describe as a jolt of pure energy that has her believe she really is funny. And when that surge of power, of sureness, of knowing, sweeps over her, Addy Lipton is not just funny, Addy Lipton is hilarious.

"Here's Brian Logan, the lovely man who built this stage, ladies and gentlemen, and a man who not only has a lovely butt crack, but who also once told a bartender in this very bar that her dress was so beautiful he wanted to talk her out of it."

Addy is unstoppable. She talks over the laughter. She improvises. And when her sister comes up to thank everyone for supporting the bar, Addy tells the crowd that a really good time for this woman, her own flesh and blood, the sister who taught her how to steal beer from the back of their parents' refrigerator and jump-start their father's old

Buick after curfew, is restocking the toilet paper in the bathrooms and making certain her dogs get their worm pills.

"And my sister wonders why she is single," Addy says, kissing the poodle's cigar.

So it goes for ten minutes until the poodle spots her owner, leaps from the stage, dislodges her cigar hat, and Addy gives the band a thumbs-up and falls from the stage into her sister's arms.

"Oh my God!" Hell exclaims. "You are funny. You are **really funny**."

"I had two drinks in the kitchen before I drove over."

"That never made you funny before."

"Well, I have to say I feel a little bit like Sally Field. You know, 'They love me. They really love me.' "

"We all loved you, Addy, holy cow, what you did here, the clown gig, the publicity—there are two newspaper reporters here and last night I got a call from **Midwest Living** asking if they could do an update because they heard about the renovations."

"I sent them an e-mail."

"Keep this up and you will get canonized before the night is over," Hell says, hugging her.

"Wait," Addy says, before they pull apart. "Is Lucky here?"

"Is he ever."

"What does that mean?"

It means, Hell replies, he looks hot and Bob One looks hot and they have been mingling and laughing and Lucky is not limping, and something else.

Something else?

Ron is here also.

Addy pulls off her big red nose and her clown hair all at once and wails, "Now what am I supposed to do?"

"Tend bar and have fun like everyone else here," Hell tells her, spinning her toward the bar while the band blasts. "It's a mob scene in here, Addy!"

"Fun," Addy wants to snort, is a really ridiculous word for slave labor but she wiggles through the crowd to slide behind the bar anyway, tugs off her clown shoes, sets her wig and nose behind the cash register, and starts pouring drinks with the sudden realization that the bar will protect her from the dance floor, from Lucky and Ron, from anything but a very short conversation with either one of them about whether they want beer or wine. And it will protect her from the suspicious glances of all the men and women in the bar who know about the divorce papers, have had a child in her class or a son or daughter who hung out with Mitchell, or heard some wicked gossip about whatever in the hell is going on around the cul-de-sac.

Lucky waves to her once while she is mixing two Bloody Marys and something called a Cadaver that has so much booze in it, it really will be a wonder if the person drinking it survives. Addy catches his eye, smiles, and without thinking waves him over to the bar. Lucky looks at her, points to himself, looks around and then mouths, "Me?" which makes her laugh. Addy nods and it takes so long for Lucky to make his way to the waitress station at the bar that Addy forgets about him until Hell kicks her in the back of the leg and orders, "Look up, dumbass."

"I like your outfit," he tells her as she

leans in to talk with him because the noise level in the bar is close to that of a jet taking off.

"Very funny."

"No, you were funny. I had no idea."

Addy looks at him with her big clown eyes and says, "Lucky, **no one** knew. This one is not your fault."

Lucky thinks he is supposed to smile, and he tries to smile, but what Addy said makes him wonder what else he doesn't know about. He is suddenly unable to speak, unable to move, and unable to stop looking at Addy.

And Addy sees that in some way she has wounded him. She sees that he is hurting beyond all the other hurt that he has already embraced, because she knows this look and she knows it is supposed to be her turn to say something and she throws up her clown hands because the partygoers are backed up four deep on her side of the bar and because Lucky needs to figure out for himself that she did not mean to hurt him. She turns to walk away just as Lucky manages to say, "Save a dance for me."

" 'A dance,' " she repeats as her heart

thumps wildly. "One dance," Addy manages to say, "has your name on it, Lucky."

When Ron parks himself at her end of the bar not more than five minutes later and asks her the same thing—**save a dance for me**—Addy wants to throw her wig back on and vanish forever into the increasingly wild crowd.

Dance? she thinks. **I should be flinging myself off a bridge if there only was a bridge in this city.**

"I'll try," she lies.

"Are we still on for breakfast?"

"Yes, we are. Let me buy you a drink as collateral."

"Before you rush off, can I just say you look ravishing tonight, Blinky."

Addy can't help herself. She starts laughing because she has been so busy she has forgotten she looks like a clown.

"What, this old thing?" And she gestures at the fat purple buttons and floppy striped pants.

Hell backs into her just as she is about to

say something else stupid and says, "Crank it, clown. Stop flirting with the customers."

"Busted," Addy tells Ron, and she is thinking how she now owes Hell one for rescuing her just as Hell slides back over and asks her if she can handle things for a while because she wants to mingle, check out the back of the bar, maybe even try and squeeze in a dance with Bob One.

Go, Addy motions, as she throws bartender Greg an "Are you okay?" look, as the crowd slows and then accelerates and the Sweat-Hers belly up to the bar, along with half the teachers from her school, people from the grocery store, all the neighbors, and then the local cops who come in quietly, as if everyone wouldn't notice anyway, and tell Greg they just want to make certain there isn't going to be any more dancing in the streets like there was a few months back when news got back to them about a rumba or something.

"Oh, for crying out loud." Greg laughs at the cops. "You just came in to see the place. You know there isn't any traffic down here

after 8 p.m. and I bet your wives or girlfriends are back in here someplace."

"The women in this town are more dangerous lately than this bar," one big cop says.

"Is that so?" Greg asks.

"Is that clown back there Mrs. Lipton?"

"Yes, that is Addy Lipton, the funniest
woman this side of the Mississippi River.
Don't you recognize her?"

"She was my teacher a long time ago but I
heard she's got all the men in Parker—except
me, of course—running scared because of
her divorce and her band of merry man-
haters."

Greg is so happy Addy cannot hear this
conversation that he almost forgets himself
and offers the boys in blue a free glass of
beer.

"When was the last time you did something grand and wonderful for a woman?"
he asks them. "When was the last time you
really listened? Planned a terrific date? Did
something you know she wants you to do?
Or just stopped taking her for granted?"

The cops are speechless.

"Look around," Greg suggests. "Do you

see any unhappy men and women in this place tonight?"

The cops do look around. They see women dancing as if they have swallowed some kind of loss-of-inhibition pill. They see women dancing with men. They see women dancing with each other. They see a female clown tending bar, a lady sitting on top of the pool table with a poodle in her lap, a group of men who look like old hippies wearing new sandals standing in a circle waving cigars at each other and occasionally bumping shoulders. They see the owner of the bar slow-dancing with a man to a song that is most definitely not a slow dance.

The cops do not so much leave as back out of the bar.

"What was that all about?" Addy wonders as the crowd starts to thin a bit.

"They wanted to make sure we were not going to dance in the street again," Greg tells her.

"What did you tell them?"

"I told them everyone in here was high on the free drugs we passed out earlier so it would be too hard for us to dance outside this evening. Half the men are still standing against the wall in here and afraid to dance anyway."

"Some things never change," Addy agrees as she looks up to see the women dancing, the men talking, and the poodle pausing for a nice long bark at the band, who have launched into some kind of demented polka.

Later, much, much later, after there is yet another small dance in the street organized by Greg to taunt the police officers, after the band has packed up and left, after every member of the male gang and every member of the female gang has noisily departed, Hell sneaks up behind Addy, grabs her, and asks if she wouldn't mind locking up.

"Why? Because you see I have like three seconds of energy left?"

"I've invited Bob over for a while and he's outside waiting for me."

"Does this mean . . ."

Hell puts up her hands. She tells her sister this part, whatever might happen tonight, whatever might not happen, may not be her business.

"Go!" Addy urges, shaking her hands at her sister. "Just remember that men are evil."

When she leaves the First National at 2:30 a.m., Addy waves to Greg, who makes sure she gets into her car as he locks the back door, and then she drives away, weary, exhausted, so tired she has every window in the car rolled down so that she can stay awake the few minutes it will take her to get home.

There is no way for Lucky to sneak into the cul-de-sac without her noticing, without her wondering if he followed her, which he did to make certain she was safe but Lucky Lipton does not care. He pulls into Bob's garage, shuts the door, does not turn on any lights in the house that he now knows intimately. He watches through the window as Addy moves through **her** house—a light on here, this one off, the sound of the door locking through his open window, her lovely feet climbing the stairs, the soft noises from the bathroom as she takes off her clown makeup and water splashes against the mirror and leaves those long streaks that look like jet marks in the sky, the way she kicks her feet against the side of the bed when she rolls over on her side.

Her side.

His side.

Their bed.

Lucky stands at the window knowing Bob will not be coming home, alone, thinking, saddened by the distance—yards, really, but more like miles and miles that separate him from Addy. When he thinks she might be asleep, he moves into the kitchen. He takes out his pen.

And the very moment he puts his pen on the paper, Addy rolls over to his side of the bed, circles her arms around the pillow that was once the nighttime home for Lucky's head, and wonders if Lucky went home alone.

FORTY-THREE
What I thought Addy was thinking . . .

The last light goes off and I wonder if she is even thinking about me.

She is probably not thinking about me. Addy is probably thinking about that guy who was at the other end of the bar.

Addy probably thinks about me less and less every day.

FORTY-FOUR
Bombastic items of affection . . .

The package arrives as planned, three days following the big blowout at the First National, a day after Hell finally admits there was no fornication going on the morning following that lively event but something close to it did happen and that if Addy does not see Bob One's car very often in his own driveway it's because he may be at Hell's house working his way through the last thirty-nine steps of foreplay. The package arrives just as Addy finishes a busy morning trying not to panic about all the loose ends in her life and the looming first day of school.

Sure, it's been a productive spring and summer, Addy is trying to convince herself, as she circles the bottom floor of her house, pacing as if she is a prisoner in solitary confinement.

Painted house.

Filed divorce papers.

Met birth mother.

Launched three new careers—bartender, lounge manager, stand-up comic.

Quit smoking.

Cut back on drinking.

Kissed a man who did not have to kiss me.

Beefed up the workout program.

Flirted.

Finished two rounds of acupuncture.

Did not yell at the therapist.

Lost sight of the beach in paradise but stayed busy.

And yet, Addy is whispering to herself . . . and yet Lucky is stuck in neutral, she has a breakfast date—a date!—looming, Mitchell has not called for a week, her sister has fallen off the male-bashing wagon and is probably making love at this very moment to Lucky's divorced roommate, there are hours of lesson plans to finish and . . .

. . . And there's a knock at the door.

It's the FedEx woman, bright and spry in her black tennis shoes, who also has the most terrific truck-backing skills that Addy has ever witnessed. She can swerve around the curb, past the trees, and end up so close to the front door that if the steering wheel was on the right side she would never have to get out of the truck.

It's a small box, handed over with a smile, no need for a signature.

It is a box within a box. The second box is hand-painted in swirls of reds, oranges, and yellows. Clown colors, Addy thinks and laughs out loud. She opens the box on her front porch in full view of the far end of the cul-de-sac and whoever might be peering out of the house next door—Lucky or Bob One or whatever tawdry woman might be getting dressed in one of the bedrooms.

The tissue paper inside the box is as soft as silk and it is the color of an oceanfront summer sky. Inside is an envelope, painted in the same clown colors, swirls that are arranged so they look as if they are dancing with each other.

And inside the bright envelope is a gift

certificate to the Pittsburgh Comedy Cellar for a three-day introductory class that will be held for comedienne wannabes Thanksgiving weekend. And stapled to the back of that is a reservation for the adjacent hotel with a meal allowance in its restaurants and behind that is a note.

> Addy,
>   I never knew about this and I never knew about a lot of things. But I am a good student and you should know that I always want you to be happy—with me or without me. Please accept this gift from me, go follow your dream and make other people smile and laugh as much as you have made me laugh and smile.
>
> Lucky

Addy drops to the step and clutches the papers against her chest. She is overwhelmed by a sheet of emotion that she can feel billowing throughout her entire body. The papers against the skin of her neck feel like a lover's kiss and very gently she takes out the soft tissue paper and uses it to wipe her nose.

Because she is crying.

Because she is happy and sad at the same moment.

Because she is confused.

Because she has a second thought that has been slowly rising inside of her for days, a week, maybe longer as she has watched Lucky rotate his life in a direction that she did not even know existed. Addy Lipton has watched Lucky fall, get up, fall again, then roll around in his own krap and get back up yet again. She has seen him cry and whine, shave his head, grow a sexy beard, empty the garage, and hold the birth mother of their son tenderly inside of his large arms as if the woman would break if he moved too fast.

Addy props the tissue under her nose as she bends her head. She thinks about the connections a marriage brings between a man and a woman. It is not just a day or a lavish event that gives you an anniversary that you may or may not remember as the years pass and everything slides south. It's the way you think and breathe and raise a child. It's the way you put the bread on the left side of the toaster because that's where he likes it. It's the right side of the bed where you feel safer because he's on the left, the wonderful simplicity of habits and schedules, the grip of panic when he's late coming home from work. It's the sound of bare feet on the kitchen floor in the middle of the night, the laughter behind the garage door.

And suddenly Addy is sobbing like a baby and not realizing that her face is becoming a rainbow because the silky tissue paper is soaked with her tears and colors are running down her face. When she impulsively gets up, clutching the package, the certificates, the note, and walks the few steps to Bob One's house and knocks on the door, Lucky takes one look at her and begins laughing, which snaps her back from her momentary lapse down marriage lane.

"I'm crying and you are laughing," she accuses.

"Addy, you have to see what has happened. I'm not laughing at you, just at your face."

Lucky pulls her into the small bathroom

off the kitchen and when she looks up and sees her face she cannot help but laugh too.

"Holy shit, I look like the gift paper."

"No," Lucky corrects, standing behind her and looking into the mirror over the top of her head. "You look like a clown."

Addy looks into the mirror and then into his eyes, smiles, and turns around.

"Lucky, this was so sweet. I have wanted to go to this school for so long. How did you find out?"

"The same way I find out most things. I talked to Hell about it. And then I did some Internet research. Believe me, I am too much of a dumbass to have figured this out totally by myself."

"Thank you, it was very sweet. Can we talk for a little bit?"

"If you promise to try and not yell at me like you did when we had coffee."

"I am taking a day off from yelling. Let me wash my face. Let's just sit for a few minutes."

Lucky feels as if he might lose his breakfast. His stomach is lurching like a baby volcano and he is trying hard to do the calming breaths that his acupuncturist has taught him. He's also saying "Don't blow it" over and over inside his mind.

"Coffee?" he asks in a not-so-firm voice when Addy comes out of the bathroom.

"I had my one cup already, blood pressure, you know. Just a glass of water to make up for the recent drop in my liquid level because of the tears."

They sit, Addy on one side of the table, and Lucky on the other. No touching. Legs tucked in their proper channels. They ask each other if everything is okay, if the bills are being paid, if the house needs anything, if Mitchell has called yet about what has turned into an extended visit by his birth mother, about Lucky's back, about Bob and Hell, and—by the third glass of water— about everything but the divorce.

And then Lucky takes a leap that might kill an Olympic high jumper. He decides to empty his heart.

"Addy—about the divorce . . . Couldn't we just stop the whole damn thing and start over? I love you, Addy, I've been thoughtless and selfish. I took you and everything I had for granted. And as bizarre as it seems, I am now grateful for what happened in our driveway."

Addy's stomach lurches. She has never been more confused in her life. One side of her wants to get up and smack Lucky upside the head, another part wants to lean over and touch his hand again. And she wants to do that as badly as she wants to reach up and smack her own head.

"Lucky, most days lately I feel as if I have been dragged behind a car, but I've made up my mind about this—"

Lucky stops her. He centers himself in his chair. He tells her it is both true and not true that people don't change. "Parts of me," he tells her, "will always just be Lucky. But other parts are changing, they **have** changed. I'll never be the way I was." He tells her that he also has his own secret dreams, things he has always wanted to do and be. He has always been terrified, he tells her, that he would fail, just like he failed in college, so he too has kept his wildest dreams to himself.

Addy is now afraid to breathe. Her right

hand is clutching the water glass so tightly that it has turned white past her wrist.

"Like what?" she asks in a voice just above a whisper.

"Don't laugh, okay?" he asks.

"I will try not to."

"And please try not to be mad when I tell you this, just listen for a second, please?"

Addy nods her head up and down, searches for a breath, can't find it.

"Addy, I have decided to retire early. I have all the figures, the paperwork is in, and there is more than enough in the retirement to keep me, and hopefully us, afloat. My medical insurance will continue and all the bills will be paid for with my back mess for the rest of my life."

Addy opens her eyes a little bit wider.

"I've applied for the assistant soccer coaching job at the junior college and I'm probably a shoo-in for it as they called and asked me to apply for it," he goes on, in a rush. "They also want me to do summer camps, design a program that can develop players and teams throughout the region to establish this part of Pennsylvania as a soccer nirvana and . . . and . . ." He falters.

"There's more?"

"It's probably the most important thing besides not getting a divorce and making sure Mitchell is going to be taken care of."

Inside, Addy has just yelled, "Holy shit!" but on the outside she says nothing. She feels her lively flow of blood pounding against frightened arteries as if a punk rock band is starting up.

"I've been waiting for you to ask me about The Kingdom of Krap stuff," Lucky says with a smile. "Don't you wonder where it has all gone?"

"I was so happy you were making an operating room out of the garage because we both seem to need one every other day that I forgot to ask."

"Very funny. I rented out a really nice heated storage space, put the car in there and I've been working on it by the way, and I also built a studio inside of the storage space, which is kind of a work in progress."

"A studio?"

"Don't faint or anything but my dream

has always been to take some art classes. I'm
going to take a welding class in the fall and
see if I can do something with all the krap
from the Kingdom because, well, people
have asked about it, so I'm working on de-
signs and stuff."

Addy is wondering if she got down on her
hands and knees right now and crawled out
of the kitchen if she could even make it to
her front door.

"Lucky," she manages to stammer. "I
don't know what to say."

"It's a lot, I know," he admits. "But that's
why I haven't done anything with those
damn divorce papers, Addy."

Anything else?

Addy wants to know if he's been interning
with a brain surgeon, dating an actress on
the side, or working with a tenor from the
Pittsburgh Opera. **Have you been injected
with some new drug, Lucky? Has Bob
One enrolled you in some kind of speed-
dating course? Have you already been to
paradise without me?**

But she doesn't say that. Addy doesn't say
thanks for sharing or **of course now we**

won't get divorced. Addy just gets to her feet. She shakes her head, tells Lucky she feels as if she just swallowed an elephant and that she needs to think.

Before she hits the door, however, she walks back, grabs the gift off the table, says, "I'll call you," then bolts like a terrified mare across the yard.

FORTY-FIVE
Southwestern symphony for one . . .

Dr. Sanchez sees Addy pull up in front of her clinic and hollers from the balcony that she should come around the back, up the stairs, grab something to drink on the way there. She thinks, but does not say, that Addy must have set a new land-speed record driving from her house on the other side of town.

"I'm having a bit of a crisis and my therapist is camping in some wilderness park of all things," Addy had said when she called, almost shouting into the answering machine.

Dr. Sanchez had picked up the phone the moment she heard Addy's voice. "I'm here,

Addy. Come right over. I'm home alone. We'll talk."

This miraculous kindhearted physician, who will not only make house calls but let you make one to her house as well, is one of the blessings of Parker. This was Addy's thought as she drove without blinking from the cul-de-sac following her encounter with Lucky.

Astounding, full-of-surprises Lucky.

Addy knew she needed to talk and surely not to Hell, the damned traitor, who must have known at least one of Lucky's five hundred secrets because there could be absolutely no doubt Bob One had whispered them in her right ear while nuzzling her neck as the dogs were contentedly sleeping at the foot of her bed.

Damn Hell.

Damn Bob.

Damn Lucky.

Damn Parker. Well, most of Parker.

Damn divorce.

Damn marriage.

Damn transformation.

Damn everything and everyone except

the voice of Margarite Sanchez yelling from the back of her home as Addy enters something that can only be described as another world, an oasis, an island surrounded by the Sea of Parker. The entire top of the clinic is a Southwestern paradise that is decorated in deep, rich reds and blues. Addy passes through a bright red door and follows the doctor's voice past a cactus garden that sits under a huge window framed in old barn wood. There are terra-cotta pots everywhere, hand-woven blankets on the wall. The scent of sage is so thick it seems as if Addy is walking in the middle of a blooming spring desert and when she passes through the kitchen with its tin cupboard doors and orange tile floor she wonders how this secret world of Dr. Sanchez was created.

"Here!" shouts Sanchez, waving from the balcony which is an extension of the oasis with its tiny waterfall, piles of adobe bricks arranged to hold even more flowering desert plants, and a table covered in bright colored tiles designed to look like a mountain landscape.

"This place is amazing," Addy says, momentarily forgetting her crisis. "You'd never know this was up here, it's like— Wow, Sanchez, just wow."

"Sit," the doctor commands. "Take off your sandals. My partner and I love the Southwest. We'll probably end up there, but for now, this is home, this is our paradise."

The word "paradise" throws Addy back into her chair as if she has just been hit by a flying boulder.

"Paradise," she moans. "Oh, you need me here like you need a call at midnight for a broken arm."

Sanchez smiles, pours some iced tea from her cactus-shaped pitcher, asks if Addy wants some. Then she tells Addy that she is more than a broken arm, more than a patient, more than just the wild homewrecker from Parker who has the entire town, especially the men, shaking in their tennis shoes, which, of course, are the preferred footwear in this part of the world.

"You are a sister, do you know that, Addy? You're a woman who needs to talk, someone who basically has the same heart, someone who has made a huge difference in so many lives."

Addy thinks this, as she knows about the common denominators all women share. But she tells Sanchez that suddenly she is not so sure of so many other things. She tells Sanchez the story of the clown box Lucky gave her and the conversation that followed and how she looked at Lucky, listened to him without speaking, and how she ran from Bob's house as if she had seen a ghost, a resurrected dead friend, someone she maybe never knew and surely doesn't know now.

"Did you like what you saw?" Sanchez asks her, gently.

"It was sort of scary and I've filed for divorce and made up my mind and there is this huge thought that clouds everything and it's that people really don't change that much and what happens if I say, 'Okay, let's stay married,' and then in three weeks the krap is all moved back to the old Kingdom?"

Sanchez blows out a soft wisp of air.

"My partner has this disgusting habit of spitting her toothpaste all over the damn sink," Sanchez confides to Addy. "It drives me nuts. I tell her just about every day to stop and just about every day she spits toothpaste all over the sink, but then sometimes I hear her up here when I am working late and she pounds three times on the floor to let me know she is making dinner, and then pounds again to let me know she is drawing me a bath, and then again to let me know she is going to come down and get me if I do not stop working. When that happens and she is so good to me, I think that if she wanted to she could spit her toothpaste all over the floor and in my face and anywhere else she ever wants."

"You love her."

"More than I ever thought it was possible to love someone."

"But you both work at it."

"Lucky appears to be working at it," Sanchez reminded her.

"But I can't seem to forget and forgive. It's as if the nicer he is to me, the more pissed off I get, the more I hang onto the bad memories."

"It's because this was not in your plan.

You were done and ready to move on. And then Lucky changed the plan."

"I am so damn confused!" Addy wails. "He has refused to sign the papers or get an attorney, and so many parts of me feel as if they have already moved on, but then a wonderful thought from the past gets resurrected, or he sends me to clown school, or I see him and my heart flutters . . . just a bit."

Sanchez listens as Addy recounts her ride, from the almost-garage-door bashing, through the surgery and the canceled trip to paradise. Addy tells her about Mitchell, his birth mother, the kiss with a stranger, and the looming date with him.

"Well?" Addy asks, when she finishes.

The good doctor smiles. She leans forward, takes Addy's hands, and tells her that all therapists do is listen. Maybe they direct a conversation, maybe they ask a few hard questions, but the trick is to always let the patient, who is in this case also a friend, answer the question.

"Addy, you know that any relationship is like a frigging seesaw," Sanchez shares. "One day it's up and the next it's down. What I see as a woman, and also as a doctor, is that people just get lazy. They forget how much work is involved in relationships. They take each other for granted, they stop being romantic, they gain emotional weight."

And that emotional weight, Sanchez says from her own in-and-out-of-love experiences, including a horrid divorce that took her breath away for a very long time, can either smother a relationship or bring it back to life.

"Bring it back to life? How is that possible?"

"Think of it as a kick in the head. Or, in Lucky's case, a hard fall on the base of his spine and his ass. But it seems to me that the moment he fell he started getting up again."

Addy thinks about that. She thinks about the up-and-down seesaw of his life and hers since the big fall, since that day she told him about her own tired heart, since the moment almost every aspect of her own life has changed.

Then Sanchez clasps Addy's hands really hard and says, "Addy, oh, Addy, you also know that it wasn't just Lucky's fault. It is rarely just one person who unbalances the up-and-down ride unless he is a cheating bastard or has some severe emotional problems or shoots at the dog after a wild night of drinking. We all get tired and give up sometimes, Addy darling, and when that happens the seesaw drags, a wall replaces it and pretty soon it is just easier to walk away and start over. Climbing over the wall, tearing it down, jumping back on the seesaw—it suddenly all just seems too damn hard, impossible, and not worth the effort."

"So?" Addy asks.

"So, Addy, you have to decide, now that Lucky has given you another chance, whether there is enough left for you to hang on. This is not easy shit, baby. Do you love him, Addy?"

Do I love him? Do I think we can hang on for the ride? Can I see him now and not close my eyes and remember the fat pig who didn't just spit in the sink but in The Kingdom of Krap, on the patio, and God knows where else? Can I forgive him for letting me slip away? Can I forgive myself **for letting him slip away and into**

the middle cushion on the couch that I had to replace after I threw him out because of the dent from his big ass? Can I walk off this anger? Can I just move on?

"This is so damn hard, Sanchez. I feel like I have one foot on one side of the Lipton Line and the other foot on the other side," Addy says, fighting back tears. "Sometimes I am so tired I just don't know if I have the energy to let him back in, to acknowledge his progress or lack of progress, to bother to see if I still love him."

And there is the troubling thought of the breakfast date that looms like an appointment for a benchmark colonoscopy. "And my date!" Addy wails.

"Addy, you are a little fast with the breakfast date and all," Sanchez says with a smile. "Everyone in Parker knows he kissed you. And apparently you kissed him right back."

The pitfall of Parker, Addy remembers. The lovely community where something happens on one side of town and before you even finish doing it the people on the other side of town know all about it.

"It's too much," Addy admits. "I need to

clear out my own Kingdom of Krap before I foist it on someone else. I'd probably spend the breakfast non-date talking about nothing but my own damn divorce. It's not a real date and I may not have the guts to go through with it, anyway."

See, Sanchez tells her, see how just talking out loud makes you come up with your own answers? See how pausing in the middle of a marathon to discuss emotions is a really good way to recharge?

Addy thinks she sees. She thinks that maybe it is a good thing that Lucky has not signed any papers and that he is trying so hard and that the little flutter she has felt a few times during the past few weeks keeps moving through her heart like a remembered song, a movement from the past, an old black-and-white photograph. She suddenly sees something fine and exciting might possibly be the last rising spark from what was once a wildfire that just slowly blew out because neither party had enough energy to keep it blazing.

See, the very wise Dr. Sanchez says, how time is such a wonderful healer, Addy?

Time to close your eyes, open them slowly, and see who this new Lucky Lipton is becoming.

On the way back home Addy stops impulsively at the office supply store, just after she leaves Ron a voice mail to cancel their date. There she browses for a very long time through the art materials section. And she discovers a beautiful leather-bound sketch pad that she purchases as a surprise gift for Lucky with the intention of walking it over to Bob's with a short apology and then with nothing else at all planned.

Anything goes.

The sky is the limit.

Let it rip.

Walk naked into a sandstorm.

Think positive.

But when Addy Lipton pulls into the cul-de-sac, stops her Toyota just inches from Lucky's Folly, not even thinking about the garage door, she notices that someone has left a note taped to the front door. With the sketchbook tucked under her arm, Addy opens it.

You win, Addy.
You can have your divorce.
Lucky.

And then the sketchbook drops to the edge of the front step where it looks as if it is trying to decide if it should fall off the edge or just rest there—waiting for whatever miracle or disaster is supposed to happen next.

FORTY-SIX
What I should have said
to Addy · · ·

You can't treat me like shit anymore, Addy.

I was a fool but I am not a fool anymore and I deserve to be treated as if I was trying. I've earned the right to be treated with a little bit of dignity, with the acknowledgment that it wasn't always a mess.

You can have your divorce.

FORTY-SEVEN
Jimmy Beam's valley of tears · · ·

The weight of the divorce papers, when they fall from the folder, through Addy's fingers, and onto her lap, is so much heavier than she expected. There are so many pieces of paper, none of which Addy has bothered to read, that she has been piling one after another in the folder that she has kept on the kitchen counter since the day she filed for divorce.

It is close to midnight and Addy has shut the blinds, locked the doors, turned off all the lights in the house except the one on the little table she has left on almost constantly, especially in fall and winter, since the very first day she called it home years and years ago. "There's just something about always seeing that light on," she remembers telling Lucky. "It makes me feel like someone is always waiting up to make sure I get home safe."

Lucky.

Goddamned Lucky and his note on the door and the unearthly silence she has experienced in the twenty-four hours since she discovered it. She has not seen Lucky leave Bob's house. She has not left the house. The Zelands have come and gone but no one else on the entire cul-de-sac has come home or gone out. It's as if the world has temporarily stopped.

Bob One and Hell are shopping for stemware in Pittsburgh to match the new décor of the First National as if they are about to be married. They have not even been notified about Lucky's decision. The Sweat-Hers have been sucked up into the last-week-before-school-starts mania that overtakes Parker every year as if someone has ridden through the town on horseback and passed around the plague. The teachers are all hunkered down with lesson plans, Mitchell is way past due for a phone call, and it's been so quiet at the bar that Addy was told not to bother to come in for the rest of the week.

Temporarily ignoring her heart-induced one-drink-a-day rule, Addy has just poured her second glass of Jim Beam, which she decides must have been originally distilled by a crazed and bitter man whose tastebuds were blown off in the Civil War. The Jim Beam is also the reason why every single one of the divorce papers have just cascaded onto her lap.

The soon-to-be-former Mrs. Lipton is tipsy, not drunk, but just about a half a glass away from it.

"Well, okay now, Mr. Lucky, let's just see what's in this mountain of legal crapola that has been drifting from my attorney's office and into this file all these weeks," Addy says out loud as if Lucky were sitting across from her in his usual dining-room-table position—elbows on the table, one foot on Mitchell's chair, the other resting on the curved support leg beneath the center as if the whole damn thing will tip over if he shifts his weight.

When Addy pulls them out of her lap she taps the papers on the table so they will all fall into place and then she counts them one at a time and turns them over—all twenty-one pieces of paper—taps them again, and begins reading after she starts her second glass of whiskey, rolls it around inside her mouth, swallows it and shakes her head at the same moment as if she's just taken in something that should have been flushed down the toilet.

Twenty-eight years equals twenty-one pages.

Addy wants to feel nothing as she reads through those twenty-one pages. She wants to be bold and brave. She wants to be a disinterested third party. She wants to read every line of the sample pages her attorney has drawn up. She wants to know how this divorce proceeding will proceed. She wants to make certain she does not give away the farm, that she is protected, that whatever Mr. Lipton and Mrs. Lipton have managed to commingle for the past 300-plus months can be separated by the hammer of a judge's pen. She wants to know everything. She wants to be in command. She does not want to fall out of the chair.

The first page is a swirl of names and words. **Commonwealth of Pennsylvania. Petitioner. Respondent. Social Security numbers. Irrevocably broken.**

Sip of whiskey.

Assets of the parties. Encumbrances and debts. Potential written marital agreement.

Sip of whiskey.

No minor children. Notice of objection. Listing of assets. Changing of economic circumstances. Violating criminal statutes.

Sip of whiskey.

Attorney fees. Disobedience of court orders. Stipulated and agreed. Clerk of Courts. Restrictions of 90 days.

More whiskey.

Other properties. Personal belongings. Household furniture. Responsibility for payment. Disclosed assets. Life insurance policies. Future interpretation. Mutual releases.

Whiskey.

Suggested settlement. Papers void until final negotiations.
Final judgment.
Last sip of whiskey.

Addy looks toward the counter where she has left Mr. Jimmy Beam sitting so proudly next to the glass canister that is full of cookies that she suddenly realizes must be so old they are multiplying like rabbits inside of the jar. In another world, one now apparently passed, Lucky would have eaten every cookie and perhaps licked out the jar.

Can I make it to the counter for more whiskey?

Addy sets the papers on the table, takes in a very large breath of air, pushes back from the table and gets up very, very carefully, keeping her hands on its top. She wobbles to the counter and when she gets there realizes she has forgotten her glass. Too late to go back. The refrigerator, with its ice tray, looms. Addy lunges and when she does not fall is given courage by this simple fact. The freezer opens quickly and the blast of frigid air makes her laugh. The three ice cubes fit tidily in her hand and she licks them as she hops back to the table.

The papers are tapped back into place and Addy puts them in what she thinks is a very lovely and professional manner back inside of the folder which she intends to place under her arm and take up to her bedroom where she will make many, many notes about what she has to do so she can get on with her life.

Sip of whiskey.

But this time when she tries to get up her left knee says **no, no, no** and she slides back into her chair.

Maybe just a little more whiskey . . .

When Addy looks up she sees the room across from the dining room that is probably still Mitchell's bedroom because he will undoubtedly come home sometime before the end of the century but that was last used as a recovery room for Lucky, her soon-to-be-ex-husband, after he fell and broke his sorry ass.

Just one more sip.

I can make it up the steps or maybe anywhere.

Sip of whiskey.

Up she goes. Standing. Glass in hand. Papers under arm. Whoa. Just a little wobbly.

The door. So close. **I can get to Lucky's bed.** Spilling some whiskey. **The dog will get it. Oh, no, the dog is dead. Barney is dead. Oh, Barney.**

The bed. The lovely bed.

Glass is on the floor.

The file of divorce papers is firmly in her hands. Addy scoots onto the bed, opens the folder, and throws it as if it is a paper airplane through the door. She watches it land on its belly out in the dining room. **Don't need you. Nope.**

All that's left between us are just these pages. Just this shit. Just this fucking shit.

Addy moves the papers in between her fingers and they do not feel like the disastrous pages of her married life but they feel soft, silky, fine. She spreads them around on her lap so that she is covered in her divorce papers. She picks up one piece, kisses it, and then another until she has kissed all twenty-one pages.

Then she holds the final page to her face and she breathes it in as if she is inhaling something that will cure her of a disease, something that smells like summer wind, something that she loves to keep close to her.

When Addy starts to cry she uses the papers to catch her tears. She cries like a drunk, like a woman who has lost an only child, like a wife who just realizes that something horrible is about to happen and there is nothing she can do to stop it. The tears come as if they have been waiting for a very long time to fall down her face and onto the pages, so ruthlessly black-and-white, that have been piled up by the cookie jar for so many weeks.

So many pages. So many weeks.

And when Addy falls asleep, when she passes through that thin veil that separated her for the past hour from just being tipsy into being drunk as a skunk, the very last page she uses to wipe her eyes is the one that says **irrevocably broken**.

FORTY-EIGHT
A high-tide swim through reality . . .

There is something about the hot tub that inspires confession, openness, and bouts of personal revelation that can be exceeded only by large quantities of alcohol or illegal drugs. When the Sweat-Hers first began attending the Y class that has transformed them in so many ways, they would afterwards strip off their wet clothing, take a quick shower to rinse off the sweat and lotion, put on bathing suits, and then climb very shyly into the soothing warm fingers of the high-powered tub that they have nicknamed Sweet Aunt Betty.

Now, months and pounds away from those initial weeks when the women were borderline prudish when it came to stripping in front of each other, they never hesitate to jump into Sweet Aunt Betty naked.

Hell does not care that she is the one who has lost the least weight and still has a stomach that looks like a miniature beer belly that could decrease considerably if only she would stop drinking full-carb beer. Debra couldn't care less that her once lovely and alert 38C breasts have decided to surrender to gravity. Malibu Heidi cannot seem to get rid of her chorister arms, that hangie-down surge of flesh that ripples on her upper arm. Lee proudly displays her billowy thighs and the little dips that will probably never go away unless she has them sucked out. Even Addy has the stomach thing going on which she knows may or may not go away depending on her resolve to stay away from Jack Daniels, the Vodka sisters, the lovely grapes from Chile, and those cheese and crackers which she considers to be an entire unrecognized food group.

Hell is leading a rowdy discussion on their progress as friends, athletes, and naked sisters in sweat. And because Addy has been the center of so many hot-water discussions,

Addy has come up with this great idea that
each one of them should reveal something
that might be considered a secret. Something, Hell instructs as if she is in charge of
the entire world, each has always been afraid
to even whisper out loud, something that
may for a moment take the spotlight off
Addy, who has told everyone she can think
of that Lucky has finally agreed to the divorce and that they have a joint meeting set
up with her attorney in three weeks.

Three weeks.

Two days after **the** social event of the year
in Parker—the annual community shindig
at the conference center near the mall.

Five weeks before Mitchell shows up during fall break and wants to know where he is
supposed to stay—what with the separation
and everything.

"Go first, Ms. Big Mouth," Addy tells her
sister whom she cannot stay mad at for more
than a short assembly of hours even if the
traitor is now openly sleeping with Lucky's
roommate. "This is your idea and I sure as
hell don't have anything else to share with all
of you or anyone else who lives in Parker.

These people know when I change under-wear, for crying out loud."

And the rest of Parker, the Sweat-Hers all point out, knows **everything** that happens not only to Addy but to everyone else.

"That's part of the charm of this little city," Debra shares. "You have to admit, Addy. This has been a terrific place to raise Mitchell, even when people are looking in your front windows all the time."

Yes, and yes again, Addy agrees, but the task at hand, as assigned by Ms. Know-It-All, is about the secrets no one in nosey Parker has yet uncovered. Spill your guts, Addy commands, splashing under the bub-bles in this intoxicating tub. Throw your own divorce papers all over the floor so we can walk on them.

There is a pause then when everyone stares at Addy as if each wants to say some-thing but has suddenly been struck by a dis-ease that prevents her from finding the right words. Finally, Lee kicks up a wave with her newly painted toenails, both feet at once, and announces she is bold enough to go first.

"Okay, Hell, here you go," she says, looking right at Hell, who has begun to slide down just a bit in the tub. "This has been one heck of a summer and if we can't share what is left in our hearts, then we are nothing."

Nothing, Lee repeats, and then encourages everyone to just follow after her. Let it go, she says. Here we are with our sisters, with the women we would call if we fell down face-first or were captured alive or imprisoned and could make just one phone call. Here we are with Addy who has been flipped and trampled and who has had the courage to act on a simple desire in her own heart. We all know enough about therapy to know this is healthy. It is good for all sides of our hearts to be open, to say it, to just take our desires and our needs out from the bottom of the shoebox that we have hidden in the back of the closet.

"So," Lee sighs, looking up, as if an angel is going to fly into the room and save her or tell her what to say. "We are naked on the outside, so we might as well be naked on the inside, because summer is over and everything is changing again and we are going to be busy and, well, just who knows, who the hell knows."

Everyone takes in a breath. It is unorchestrated but something they have learned how to do as Sweat-Hers. Something they know will fill them up, cleanse them, and spread the oxygen into the places that need it.

And just like in grade school, at summer camp, during sixth grade, the first few days of high school, the night of the first date—when someone takes the first step, everyone else seems to fall into place. When someone goes first, it is so easy to go second or third or fourth. It is so easy to start when someone else has already cleared away the debris so you can follow their path.

"I'm afraid I may have been too harsh about not wanting to get married, not wanting to step into another serious relationship," Lee confesses first. "I think I may not be designed to be married, but if I don't let go a little bit, if I keep clinging to this idea that I will never have a relationship again, then that is what I will have—no relationship. This group, the way Addy has stepped up to the plate and initiated changes, have made me think that I have been too rigid, too closed, too unwilling to just try it again."

The first confession unleashes a riptide of talking that threatens to create a flood in the tub room.

Debra admits for the very first time that her seemingly perfect life is awash in so much sacrifice that this class and an occasional visit to the First National are the only times when she can even think about herself. "It is time," she says without hesitation, "to give away some of what I do, to admit that I need more for myself, to ask my husband to be more than twenty-five percent invested in all the events and schedules and decisions that befall a family of six and an extended family that sometimes seems to number in the thousands."

Just as Debra finishes her last sentence, Malibu Heidi pipes up and reveals that she is sick of listening to herself.

"Oh, I never even told you this but I legally changed my name a month ago to Malibu and now I wish I would have changed it to Casper or Vero Beach or Seattle or whatever pops into my head sometime in the next thirty minutes," she almost shouts. "And that terrifies me. I'm never frigging satisfied. I am working on admitting that I change every five seconds and that it's okay and if I want to change my name three times a year, so what."

So the heck what.

Hell laughs when she starts talking. She says she's got such a big mouth, such a swagger, such an attitude, it's a wonder any of the women, her sister included, can stand to be in the same room with her. Being naked together in the biggest bathtub in Parker is another issue entirely.

"I just leap and before I am done leaping I am already looking at the next cliff to jump off of even before I realize that what I should be doing is enjoying the rest of the jump," Hell shares. "Bob is a good example. We get along great. He is the most evolved man I know. And already I am thinking up excuses why we shouldn't be together."

"Evolved?" Addy snorts.

"He is remarkable, Addy. Smart, working on his shit, trying new things, open, kind. And all I seem to be doing is making up excuses why we shouldn't be a couple."

And you, Addy? they say. **What is your secret of the week? Are there any left?**

Addy remembers how she wanted to slip under the water just a few months ago when these women asked her if she loved Lucky. She remembers how that one question spun her entire life around.

"Before I kneel in front of you all in humble gratitude, which would expose my breasts and probably half my flabby stomach, I want to say thank you for this," Addy begins.

"This?" Malibu asks because she is Malibu and cannot wait.

"This honesty. This acceptance, this warm pool of neutrality that allows us to, well, bare it all."

"Come on!" they all say at once, dismissing any thought that would direct them to any place other than where they are at right this second.

Addy tells them what she has to say may take a while. They all wave their hands as if they were being attacked by a swarm of late-summer flies. **Go on. Take your time. Hell can throw that towel bin against the door again if we need to stay in here all night.**

First, Addy asks for forgiveness from her sister. Her sister who always comes on the first ring, who supports all of her wild-ass decisions. Who is planted so deeply in her heart that Addy would die without her.

"I was so pissed when you started dating Bob. That was so selfish and part of my own insecurity," Addy shares. "I was miserable with a man and so I thought you should be miserable, too. I'm sorry."

And Addy says she knows she has shaken up Parker, caused other women to think about their relationships, and that some of those women may be making decisions they might never have made.

"Stop right there," Debra demands. "You are getting off track here, Addy. We are all smart women. In the end, we are each re-sponsible for our own decisions. Nothing

but good has happened this spring and summer and you are skirting the initial question.
We need your secret."

The secret.

Addy sinks just about an inch into the
bubbles and they all notice.

Sit up, they say.

This is no time to drown.

Say it.

There is no way you are going under.

Not with us here.

Talk.

Addy kicks against all the currents that
she's certain are trying to drag her under. She
floats back into her position between Debra
and Lee and thinks for just a second about
the miracle of female friendships, about surviving so many near-drownings, about how
she has never really felt alone—lonely yes,
but alone, never.

She tells them first about Lucky's gift of
the comedy school and the way she cried
and how the tissue paper ran down her face
and how she instinctively walked across the
yard to thank Lucky who then shared with

her more in thirty-eight minutes than he had shared with her in the past ten years.

"I could barely speak and he just seemed so different but then at the very end I looked at him and I just didn't know if it was just some kind of trick to win me back because he has changed so much and I ended up running, all but screaming, from Bob's house."

Then, Addy says, then she thought better of it and here is where the big secret comes in.

"My heart opened," Addy confesses. "It was as if someone had jammed a wedge in there and was determined to keep it from closing again and I thought, well, hell, we have been married so damn long and he wanted to take me to paradise and maybe that would have changed everything and here he is baring his own soul and I should at least acknowledge that as I continue to tremble."

But then he gave up.

In just that little bit of time, as I wavered he gave up. He left me that note and now I have no choice. I had a choice, Addy shares, I could have stopped the divorce, but now I have a lump in my heart the size of one of his damn soccer balls and I want to slap him upside the head all over again.

Well, screw Lucky.

To hell with him.

Who cares if he shaved his head and retired early.

So what if he was sensitive for three whole months.

Whatever about the soccer and the birdbath.

Artist schmartist.

The secrets blend together then and raise the temperature of the Sweat-Hers' own personal bathtub so much that the women notice tiny beads of perspiration running down each other's face.

"Can't be tears," Hell says, with a bit of swagger in her voice. "Only men would cry after something like this."

And they laugh, finally, and decide that the war must go on and that they should go en masse to the Fall Festival wine-tasting, but only after they have gathered at Hell's house with the rest of their gang for a strategy session where they will encourage whoever needs encouraging and where the women of Parker will rise up in solidarity against all evil and all things testosterone, unless, of course, they are feeling extremely generous and extraordinarily forgiving.

FORTY-NINE
What I thought Addy was thinking · · ·

She never called. Never came over. Never said a word.

I was thinking that she might be thinking we could at least try again as a couple, you know, not just as a her or a me.

But she never called.

FIFTY
Scarlet letters and a ship of fools . . .

The letters start to come about three seconds after the Sweat-Hers have once again declared war on the men of Parker. It is as if, Malibu tells them all during a volley of phone calls, there was a spy at the Y who was listening outside of the damn door.

"What is going on?" Hell wants to know, and of course, the only thing they can think of is that the men of Parker, the husbands and boyfriends, have hired relationship consultants.

"Like we could have predicted this," is what everyone tells Hell. "Like anything that a man does should ever startle or alarm us. Maybe they are still pissed off because of

how we ambushed them before the barbecue."

Alarmed is what Addy is for certain and
also pissed off which she takes as a good sign
lest she pout and cry over her divorce papers
and what should have been, could have
been, and will now never be, which is probably a good thing—at least for this one day.

Yet even as they waged war, the women
started receiving beautiful, lovely, gorgeous
handwritten letters from the men in their
lives. Letters tucked inside scented pastel envelopes and delivered by the same UPS guy
who brings them Steeler tickets, junk they
order from eBay, back-order items from the
mall, and the same twenty-six articles of
clothing they have all been purchasing from
the J.C. Penney catalogue since they were
in high school. Each of these letters is ad-
dressed to them in handwriting that they all
describe as artistic, flowing, a work of art.
And what is inside of these letters, which so
far have arrived at twelve-hour intervals to
each one of them, is sort of like a thank-you
note.

"Read yours," Addy calls to tell Hell.

"Mine is from Lucky. It just says, 'Thanks for the memories.'"

"That's so short it's hardly a letter," Hell agrees. "Mine says, 'Thank you, Hell, for not judging my past, for seeing who I am now, for being willing to give me another chance.'"

Addy thinks for a moment. She then tells Hell that the notes the other Sweat-Hers have received have been brief also—and then the third and the fourth—

"Addy, this isn't like a mystery or something," Hell tells her sister. "Maybe the men are just being nice. Isn't that what we want?"

"Hell, can you come over here right now? And swing by first and pick up Malibu's letters, anyone's letters you can get your hands on. Can you bring them all over here?"

"Sure, but really . . ."

"Really, my ass. Hell, you have been riding the line with all of this Bob One stuff and oh sure, this is really nice to get a letter and all, but what if the same person is writing **all** of them? What if they were really not that sincere?"

"I'm on my way," Hell announces instantly and in twenty-three minutes she is standing in Addy's kitchen just as the phone rings.

"Mitchell," Addy says, motioning to Hell to sit down. "Honey, I've been waiting for you to call. Hold on."

She instructs Hell to spread all the letters out while she talks to Mitchell, who is calling to find out what is going on.

"Your aunt is here. We are just going to have some coffee and talk about the Fall Festival we all go to every year."

Hell can hear Mitchell laugh from across the room.

"It's not a festival, it's more like the Parker wine-tasting of the year," Mitchell says. "Remember who had to drive everyone home last year? Just be careful because I won't be there this year."

"Stop acting like my dad."

"Wreck the car and your insurance rates will go up," he warns his mother, laughing "And hey, what's the latest on you and **my** dad?"

Shit, Addy thinks, **I hate this part. I hate standing here in the kitchen where**

we used to play catch with sugar cookies and loaves of bread and where Mitchell once walked in on us going at it on the kitchen floor when we thought he was spending the night across the street and telling him it's all really over.

"We have an appointment in a couple of weeks to finalize a few things," she tells him. "And then it will just take a few months for this thing to wind its way through the courts."

"And then you'll be divorced." Mitchell says it as a statement of fact and not as a question.

"Yes, Mitchell."

"Mom, is this really what you want?"

"I suppose."

"Well, Dad told me he's getting an apartment over by the river, with an extra room he will set up for visits and stuff because he wants you to keep the house and the neighborhood. You know how people always freak out after a divorce and friends pick sides and stuff. Dad doesn't want you to have to go through all of that."

"Oh."

"Mom, are you okay?"

Am I okay? My nineteen-year-old son is giving me marital advice. I'm getting mysterious letters every twelve hours. We have to plan a Parker counterattack. I canceled my breakfast date. The garage is empty. I jumped off a cliff and now I have to try and figure out how to land when I get close to the rocky bottom, which seems to be getting closer and closer every day.

"I'm fine," she lies like a good mother. "School is starting and you know what that does. It's been quite a summer, baby."

Mitchell talks then about his birth mother Melissa while Hell stares at the letters and then looks at her sister, who is walking in small circles around her kitchen.

Melissa is nice, he says. She told Mitchell everything and they went for a few walks and they shared a few meals and she asked him lots of questions about how he was raised and she told him all about her parents and what she does and she showed him photographs of her house and husband.

"She's nice, Mom, and she said that she was totally wowed by how kind you were to her and how it made her realize that she had made the right choice when she gave me up," Mitchell shares, and his voice cracks just a bit when he says the words "gave me up."

"She didn't really give you up," Addy corrects, very gently. "She gave you to us. And she did that because she loved you, and because she wanted you to have the very best chance at everything."

Addy has often thought of that moment when the decision was made. When a sixteen-year-old Melissa stood alone in the quiet of a house that was not accepting and forgiving and moved her hands, fingertips to fingertips, across her stomach, the warm place where Mitchell was already living, when she decided to "give him up." **Up to me, up to Lucky, up into our lives where we longed to touch the face of a baby, boy or girl, who would become our child, our life, the center of our hearts.** How often she had yearned to take that Melissa, the frightened and lonely young girl, not much younger than Mitchell at this very moment, into her arms and cradle her like a baby herself, to whisper in her ear that everything would be all right, that Mitchell would be loved so fiercely and so tenderly that it would be as if Addy had given birth to him herself.

"I know that, Mom, but I get a little sad when I think about how hard it must have been for her," Mitchell says. "It was really brave for her to do what she did. She made me think of that, Mom, she made me cry and I let her hug me and put her arms around me and she cried for such a long time, Mom. Oh, Mom, she just cried and cried."

Addy cannot breathe. **My son is thinking and feeling. He has emotions that are growing as fast as his body did in sixth grade. He is whole and kind and he has a tender, open heart. My Mitchell has a heart.**

"Mitchell, you know it is fine with your father and me if you want her to be a part of your life. Anything you want is fine with us. This is big stuff."

Mitchell smiles and he wishes his mother could see him. He smiles because it is just so like her to focus on him or his dad or all the kids in her class—anyone but herself. He also knows that no matter what she says she is not fine because his dad sure is not fine.

"Mom, you know I am glad she gave me up so you could adopt me," Mitchell says quietly, as if he has been rehearsing this conversation and wants to remember his lines. "Don't worry about me."

Addy reaches for a chair and sinks into it as she finishes this conversation with the strange boy on the other end of the phone who almost sounds like a man and who has the same voice as her son. Her son, the sassy kid who crawled in and out of the basement window after curfew, who drank all the beer in the refrigerator one night when he thought she would not notice, and who got two speeding tickets within a twelve-hour span when he was sixteen years old and then almost made her commit a felony herself.

"Astonishing," Addy tells Hell when she finally hangs up. "You wonder every moment of their little lives if you are going to first kill them—by holding them improperly, then psychologically ruin them by saying the wrong thing or not giving them what they want, and finally by throwing them to the lions when you send them off like this—and, miracle of miracles, they turn into warm, loving, kind human beings who actually care about you. Whoever knew it was possible?"

Hell is sitting next to her sister and now she grabs her hands, spinning her so that their knees are touching, so that she can look directly into Addy's eyes, so that Addy can go nowhere, so that she will **listen**.

And Hell tells her that she was always and will always be a good mother. Hell tells her that it was a total joy to watch Mitchell come into Addy's life and see Addy grow as a woman and as a mother. It was and continues to be a gift in her life to be an auntie, to be a part of something as wonderful as Mitchell Lipton, and then Hell says, Sister, **I know.**

"What do you know?" Addy whispers.

"I know that this part of your life is really hard and that you are having second thoughts about Lucky and that he was and is just as good of a father as you were a mother. That is what I know."

"But how do you know, Hell? How in the hell do you know if you are making the wrong or right decision?"

"You don't. That is supposed to be the fun part."

"Shit, Hell, I was just looking for a little slice of paradise. That's all. Is it so much to ask for? Can't a woman have the romance and the things she wants **and** the man? Can't Lucky be my friend and my lover like he once was?"

"Everything is possible, baby. Lucky could be the real deal right now, he could be still trying to woo you back. I know you think Bob and I talk about this all of the time, but believe me, we have much better things to do."

"Scum," Addy says, leaning forward so she can fall into her sister's arms. "You are just scum, sissy."

Addy tells Hell that perhaps because Lucky took a step forward and signed the papers and because Addy cannot quite make herself move forward, because her anger constantly runs her life, it is hard for her to move off center. "Don't you think?"

"Jeezus, Addy, what I think doesn't matter! Why don't we just go over these letters and you can change your mind another thirteen times while we do that if you can stop being crazy for three seconds?

"Debra has three letters," Hell tells her sister, "the rest of us have two, and Bob Two's wife is afraid to open her second one because the first one was so sweet she thinks she might faint if she opens the next one. She thinks she is being stalked and someone is using Bob Two's name."

"Really?"

"Well, look at these. I picked up three of them on the way over so you have four, plus yours to look at."

Addy spins around, picks up the letters one by one, reads each one, runs her fingers over the exquisite lettering, sets each one down, and then moves back through them all one more time.

"What?" Hell asks more than impatiently.

"Hang on," Addy demands as she leaves the room for a second.

When she comes back, Addy has the note that came with the clown gift. She places it carefully next to the first letter, next to the second, third, and fourth, until she has compared it with all of them and then she does it one more time.

"Lucky wrote all of these letters," Addy announces.

"What do you mean?"

"Look."

Hell looks first at all the notes and then back at her sister. "They all look the same."

"Yes, they do."

"So?"

"So if Lucky is doing all of this, what does it say about the sincerity of the messages?"

"Maybe the messages are being dictated," Hell offers. "Maybe Debra's husband telling her that he has been an ass and that he agrees they should now have, what does he say here, 'equal time with specific household chores,' is something he told Lucky so Lucky could write it down and make it look nice. How many men do you know who can do calligraphy and compose a sweet message at the same time?"

" 'Specific household chores,' boy, does that have a nice sexy ring to it."

"Come on, I could hear Bob saying what he wrote in mine."

"You are gone, Hell. That man could send you one word on a piece of toilet paper and you would love it."

Hell actually blushes and this worries Addy just a bit and she asks her sister if it's serious. Have you fallen in love? What in the world is going on?

Hell says she is in heavy-like, and then not-so-deftly changes the subject so she will not be the focus of one of Addy's anti-love tirades and so she can keep a late-afternoon date with Bob, which she, of course, does not want to tell Addy about.

The two sisters drink their coffee and study the notes Lucky has written to each and every one of their women friends and they try and think about what to do next. They are clueless until Hell remembers that she forgot to hand off the Fall Festival brochure to Addy. She did not really forget, it's just that she has been terrified to do it. Maybe, she thinks, reaching into her back pocket, Addy will not flip out. And maybe also a wild sea lion will walk out of the bathroom and begin singing a song from **A Chorus Line**.

"The theme for this year's Fall Festival is Fall Paradise?" Addy shouts with a sort of laugh.

"Yes," Hell manages to snort through her coffee.

"Perfect! This is just perfect! And they're going to focus on wines from warm and humid climates and they're asking us to dress in tropical attire?"

Hell just nods her head up and down this time as Addy jumps up and starts circling the kitchen again like a sheepdog that is waiting for the gate to open.

Addy circles two, three, and then four times until she comes up with it just as Hell knew she would come up with it.

"What?" Hell asks.

When Addy turns back to the table Hell blinks once and then twice because it looks as if fire is coming out of her sister's eyes. She braces herself by placing both hands on the table and planting her feet under her chair, ready to either jump up or run or start doing the limbo in preparation for the party.

"Paradise can be invaded by pirates and wenches," Addy says, glowing. "We prep at Malibu's house as soon as possible. We do not just attend this festival with our elegant and well-written brothers but we **capture** it. We dress the part. We take it over. This will make the cul-de-sac barbecue look like a garden party."

Hell cannot help it. She temporarily forgets about Bob One's soft lips. Instead, she thinks her whack job of an almost-divorced sister is a genius and when she rises she swings herself on top of the table, shouts, "Hand over the wine, matey," laughs as if she has just seized command of a ship that has a full load of liquid spices, and then she starts laughing so hard she almost falls off of the damn table.

FIFTY-ONE
The wenches' whistling rendezvous . . .

The start of school in Parker, PA, suspends everything but breathing and perhaps preparing for bowling season and the women of Parker are having a hard time coordinating a pre-festival meeting to discuss what they will wear, how they will get there, and what to do about the letters that have now been replaced by flowers, tickets for plays and movies, and in Addy's case pieces of a puzzle that are a variety of colors, do not fit together, and have no apparent meaning to her at all.

Hell knows nothing.

The rest of the Sweat-Hers are on overload.

All the Honduras babes want to do is get together at the bar.

They all agree a plan is a dire necessity.

The men are lying low and apparently spending all their free time purchasing gifts and trying to figure out what to do to top what they did the day before to seduce or keep the women in their lives.

And the rest of Parker is holding its breath because the festival is already sold out, people have heard that the He Said–She Saids might do something wild and dangerous the night of the event, and one loopy guy who wishes his wife would yell at him so he could hang out with Lucky and the boys has put up a website so people can buy and sell tickets for Fall Paradise in Parker.

This eBay of Parker has shifted the annual event into its own stratosphere. A guy from the south side of town who bought twenty tickets for his extended family has already made five hundred dollars selling half of them to eager customers on the website. And for the first time ever, the Pittsburgh and Philadelphia newspapers and one television station are planning on covering the event.

Addy comes home from work each night, does not bother to see if Lucky is next door, and immediately falls into routines that quickly become so comfortable it seems as if she has done them for a very long time. She likes the fact that she no longer worries about what to cook for dinner. The time she saves by keeping it simple—maybe preparing a salad and grilling some tuna or a piece of chicken from the freezer—gives her more time to read, prepare for the next day, and keep her daily workout routine alive. Also, not sneaking out to the tree to smoke is saving her so much money and time she has already managed to tuck away three hundred dollars. The money will eventually take Addy Lipton on a trip to someplace warm during spring break, maybe even Costa Rica. Maybe not.

And by ignoring the upcoming meeting with the attorney that is scheduled for two days after Fall Paradise, Addy thinks she has every major problem in her life temporarily covered. She is of course kidding herself and she knows this but she also thinks that if she can limp through the next few days, if the damn girls can help her brainstorm the wine-tasting, then at least she will have some kind of edge when it comes time to sit next to Lucky in front of their attorneys and their grim smiles, mountains of papers, and the damned black pen that will be used to finalize the entire mess.

Just as she finishes rinsing off the plate, fork, knife, and glass from her eighth salad dinner in a row, Malibu calls to announce that she is making one last stab at a meeting before the festival wine-tasting.

"This is it," she announces with a huge sigh. "I am calling everyone and just telling whoever can make it to be at my house with something to share in one hour. Bring something to drink, a six-pack, pomegranate juice, or a bottle of wine."

"Who's coming?"

"I have no idea but I am sick of trying to find a time for a group meeting and this is it. Maybe everyone is just tired of the Parker War or something."

"That would be a sad day," Addy laments. "I think it's just the time of the year. We're busy and we've been lulled into submission by all the cards and gifts."

"Not you?"

"Just those damn puzzle pieces, but remember, I'm the cause of all of this and everyone else is in a different spot."

"Addy, you know that but for the grace or lack of grace of God, there we could all be," Malibu shares. "Every single woman I know has part envy and part sympathy for you. And half of us wish we had the guts to be an out lesbian like Sanchez. That doctor's the smartest chick in town."

"Are you flirting with me?" Addy laughs.

"Just bring some booze and celery or something and get over here," Malibu laughs back. "You are coming? I'd hate to make these decisions all alone."

"I'll be there, Malibu Heidi."

Addy grabs the notes from her assignment book, a glass of water, and decides to sit in the backyard for forty-five minutes before she drives over to Malibu's house. She feels strong enough to resist the temptation of the smoking tree and only wishes, as she pushes the old metal chair close to the half-baked barbecue, that the backyard looked as she has always dreamed it would look. Flower beds, high grasses, a built-in grill that includes a small fireplace, cobblestone pathways curving around to the sides of the house . . .

Maybe it doesn't matter, she thinks now. **Maybe it does matter and by the end of autumn on my tremendously free Saturdays I can have the entire backyard turned into an oasis for women's meetings. Maybe I should sell the house and get an easy-living condo. Maybe I should get an apartment, too, and then travel every summer, just get the hell out of Parker, leave my backyard to some other unsuspecting family.**

The possibilities are endless.

The decisions are endless.

The problems are endless.

The quiet on these nights is sometimes endless.

And then she hears something that makes her drop her pen and freeze. She hears something that she has not heard for so long that it takes her a few seconds to realize what she is hearing. Addy leans forward, turns toward Bob One's house, and tries to remember the last time she heard this.

Lucky whistling.

Lucky whistling like he always used to whistle when he was happy. When he hung out in The Kingdom of Krap. When he kicked the soccer ball around in the front yard with Mitchell. When he was on his way to meet with the guys. When he was sitting at the dining room table designing his latest bowling ball, washing machine, coat hanger or other piece-of-junk sculpture. And the way he used to whistle when they first met, when he didn't know she heard him, just before he knocked on the door to pick her up.

Addy almost shouts, "I can hear you!" She almost gets up and walks to the edge of the yard to see if he is working in the backyard, or whistling in the kitchen with the window open, or if he is waiting at the front door for someone else to arrive. She almost puts her hand over her heart as a cascade of marriage memories floods through her and makes her woozy with its sudden and totally unexpected fierceness.

And she thinks about the distance between her and Lucky. It is just a yard, just some bushes, a few trees, a halfhearted bed of flowers and the head-high fence that Bob One installed so he could practice for his entrance exam into a nudist colony.

Just that, Addy knows, but it may as well be the stupid-ass barrier that idiots think will keep people from trying to cross the national border. It may as well be an invisible dog fence that will shock the living hell out of her if she tries to cross over it. It may as well be the very deepest part of Lake Huron, or a river full of piranhas in the Amazon, or the black hole in the Atlantic that eats people alive.

The whistling does not stop and Addy gets up and looks toward its source one more time. Then she blows Lucky a kiss, murmurs, "Keep whistling, Lucky," and turns without saying another word toward the kitchen where she grabs a bottle of wine and just to be funny a bag of carrots before she stows her emotional Lucky baggage and meets with the wenches of Parker.

The wenches and female pirates who show up en masse.

By the time Addy gets to Malibu's small bungalow on the other side of town, which is only about fifteen minutes away, there are cars parked up and down both sides of the street, bottles of beer, water, wine, and juice crowding coolers on the front step, women packed shoulder to shoulder in the living room and throughout the kitchen, and enough food to feed a third-world country for a solid week.

Women, they all agree, are beyond awesome. Women somehow always manage to pull out all the stops and get there and do it and be and sacrifice and eventually figure it all out.

Figuring it all out on a school night is such a miracle that the women act as if it is a Friday night. They drink beer and eat nachos and savor stories of the gifts and letters they have received and the thought that the bridge is about to give way because there is no way in hell the men can keep holding it up. There is no way they know what will happen next, how they will fulfill their promises—to really fix the sink, actually pay for the art lessons the women want, and do something tangible instead of throwing dreams into the air without any real concern for where and if they might ever land. More likely, the women all joke, you could put an eye out from the falling dream debris.

The discussion about what to wear and how to act during Fall Paradise is soon eclipsed by a swell of anger, a chance to vent, a wavering doubt about the sincerity of pastel envelopes when the garbage cans are full and about gift certificates for sexy underwear when someone needs to take a vanload of kids to soccer practice.

Addy is so quiet during this conversation that she barely moves. She occasionally looks over at Hell who is almost as quiet but who may have had a bad date with Bob One because she occasionally says "No shit," or runs to grab a beer out of the cooler, takes a sip, and then passes it to the woman who requested it in the first place.

Finally, Addy thinks, she understands. She thinks she has this vague memory of some nice weeks at the end of summer years

ago when she had so much free time and
everything was caught up and then school
started again and the pace of living went
into warp speed and the dishes piled up and
the now dead dog looked within a few weeks
as if he was starving and she was once again
living on five hours of sleep a night while
The Kingdom of Krap filled up and bowling
started and who the hell knows what else.

"Listen," Addy finally manages to blurt
out. "I think happiness is a bit cyclic, especially in Parker."

"No shit!" about half of the women yell.

"We are coming off of summer when lots
of us are around all of the time and when
things are easier, and I sort of feel responsi-
ble for this meeting and lots of everything
else because I just stopped and declared that
it shouldn't be cyclic, that we should draw
some lines in the sand, that whatever kind of
relationship we are in—man, woman, partner, donkey—whomever or whatever we
chose to love—well, there should always be
a hint of paradise."

The women are all listening. Addy, to
many of them, has become a heroine. The

Parker woman who was the last on their list of Possible Divorcées. The teacher from heaven. The Mom of the Year. Lucky's lover. Mitchell's wonderful launching pad. Hell's heart.

The women shake their heads and say that is why they are at Malibu's house on a weeknight when they should be home punching out morning lunch bags, going over their notes for work, and maybe doing something as lavish as taking a five-minute shower, preparing coffee for the morning, and deciding what they want to wear for work without being interrupted by a man, beast, or child.

So?

So what do we do now?

So how can we demand follow-through from these letter writers?

So how do we keep dancing naked while balancing everything, every single thing on our shoulders?

So how do we make sure we can cash in all those pieces of paper we have been getting?

So how do we keep an eraser off the lines we have drawn this summer?

Addy wishes Sanchez would walk through the door dressed in a fairy godmother outfit and answer all these questions. When that does not happen, she closes her eyes. She tells these women the first thing that comes into her head. She tells them the truth.

It is never **always** easy. If you just think about it, though, you will always know what to do. And if your heart is torn, just pause for a second. If you loved this man enough to marry him or sleep with him there has to be a shard of something good left. You can start over anytime if you are both okay with that, if it is not too late, if you can keep your damn foot on that line. But think hard about your **ifs**. Make certain you have the stamina. Make sure you are not too damned exhausted and that your heart is full of not only love, but courage, too.

And one more thing.

"Why not have fun at the Fall Paradise?" Addy finally says. "Why not show these guys before the winter freezes us in that we are never going back to the way things were, that we always have each other, that they had better pay up and keep their promises? Why the hell not?"

Then the women leave, some of them so late they will go to work or to drop kids off at school in the morning in the same clothes they wore while at Malibu's house. They each have an idea for what to wear to Fall Paradise, how they will tell the men they are not going to actually attend this event with them, but may meet and actually speak to them during the party, and how all bets and promises are going to be called in very, very soon.

So, boys, in other words you had better kick ass and pull out all the stops because if your promises are empty it may be a long time before you whistle again.

A very long time.

FIFTY-TWO
Riptide showdown at the Fall Paradise corral . . .

Wine, they say, is the nectar of the gods and goddesses. It is the sweet fruit of life that has cascaded through hand-carved tumblers and goblets, into metal cups, then crystal and glass from one ancient civilization to the next. But the early wine drinkers and grape lovers from the villages around the Caspian, Red, Black, and Mediterranean seas have nothing on the extraordinary connoisseurs who call Parker, PA, home.

The eclectic wine drinkers of this nonchalant-appearing town have helped put it on wine maps that are distributed by the Pennsylvania Board of Tourism, which proclaims, "Bountiful, polished, yet casual wine stores, the extraordinary First National

Wine & Cigar Bar, tastings and numerous events, all are part of the annual Fall Festival that draws sellers and cellars from throughout the world and is a sellout every year."

Parker is **the** place to be for an entire week every September when gas stations, grocery stores, restaurants, the Little League Parents' Association, eight churches, and just about every other person in the community sells something that has to do with wine, sponsors a wine-tasting, drinks a lot of wine, buys a lot of wine, and does everything he or she or it can to blow the hick-town image of a place that looks as if it should have been called Mayberry.

The Fall Paradise activities kick off on Monday evening with a barrel-uncorking ceremony at the First National. Hell, who helped organize the first event four years ago, taps Addy—the new local comedienne—to begin preparing for her upcoming November comedy-school debut by being the Mistress of Ceremonies for the uncorking, which usually lasts at least ten minutes and is really just a good reason to sample the donated wine, this year from a vineyard in southern Arizona, of all places, one of many wineries that are lined up to become part of what is now a fairly serious and prestigious wine event.

"Go figure," Hell gloats to Addy after they have filled and passed out 245 glasses, the occupancy limit for the bar. "Remember when we started this damn wine party? Didn't we just want some free samples?"

"Well, here is a big piece of news. Watch out what you wish for because you may just get it."

"No kidding. You start with wine, ask for a divorce, think you need a boyfriend, and **bam**. The whole town is suddenly filled with winos, there's divorce papers on the dining room table, and a guy's size twelves under the damn bed."

"Let's drink to that," Addy said, handing her one of the two last glasses of wine from the opening-night barrel.

And that was just the beginning.

There was a grape stomp, a small parade that included half the grade-school population dressed up as long, cascading vines which were really ropes painted brown, a mess of goofy adults appearing as individual red, green, and black grapes, the high school marching band, floats from all the bars and restaurants, all followed by an outdoor chicken fry where beer was not allowed and all of this leading up to the Saturday night event that unsuspecting non-Parkerites thought was a grand wine-tasting event that included live music, gourmet food, dancing, demonstrations and discussions with wine-makers from throughout the world, and a chance to purchase wine at prices that would knock the wineglass out of the hand of any-one living in Manhattan or San Francisco.

Most of these celebrants did not know about the pirates and wenches. They were not privy to the He Said–She Saids, they would not know a Sweat-Her if one wrapped herself over their shoulders.

And so after a week of wine frivolity, of many Parkerites coming in to volunteer to work at Festival events, it comes as no sur-prise to see dozens and dozens and then hundreds of men and women dressed up in floral shirts, flip-flops, and faded shorts from summers past and each one of these tropical gems streaming toward the quaint convention center as if this sort of thing were an everyday occurrence.

It took those in the know a while to realize that this year most of the initial attendees were men. Men whose legs had already flipped back to the white side. Men who wore geeky plastic leis around their necks. Men who had donned straw cowboy hats. Men who at first huddled in groups trying to figure out what the absentee women were up to and men who were almost too busy talking to realize that Lucky Lipton had walked in wearing a kilt.

What the hell, Lucky?

Mr. Lipton, who has been working out almost as hard as his soon-to-be-ex wife, looks a few steps on the other side of adorable. It's a kilt that he obviously special-ordered, because it's a rainbow of colors, tropical surely, and his loose-fitting silk shirt is a deep blue and brings out the subtle light spots in his eyes that Addy once, a very long time ago, discovered when she loved to kiss his eyes.

"Buddy," Bob One says with a smile, "you are definitely the stud."

"Thank you. And by the way, where are the ladies?"

"Wish we knew," Bob Two laments. "I for one wish this war thing would slide to a halt."

"We are dealing with **women,** you know," Bob One reminds him. "Hell has not spilled her guts in weeks, and if we stand around here and try to figure out what they might be doing they could run out of wine over there."

The men nod and begin to turn and suddenly the world in front of them changes and shifts and they become rooted in place as the doors are flung open and the women of Parker do not so much walk as fly, saunter, parade, leap, and swagger into Fall Paradise as if they owned the damn place. Lucky and Bob One lose count after twenty-four women enter. The three hundred or so others who are about to take a sip of wine freeze in place as if they have suddenly been led into a walk-in cooler. Two photographers gasp and then start taking pictures as if their cameras were machine guns.

The women, the lovely Parker women,

are dressed as pirates and there are more pirates and there are women who look like the pirates' whores and Addy is a hooker and Hell is a pirate and they are leading the brigade and running throughout the conference center, which has been decorated to look like a tropical vineyard, laughing and yelling to the thunderous applause that echoes across the top of the room like the crack of a cannon being fired offshore from the bow of a ship that is escaping with all the gold.

While everyone else stands motionless, the women run to the tables and fill their glasses, take a sip, wipe off their chins with the sleeves of their blouses and jackets, and then begin streaming toward the group of men, who all look as if they have just been caught in the scorching beam of some high-powered searchlight.

"Holy shit," Bob Two mutters. "Do we run or open our arms?"

"I would say stand still," Lucky advises. "They sort of look as if they are in charge here."

"My God, they look . . . hot," Bob One

says in a half-whisper that sounds sexy even
to his friends.

The men stand where they are, temporarily immobile, with their glasses hanging
from their fingers. If someone sneezed, all
the glasses would fall to the ground and
shatter at once.

The women are laughing, clearly having
fun. They are talking, slapping each other on
the arms, playing with their swords and
knives—plastic, the men hope. And they are
being followed by the photographers and the
very happy-looking television reporter who
is witnessing something she never intended
to see while at the Parker Fall Festival.

"Roll!" the reporter yells. "My God, this
will go national. Look at these women.
Roll," she orders her male cameraman, "or
I'll make them turn on you and get out my
own sword."

Months and years later when this night is
recounted and remembered in Parker and at
various other locations throughout the universe, the stories of what happened next will
twist and turn depending on who is speaking,
who is remembering, who was there, and

who was not. There will be archived footage from a KCLP Pittsburgh reporter. There will be all the photos in the local and regional newspapers and the photos in the much-loved society pages. There will be the laminated **People** magazine spread, the seemingly constant talk shows for some of the women and a few of the men, and stunned, and often garbled, second- and third-hand phone conversations between mothers, aunts, old high school and college friends that still seem to be ricocheting throughout the entire world.

But first the men had to stand still for a very long time.

They had to stand still while the women charmed the other wine-tasting patrons and the wine cellar representatives. The men stood without drinking or moving while the women filled their glasses at least three times and strolled around the borders of Fall Paradise, and then the men shifted just a bit, the foot-to-foot kind of shifting that we all do when we need to move but we're pretty certain we may be shot if we move the wrong way.

Finally, with cameras blazing, the women

began moving toward the men as if it was the perfect moment, the right time, the very instant they had to do it.

Glasses full.

Swords and knives in hands.

Boots and sandals stomping.

Eyes on fire.

Hearts pounding.

And way behind all of that a smile tucked inside of a laugh that knows for certain the men are either terrified or ready to laugh out loud, too.

And if the men only knew that the women have absolutely no plan at all, and really just wanted to scare the living hell out of them, and possibly get them to admit that they have no idea what they are doing either, it is very possible that the men might also be jumping around with sharp objects in their hands.

But they are not and so the women have the upper and the lower hand and they begin to circle the men. They walk slowly with a glass in one hand and a plastic sword or knife in the other and they know they look ridiculous and quite possibly insane but they could also care less.

Addy begins to wonder, as she walks with her friends, what in the hell she is doing in this circle because she has already made her decision, the motion now seconded by Lucky, and she is no longer waiting for another answer but there is something about the way Lucky looks in a kilt that keeps her in the circle. It's the damn kilt and his legs sticking out like those of a strong bird and the sudden resurrection of his smile the way she remembers it from all those years ago when she first met him, when there was never any need for questions or doubt or suspicion or anger.

Malibu Heidi, of all people, begins talking first. She tells the men that they will not get any wine until they have answered the specific and very important questions from the women in their lives who need the answers.

"We have captured all your promises, all your notes, everything you have sent us and we need to know when, if ever, you plan on doing more than just writing about them," she announces with her sword resting on the tip of her black pirate boot. "And now, as you see, we have also captured you and we will wait, we will drink all the wine, we will stand here forever until we know the answers to these questions."

The men seem a bit panicked. They all remember what they wrote and what they promised and they cannot for the life of them, not even to save their own lives in this very public arena, think of what to do next.

When Lucky sets down his empty wineglass and moves forward first, smiling as broadly as Addy has ever seen him smile, there is not a whisper, a sigh, a breath of anything moving throughout Fall Paradise. There is a sudden burst of calm as Lucky moves forward, as he gets down on one knee in front of Addy, as he slips the wineglass out of her hand, sets it carefully on the floor, and then takes her hands in his own.

Addy feels a swirl of something liquid, something that starts in her ankles and moves through both legs, into her stomach, around her uterus, through her heart, and into the back of her throat that is like the sweet pounding of some ancient music. She knows that if she closes her eyes she will fall over. Addy Lipton will faint for the first time in her life. **Am I breathing? Am I alive? Is this really happening?**

The crowd moves in. Lucky's swift movement has shaken the paralysis off of his friends and now the circle around Addy and Lucky is huge. The camera people have jumped on top of chairs. The reporter is crawling on her hands and knees, totally ruining her black nylons, so she can get closer, so she can hear what is happening. Everyone holds their breath.

"Oh, my lovely wench," Lucky begins. "Forgive my impertinence and please accept my apologies for my actions prior to this moment, during the past ten years, and for every moment before that when I failed you. Men, as you know, are the weaker sex, we need help and guidance. We need to pause at the door every day and to ask ourselves if we have done the right thing, if we have kept our promises, if we have even bothered to take into account the wishes of the women whom we love so very much."

The writer from Pittsburgh is writing so fast she is forgetting to watch the crowd. The crowd that is melting. The swords and knives that have tumbled to the ground. The sounds of hearts beating so fast a tidal wave could erupt from the sudden sway of all the bodies leaning, listening, longing.

"Lucky . . ." Addy sputters.

"Let me finish, my darling, please, give me this one last chance, I beg of you."

Hell has to bite her tongue to keep from saying out loud, **I love it when men beg**. For once, to her own surprise, she manages to keep quiet.

"I know I failed you many times but I just have to say it was because I didn't know any better, because I stopped believing in myself, because I got lazy and it took that stupid fall in the driveway, your complete honesty, the idea that I could lose everything I ever loved and wanted, to make me realize I have a part in all of this, too," Lucky explains. "A relationship needs care. It needs to be fed and watered with laughter and excitement and love just like a child. But this paradise that we were headed toward, Addy, I think this paradise is right here, right in this place, right now."

Addy is crying. She wants so much to put her hands on Lucky's face, to believe him, to bend down and kiss him.

"Lucky, it wasn't all you, not always," she begins. "It was so easy to be tired, to just be so damned tired, and I never meant to hurt you with the divorce but it was just that it looked as if nothing would change."

"I understand."

"The pieces of the puzzle that you have been sending me, Lucky, what is that all about, what kind of promise is that?"

Lucky drops his hand toward his crotch, the crowd takes in enough air to launch a parachute, and he holds up his other hand as if to tell them, **Wait just a second,** then he reaches into his secret kilt pocket and pulls out something that he slowly holds up so that Addy can see. The crowd edges closer. Addy bends down just a bit to take the photograph out of his hand and when she realizes what it is she puts her hand to her mouth.

"Our one-night honeymoon, that day we walked on the beach . . ." Addy says, remembering how one day could have been a thousand because it had been so wonderful, so uncomplicated and perfect, so damn sweet.

"Those puzzle pieces are from this photograph and the last piece would have said this, Addy, it would have said that the puzzle pieces of our marriage are the same but it is now time to rearrange them to form a new picture, something wild and beautiful and always growing, and I would never have thought of that without the divorce papers, without you being brave enough to demand a change, to demand a new picture of our marriage."

The men are crying and the women are crying and the wine vendors are crying and all the photographers too. The Pitts-burgh reporter is crying and she will later dump her boyfriend and write a note to herself listing what she will now demand from a relationship, a note she will keep for a very long time until she meets a wonderful man and elopes with him to Costa Rica of all places.

But before that, before relationships in Parker, PA, are forever altered by what is happening on the floor of the Fall Paradise wine-tasting event, before the talk shows, and the club that forms in the weeks following the wine bash, before kilt sales explode throughout the country, before Mitchell hears about what his parents have done and then sees them on the evening news and later drives them to an **Oprah** show in Chicago, before the larger convention center is built and the Parker Fall Festival events explode into twice-a-year happenings, before lovers flock to Parker to get marriage licenses, and boutiques focusing on anything having to do with paradise and romance blossom through the city, before all of that and so much more, Addy Lipton leans forward.

Addy leans forward and she forgets about her weariness and her high blood pressure and her permanently partially disabled husband. She forgets about the smoking tree and The Kingdom of Krap. Addy forgets about the sandy beaches of Costa Rica and what dozens of bowling balls look like piled on top of each other. She forgets about sweat socks and the boxer shorts tossed next to the toilet. All she can think about is what she might look like now that she is thin again when she puts on the red nightgown with the purple trim and is lying in the very center of their bed when Lucky comes up the steps in his kilt.

Then Addy Lipton leans over and kisses Lucky Lipton in front of hundreds of people who begin screaming, hollering, and kissing each other as dozens of intimate conversations break out between pirates, wenches, and men dressed to kill in floral shirts that are surely a sign of paradise to come.

FIFTY-THREE
What I know Addy is thinking · · ·

This is it, Lucky Lipton. You are evolving and changing and I like what I see. But this new puzzle of your marriage had better be more of a priority than your new career, your bowling balls, and the damned antique car.

I get it, Addy. I am in paradise now and I have no intention of ever leaving it again. And hey, Addy—isn't it something how paradise can be right there an inch away, breathing in your ear, living in your house, and you don't even recognize it?

I love you, Addy Lipton. Now please take off your blouse.

EPILOGUE

After the last bottle of wine had been emptied at the soon-to-be-infamous Parker Fall Paradise celebration, which turned out to be not so much a wine-tasting as a city-sized reconciliation (at least for one night), Parker seemed to glow for days.

Lucky went home with Addy, and everything Addy dreamed about while he knelt on the floor in his kilt happened—only for much longer than she had anticipated. Lucky moved back into their home immediately and under a set of guidelines that both Lucky and Addy agreed upon during a late-night rendezvous under the smoking tree which has since felt smoke, but not from a cigarette or cigar.

By the end of November, Lucky had finalized all his paperwork for early retirement, enrolled in welding school, finished three sculptures in his new art studio/workshop, and gotten the coaching job.

Addy went to her comedy school, graduated fifth in her class, and, driving home from her last class, had an epiphany that didn't change the course of her life but the course of the lucky students who are now able to enroll in her series of classes at Parker Community College called Giggles where she teaches Joke-Telling 101, How to Laugh at Least Twenty Times a Day, and Eat Drink and Be Merry Because You Still Live in Parker. She also decided she was sick and tired of living on the cul-de-sac, did not have the energy to redo the house the way she has always dreamed, and in a moment of utter honesty admitted she kind of missed The Kingdom of Krap.

Addy's blood pressure is stabilized and although she may have to take medication for the rest of her life she thinks it's a small price to pay for not having a stroke. Lucky's back will always give him some pain but losing sixty-nine pounds, following a toning and weight-lifting program, and finally doing something that he has always dreamed about has helped him cope with a stabbing pain that is every day now more like a bothersome wild tingle.

The Liptons recently purchased eight acres of land on the far side of town from a farmer who happened to stumble into Fall Paradise and has never been the same since. When he is not helping to plow fields while wearing a back brace, Lucky is supervising construction of an 1,800-square-foot house and detached artist's studio that are totally environmentally friendly. There will eventually be a small library, a huge master suite, and a large, light-filled kitchen/living room, as well as a bedroom for Mitchell. The backyard barbecue area has already been completed by Lucky himself.

The Liptons also agreed to attend six months of counseling with a new therapist who wanted to release them after the second visit, but much to her complete joy they refused to suspend the sessions, lest they slide back into their old routines and break another back or heart.

Mitchell is edging his way toward his college degree, has had three girlfriends and two more speeding tickets, and has visited with his birth mother twice. He is also excited about being a big brother, as Melissa and her husband have decided to adopt at least one child, maybe more. He was not embarrassed by his parents' brief brush with fame but the night he caught them naked in the backyard was almost too much and he now announces his entrance with loud beeping and several pre-arrival phone calls.

Hell and Bob One gave it a good try but the relationship did not last past the first Christmas. Hell, to her credit, told Bob she was just not meant to be with one man and although they remain friends he has been reluctant to date anyone else. Bob told Lucky last week that he will always love Hell and if that means from a distance then so be it. Lucky is trying to get his friend to give it up and get on with his life and is secretly working to get him on a singles cruise where

Lucky knows Bob One will wow the women with his charm, cooking skills, and all of his new kilts.

The Sweat-Hers continue to meet and have now lost a combined total of 238 pounds. The women were recently the stars at the YWCA Health Fair and have inspired three weight-loss and exercise programs and all the classes now have a waiting list.

The Parker Paradise Dating Club was formed just a week following the Fall Paradise event. Dr. Sanchez agreed to be the professional attached to the club that is now turning heads all across the country. The rules of the club are usually specific but also change every time there is a wine-tasting or community event and someone hauls out the original rules that were scratched on the back of a cocktail napkin the night of Fall Paradise. The club's purpose is very simple. It was created by the Sweat-Hers, and by Lucky and his gang, to help couples, or a person who wants to be half of a couple, and any and every kind of couple, make certain that there is always a hint of paradise in their relationships.

At last count there were 379 men and women enrolled in the club and the upcoming spring list of events includes a seductive nightwear fashion show, classes in Latin dancing, birdhouse construction, poetry writing, couples' fly-tying, a workshop on the importance of laughter, and a class called "Fire and Ice: Foreplay for Forgetful Hearts" that was filled the day the class list was posted at The First National Wine & Cigar Bar.

And no one knows this yet but Addy has been working with the art teacher from her school, who is also a professional photographer, on a set of "Paradise in Parker" postcards. The cards will showcase the landscape, people, and places around Parker that Addy likes to say can always offer a sometimes hidden glimpse of real paradise.

PARKER PARADISE
DATING CLUB RULES
(as of last Tuesday)

1. All members must come with open minds and hearts.

2. Couples can be dating, married, thinking about a second date or about former partners.

3. Sexual preference does not matter. Everyone is welcome.

4. Due to overwhelming demand, singles are welcome and will be recognized by lovely red badges that say "Pick ME."

5. Paradise starts with fun. Make sure that is your number one intention. When the fun stops, so does everything else.

6. This is a club for openness and growing, so please park your bad attitude one town over.

7. Dues will be used for several parties each year but if you cannot

pay it's no big deal. Paradise in Parker is for everyone.

8. Take it outside. If your dating has a glitch, please leave it home.

9. Dr. Sanchez is the only one who will read suggestions dropped into the suggestion box. Feel free.

10. We are open, REALLY open, to new events, classes, adventures, and field trips.

11. Membership in this dating club means you are really cool.

12. If you do break up, get a divorce, or take a leave of absence from your relationship, we hope you realize that we will pester the living hell out of you to make sure you know what you are doing.

13. Crying is always allowed at events and meetings although we would prefer that you cry before or after. But if you can't help it, it's okay to cry whenever.

14. There will be a drawing at each

event for the "Best Dating Tip." The tips will be combined into a booklet each year that we will sell for a lot of money. Proceeds will be donated to the Parker Women's Center.

15. These rules, except for most of the numbers—especially numbers one, three, five, and eleven, and probably nine—can change at any given moment or at the next event, which will be next Thursday at the bowling alley. It's flashlight bowling so bring extra batteries.

16. It's always okay if you do not feel like dating once in a while.

17. Kilts are not mandatory.

18. Women are not allowed to bring swords or knives to any events.